Coming Home to the Cowboy

Coming Home
to the Cowboy

A Redemption Ranch Romance

Megan Ryder

TULE
PUBLISHING

Chapter One

CHASE SUMMERS LEANED against the tunnel wall leading out to the arena, thumbs hooked in the loops of his comfortable old jeans, wearing his lucky flannel shirt under the competitor's vest with his sponsors' badges decorating the lapels. He barely heard the dull roar of the crowd or the pounding country rock music as he focused on his ride. People milled about—other cowboys waiting for their rides, watching the competition, or those who had finished and were seeing who had made the next round with them. The sports medicine team pushed past Chase and ran to the arena to help one of the riders who had just gotten thrown and was slow to get up. Chase didn't go look. He couldn't afford the distraction, not this close to his ride. Couldn't let the risks mess with his head, not yet. He'd check the status later on the injury list.

It'd been a bad season so far. Bull riding was one of the most dangerous sports there was. Yeah, people complained about football. Two men lining up to attack each other in the pursuit of a ball. Not that he didn't love football or respect the game, but those men weighed a couple hundred pounds. Try putting a guy who weighed a couple hundred pounds, maybe, against a fifteen-hundred to two-thousand-pound bull who didn't play by any rules except to kick the shit out of you. Then see who had it rougher.

Despite the dangers, he'd ride the bull any day. The rush, the adrenaline, and the reward were intense. But this season there seemed to be more injuries than usual; more of the top guys were out for extended periods. The number one rider had been kicked in the face just two weeks ago and needed major reconstruction, leaving the field open for someone like Chase to catch up.

He took a deep breath, letting the smell of dirt, bull, and rawhide permeate his lungs, then he let it out slowly, expelling the thoughts of injuries like a bad odor. The scents reminded him of the ranch, the only home he'd ever known, the home he never thought he'd actually have and wouldn't have except for the generosity of his mentor and foster father, Douglas Rawlings.

J.D. McIntyre strode up next to him, his chaps and jeans coated in dirt from his fall in the ring and clapped him on the shoulder. "You up next? Who did you draw?"

"Oleander," Chase replied, nodding to his sometime traveling companion and fellow hell-raiser.

J.D. snorted. "Better you than me. That bull looks sweet and docile but turns into a righteous demon in the chute."

Chase shrugged and checked his gloves. "He's worth the points. I'll need them for the lead."

J.D. shook his head. "Well, someone had to draw him. If anyone can, it'd be you. Go beat the Brazilian and bring home the trophy. I'm out of the running for now. Damned Quick Draw tossed me in 2.8 seconds."

Chase grunted. Quick Draw was living up to his name again. But J.D. was his only other real competition outside of Antonio Pereira. Antonio was ranked number three overall, but he hadn't gotten as high-point a bull as Chase or J.D. If Chase could ride Oleander, he could take the competition from Antonio and gain serious ground in the overall rankings.

The announcer called his name to the chute.

"See you on the other side." He nodded to J.D. and strode to the ride-chute where Oleander was already being led.

Oleander was a beast of a bull, docile as most of those creatures were outside of the arena, calm, almost amiable. He was mostly white with a few splashes of black to break up the albino quality. He settled quietly in the chute, no banging against the metal walls, no fighting the handlers. Chase eyed the bull, who steadfastly ignored him as if he were bored with the proceedings, but Chase knew better.

Chase climbed the metal fencing next to the bull and handed the rope to the handler. He grabbed the opposite fence across from the bull, making sure to get a good grip, then he set his boot solidly on Oleander's back, letting the bull know he was there. He waited a few seconds, pausing to the let the bull do his customary buck, an introduction from Oleander, a preliminary howdy-do. He then slid his legs around the bull, keeping his toes pointed forward to ensure his spurs stayed away from its flanks. He warmed up the rope, checked the slack, then rubbed the rope to get the rosin sticky and hot on his glove. He punched the rosin rope away and warmed the handle to improve his grip. Then he positioned the bull rope for the ride.

Through this, Oleander stayed fairly docile, almost

3

asleep, but Chase wasn't fooled. No bull was assigned the high round of any tournament if he wasn't a tough contender, and Oleander was one of the toughest. Several competitors swore this damned beast used psychological warfare against many of the riders. No one had ever ridden him successfully; Chase was fixing to be the first.

When the rope was situated to his satisfaction, he took the final piece of wrap and slid up Oleander's back, put his feet toward the shoulder of the bull, and nodded.

The chute opened with a clang, and they were off.

Oleander came alive in a whirlwind of motion, shoulders and back arching then colliding with the ground, a move designed to jar the rider's teeth. At the same time, the bull's back end came up, and twisted to throw Chase off-balance and hopefully off his back completely, but Chase was prepared and moved with the bull. Chase kept his legs clasped around the bull's body, shifting and moving as the bull flung his body about in a ferocious attempt to dislodge the human interloper from his back. All the while, Chase waited to hear the blessed bell indicating that he had successfully made the eight seconds needed to beat the behemoth between his legs.

But all he heard was the sound of grunts and snorts, and he saw bull snot flying around them. Then, finally, the sound of victory. The bell sounded and Chase made his move to dismount, but the bull made one unexpected sideways turn and a blunted horn came straight for Chase's head.

Blinding pain.

Darkness.

CLAWING PAIN HAMMERED at his head, radiating throughout his body, but he fought the nausea and darkness to open his eyes. He expected to hear the roar of the crowd, the music thumping in the stadium. Feel the dirt they brought in for the arena. Instead, he heard only a beeping sound and saw a soft light that somehow still managed to stab his retinas.

He wasn't in the sports medicine room. This was a hospital.

He let out a groan as reality came crashing down on him, much like the body of that damned bull had.

A shadow shifted and moved from beside the bed and slowly revealed itself in the light spilling in from the hallway. His older brother, West Morgan, leaned over him, looking haggard and worn with more than a day's growth of dark stubble. Lines of exhaustion were carved into his weathered face. West wasn't his blood brother, but that had never mattered to the three teens who had found themselves on the Rawlings Ranch where the foster system had deposited them after they were deemed high-risk youth. But they had created their own odd sort of family, staying together and building bonds tighter than blood with the man who had saved them, who had been more of a father than their own sperm donors.

West laid a hand on his shoulder. "Stay still. I'll get a nurse."

Chase struggled to speak, but West had already pressed a button, and it was amazing how fast help rushed into the room. Judging by the way the young brunette checked out his brother, maybe he wasn't so surprised. Chase closed his eyes and let her check his vitals, answering her brief questions with a raspy voice raw from disuse. His mouth tasted like dirt from the ring. With one last lingering glance at West, she left the room. West pulled up a chair and held up a cup with cold water and ice chips for Chase to sip. The cool water both burned and soothed his sore throat.

Chase let his head fall back against the pillows and tried to catalog his injuries, but the pain throbbed in every part of his body, making it difficult to locate the worst of the damage.

"How long?" he croaked.

West stared at him as if memorizing his face, a muscle jumping in his jaw. "Three days. You have broken ribs, a punctured lung, bruised kidneys, and a concussion."

Chase tried to laugh but groaned again from the sharp, stabbing pain that knifed him in the chest. "Damn, that hurts."

West jumped up from the chair and started to pace the small hospital room. "Goddamn it, Chase. You had to have surgery to repair your lung and release the air or something. This isn't a laughing matter. Jesus, you could have been killed."

The door opened, and the hallway light spilled in around a woman. Tara Rawlings, West's fiancée, let out a small cry and raced to the bed, petting Chase's face gently. "Chase, you're awake. We've all been praying, and West hasn't left your side once for the past three days. Thank God you're okay."

"That remains to be seen," West growled from the foot of the bed. Tara shot him a look then continued to pamper

Chase.

"How are you feeling? Do you need anything?"

"I hope that bull knocked some sense into you." West came around the other side of the bed and leaned over the metal railing. "You almost died. I never want to get that phone call again, never want to make that long drive not knowing if my brother is going to be alive when I get here. Do you know how that feels?"

Chase stared up at what appeared to be tears in West's eyes and tried not to think about what could make his brother cry. "West, man, it's fine. I'm going to be okay. A few weeks' recovery and I'll be back in the saddle. This was sheer dumb luck that my spur got caught in the rope. It won't happen again."

West gripped the metal bar so tightly his knuckles went white. Tara reached across the bed and rubbed his shoulder, making soothing noises. "What if it's not? What if the next time you're not so lucky? And honestly, I don't think you were that lucky this time."

Chase sank against the pillow and let his eyes fall closed. Luck rarely played a role in his life—unless it was bad luck, and right now, this was the worst. Just as he was on top of the world, fucking Oleander had to take him out, leaving him on the sidelines when he could have gained some ground on the circuit. Luck wasn't for guys like him, no matter how charmed people thought he was.

Chapter Two

CHASE STUDIED THE gently sloping hills as he and West barreled down the highway, the silence in the cab a quiet comfort after the bustle of the hospital. Chase winced as the truck hit a bump in the road, the jolt sending pain shooting through his body, reminding him that a bull had used him as a punching bag just a couple of weeks ago. Healing was going to take a lot longer than he would like to acknowledge, and he'd be stuck recovering at the ranch while dealing with Tara mothering him and West acting like his father the whole time.

It had been hard enough avoiding West and his concern in the hospital, but there he could pretend to be asleep or flirt with nurses to have people around to run interference. But now, stuck in a truck cab with his brother for miles on end . . . well, Chase had no recourse but to deal with him.

Yet, West had kept his peace, instead talking about plans for the ranch, Tara's expansion into the dude ranch—or guest ranch as she preferred to call it—and West's breeding operation for the cattle. Or they listened to music quietly while Chase let the painkillers drag him into a healing doze. They chose to drive, worried about the change in altitude in flight and the lingering effects of the pneumothorax from his punctured lung. And, apparently, West wasn't going to let him hang out in a hotel room for the next several weeks, not that Chase was keen on spending the money for that.

Chase leaned back on the headrest and closed his eyes. It would be nice to recover at home. Have some nice home cooking, maybe some nursing from a couple of local girls, though he hadn't been too interested in anyone the last time he'd been home. Which was a good thing; there would be no clinging women wailing about his injuries and looking to sink their claws into him while he was down and out.

Without opening his eyes, he sighed. "I like your new truck, brother. But you could have sprung for the fancy entertainment package. I hear they have Wi-Fi now, and you can even play games and DVDs."

West snorted. "If I had known I'd be dragging your sorry ass home after you almost died, maybe I would have done that. How many more times do you plan on doing this? Should I invest in a new truck for your lazy ass?"

Chase grinned. "I didn't exactly plan this little road trip, but I sure would like to see a movie. Your music taste sucks."

West flicked off the country music station. "That's easily handled. Seriously, Chase. How many times am I going to have to do this?"

He shouldn't have complained about the music. Chase opened his eyes and glared at his brother. "You act like you've had to do this every couple of months. Sorry to pull you from shoveling shit, but I never asked you to come."

West slammed his fist into the dashboard; Chase half expected to see a crack and was impressed when it didn't appear. "Dammit, Chase. That's not the point. You never call when you get hurt. How many times have you had a concussion just this year? Or broken a bone?"

"Do you want me to call you every time I get a boo-boo? Jesus, West. I'm a grown man. I can take care of myself." Chase lounged in the passenger seat, trying to get as comfortable as his bruises would allow, and scowled at the relentless grasslands passing by.

"Hell yes, I expect you to call me. I'm your fucking brother." West gripped the steering wheel tight, his knuckles almost white with tension.

"God, you're acting like an old woman. I've taken care of myself for years. I'm a big boy. Besides, there are plenty of women who are more than happy to take care of me when I need some TLC."

Chase saw West's gaze reflected in the passenger window. His stare was steady, not angry or even hurt. "You don't have to be alone, you know. You have a family that gives a shit about you, God knows why." The last was muttered under his breath almost like a curse as West focused on the blacktop.

Chase often wondered the same thing. His whole life had been a pattern of people walking out on him, one foster family after another, only in rare cases keeping him around for more than a few months. If he lasted a whole school year with one family, it was a fucking miracle. If he'd owned a suitcase as a kid, he'd never unpack. Only Douglas had kept him around, despite Chase testing him at every turn with attitude, language, and the crazy antics he pulled. Through it all, Douglas had his back and so had West. Clearly, West *still* had his back.

Chase scrubbed his hand over his face. "Ignore me. I'm

tired and I have a headache. I'm just being an asshole."

West grinned. "Well, at least that concussion didn't change your personality."

Chase snorted. "As if a little concussion could do that."

West gave him a sideways glance. "Four could. When were you going to tell me that the medical staff was going to bench you if you got another one?"

Chase sighed. This whole debate over concussions and head injuries had bled over from football into bull riding, and it was making him crazy. He was so close to the prize, to the big money he had worked so hard for, the money that could go a long way to helping them with the upcoming tax bill on the ranch and turning things around. This was his part in the effort, and he didn't need a little headache to keep him down, not when he had a chance to gain some ground. He sucked in a breath, and the pain stabbed him in his chest.

A simple thump on the head wasn't keeping him out, not anymore. Not when they needed the money more than ever to save the only home he'd ever had.

"It's no big deal. Really, West. We've all gotten knocked around by cows before. Same thing."

"No, it's not even close. I don't climb on the back of a fucking bull and get jerked around like a washing machine. If we get hurt, it's on the job and by accident."

"And you think I do this for fun? It's my job, dammit. No different from you. I've accepted the risks."

West muttered something under his breath and, when Chase glared at him, he grunted. "You're not twenty anymore. You kept us going when things were tight, and I appreciate it. But we have a plan now, a way to be more stable without you risking your neck every week."

Chase stared out the window again, not letting on how the words hurt worse than every breath felt. How else could he help the family? What else did he have to offer if his efforts weren't needed on the rodeo circuit? Without the rodeo, he was just another cowboy, working the ranch like any other hired hand.

Who was he if he wasn't a bull rider?

A COUPLE OF hours later, West steered the truck into a turn about a mile before the ranch, next to a new sign proclaiming the place to be Redemption Ranch. The sign was wood-carved, probably by Gene Woodruff, a genius carver in town who made furniture and other art pieces but was notoriously difficult to work with and didn't often take on vanity projects. This sign was unmistakably his, simple in its design but beautiful for the detail. The words for the ranch stood out in a dark reddish wood against a lighter grained background. Two rearing horses perched on either side of the sign, their front hooves connecting with the top of the wood, manes and tails flying in the imaginary wind.

West paused the truck to let Chase study the new addition. A tiny smile flirted with the edges of West's mouth, confirming Chase's suspicions.

"They just put the sign up?"

"Yup. Guess they wanted to welcome you home in grand style." West's smile grew as he put the truck in gear and continued down the hard-packed driveway toward the house.

"Looks good. So, we're moving forward with the dude ranch idea, huh?" The tension was slowly rising, the muscles in his back and neck tightening as they got closer to the house.

"We've already had a few tours for hunting and fishing signed up, but the real guests will be here next year." West slid him another sideways glance. "And it's a guest ranch, not a dude ranch. You'd better remember it or Tara's liable to tear a strip off your hide."

Chase grinned as they pulled up to the white farmhouse. "Nice job on the cleanup. Why are we headed down here and not the main house? You don't want me near you two lovebirds?"

The front door opened and Tara came onto the porch, worry etched on her face. A pang shot through Chase as he took in the circles under her eyes and the concern he sensed that had more to do with him than the start of the new business. She quickly pasted on a grin and raced down the steps and the path to the truck and launched herself into West's arms, her legs wrapping around his waist, and kissed him as if it had been years instead of a few days since she had seen him in Cheyenne, Wyoming.

Chase slid out of the truck and slowly eased his way to the ground, testing his sprained knee, making sure it would hold his weight, before letting go of the door and taking out the cane. He hated using the damned cane, but it ensured he wouldn't hit the ground like a newborn calf, so he planted it firmly and leaned on it, scowling at the damned thing. Thank God no one was paying attention to him in those few moments it took to get adjusted to life not in motion. It had been bad enough that West had stopped every couple of hours, stretching the eleven-hour drive to almost two days to ensure Chase didn't get stiff or sore by sitting too long. They also stopped in a hotel overnight to give them time to rest instead of driving through the night or switching drivers since Chase was on painkillers. West wouldn't let Chase stop taking them so he could drive. Judging by how sore Chase's body was just from sitting, it was probably for the best.

He straightened and gently worked the kinks out of his tight muscles, feeling every single injury from that damned bull and every other one he'd ridden in the past seven years. The kissing continued, and he made kissing noises at the couple.

"Can I get me some of that?"

West shot him the finger without lifting his head from Tara's, and Chase burst out laughing. Damn, it felt good to be back with his brothers.

"And this is why West brought you here and not the main house."

He jumped at the voice, turning to see his younger brother, Ty Evans, standing a few steps away. "Jesus, Ty. You scared the hell out of me."

He took a step forward and gave him a manly hug. Ty, for his part, returned the gesture, but he treated Chase more like breakable fine china than his brother. Chase thumped on his back as a warning before releasing him. Ty grunted.

"Turnabout's fair play. You scared us all too. Getting that phone call in the middle of the night was no picnic for us either." Ty's dark gaze ran over his body, cataloging his injuries and bruises visible on his face. "How are you doing?

Really, old man?"

Chase shrugged. "I feel like a bull used me as his bitch without the sweet-talking. Otherwise, I feel like a ray of fucking sunshine. You?"

Ty grinned. "Good. No more questions about how you're feeling, what I can get you, and how I can kiss your ass? No problem. I have a half a dozen stalls that need some shit shoveled. You up for it?"

Chase swiveled his shoulders and winced as his ribs protested. "Nah, I think I'll take advantage of this vacation. Kick back on the porch, have a few beers, catch up on my reality television. Give me a week. We'll see how I feel then." He glanced around the house, seeing the riot of flowers and fresh paint on everything. "Someone has sure been busy."

Ty laughed. "You know Tara. She has a mission, and everyone's been put to work. Be careful or you'll be next. She has no mercy, not even for the sick, infirm, or lame. And you're all three."

"Hey! I resent that," she protested.

Chase turned to see Tara and West had finally broken apart and walked around the truck to come up next to them, still wrapped around each other casually, like a comfortable couple. It was nice to see his older brother relaxed and happy finally. Not that West had ever been unhappy, but now it was obvious what a difference Tara had made in his life—in all of their lives. Despite the shakeup she was creating, Chase was grateful for her presence. He reached over, ignoring the twinge in muscles that didn't want to be stretched, and tugged her close, hugging her lightly.

"Thanks for everything, sweetheart."

Tara leaned into him, releasing West and gently wrapping her arms around Chase. She pulled back and laid a hand on his cheek until he focused on her. "Don't ever do that to us again. You scared us, Chase."

He glanced over at West helplessly. West tugged her back to his side. "Stop flirting with my brother. Get your own chick, bro. This one's taken."

Chase nodded and focused on the house. "So, I'm banished from the house where I was raised, huh?"

Ty leaned into him. "Trust me. This is where you'd rather be."

Tara scowled at him. "With your knee, we thought the stairs at the main house would be difficult to manage, and the cabins are under renovations, except the one Ty is living in. Besides, they're a little too far away for you to maneuver. This house has an en suite apartment we planned for the guest ranch manager to use, once we hire them. But for now, I think it will be perfect for you."

He sighed. "The room is filled with flowers, isn't it?"

Ty grinned. "We tried to find some cheap perfume or buckle bunnies to welcome you home, but Tara refused."

"I'm not wasting my good perfume on you, and I refuse to buy the cheap stuff. It's nasty," she said from the other side of West. "Flowers will brighten the room. Help with your healing. Good feng shui."

West considered the problem for a moment. "We could always bring some shit from the barn, make it smell like what you're used to. Or you can leave your dirty clothes strewn around."

Everyone laughed, then Chase froze. "Wait, my stuff.

What happened to—"

West laid a hand on his arm. "I got your stuff from the hotel and took care of the bill. Tara brought it back with her a few days ago."

"The airlines almost wouldn't let that rank duffel past the drug-and-bomb-sniffing dogs. But your clothes are all cleaned and in your room. Except what you were wearing in the ring. We couldn't save those." Her voice trailed off with a sad glance at West.

Chase groaned. "Damn, that was my lucky shirt too."

Ty snorted. "Seriously, bro? I think we need to talk about your definition of lucky."

Chase laughed. "Yeah, maybe you're right. Well, show me my new digs for the next few weeks before I head back out. I have a belt to win."

He slowly walked to the house, leaning heavily on the cane, not missing the way his family exchanged concerned glances. He couldn't afford to get too comfortable. He was too close to his dream and the big prize money.

And there was no way could West afford to upgrade the ranch without it. They needed his money, and Chase had put his body on the line for it. They were counting on him.

Chapter Three

HAILEY BARNES SPENCER flipped the pages of the small-town newspaper to the single column of want ads.

She needed a job. Yesterday. Well, last month really when she decided to move back to Granite Junction to help her parents after her mom's mini-stroke and stint in rehab. Living at home after years being on her own, first as a wife and mother, then a single mom, was no joke, and she needed her space pronto. Too bad the only jobs available were here at the diner or with her father at the bank—not an option for her plan. And Hailey always had a plan, even if she had to deviate from it from time to time, which lately seemed to be the norm. But good plans required contingencies, and she knew how to make those too.

As she suspected, there was not much available for work, and there were only a few apartments, nothing she'd want to raise A.J. in—not when she had a house and yard for him already. She sighed and took another bite of the light and fluffy waffle. God knew how old, cantankerous Earl did it, but the man sure knew how to make the best waffles around. Probably buckets of unhealthy lard.

A young woman slid into the booth across from her, re-filling Hailey's coffee cup at the same time. "Well, I didn't expect to see you around here."

Hailey looked up into the smiling face of her old class-mate, Emma Holt. She was dressed in jeans and an Early Byrd's Diner T-shirt, with a pink apron around her waist. Her dark brown hair was pulled back into a ponytail, making her look much younger than the twenty-eight years Hailey knew her to be. Although, not having to raise a child alone may have contributed to her looking far younger than the face Hailey saw in the mirror every morning.

"I didn't know you worked here," Hailey said when the silence had dragged on a little longer than it should.

Emma laughed, the same infectious sound that had at-tracted people to her throughout their school years. "Well, that's more polite than most people say it. Usually, I hear, 'You're still working at the diner? When are you going to find something else to do with your life?' Or, 'When are you going to grow up, Emma Holt?'" She just shrugged. "It doesn't bother me. In fact, I just finished my master's in child psychology, and I'll be starting at the school in the fall as a counselor."

Hailey stared at her for a long moment, embarrassed to hear her own thoughts parroted back at her. "I'm so sorry. I didn't realize how rude that sounded. Congratulations on the degree! You've always wanted to work with kids."

"Yeah, well, being a teacher wasn't quite what I wanted to do. I taught for a few years while I finished my degree, and waitressed here to save the money for school, but I've always wanted to do more to help troubled kids. Now I can. Or I'll fail miserably and be serving up waffles for the rest of my life. But at least I tried, right?"

"Order up!" Earl bellowed from the kitchen.

"Be right there," Emma hollered back. "Let me get that order and we'll catch up. I want to hear all about you and what you've been up to. I have a break coming. Don't disappear."

The word *again* was not said but implied, considering how quickly Hailey had left after she'd found out she was pregnant with A.J. and they moved away, with infrequent visits back home. She should have known Emma wouldn't let a little thing like time get in the way of friendship. All too soon, Emma was seated across from her with a glass of Coke and a basket of fries smothered in ketchup to snack on while they talked. Looks like they were settling in for one of their high school chats.

Emma dragged a fry through the ketchup and slurped it up. "I was sorry to hear about Adam. He was a good guy. I know it's been a few years, but I haven't really seen you since it happened. How have you been?"

Hailey nodded. The familiar ache had almost completely dissipated in the four years since his death. "It's been as you would expect for the past few years, raising A.J. on my own, working full-time. I didn't get to come home very often."

Emma snorted. "Well, your father didn't make that very easy, did he?"

Hailey pasted a noncommittal smile on her face. She knew better than to get into the same old argument about her father, especially not in a public place. Word always seemed to get back to him, especially when she'd been growing up, and she didn't need to get called on the carpet for not holding up the Barnes's standard. "You know how he is. Mom came to visit when she could, but we were fine."

Emma offered her the basket of fries. Hailey shook her head; Emma shrugged and popped another one in her mouth. "I heard your mom is getting better. Are you just visiting or back for good?"

Her friend was doing more than fishing now. "Mom is home now and on the mend. What have you heard?"

A big grin crossed Emma's face and she leaned forward, ready to impart some serious gossip. "Well, the ladies from the church came in this morning after their meeting at the parish, and Lucille Turnbull mentioned that she heard from Loretta Patton you were home for good. All your stuff was in your car and everything. She saw it when she was walking her Pekingese the other day."

Hailey sat back and scowled. "How the hell did she see that? My car was parked well into the driveway. She would have had to walk almost into our backyard to look into my car."

"I wouldn't put it past her to be brazen enough to do that." Emma snorted. "Or, if she wanted to be sneaky, she could let her beast loose and then 'chase' him into your yard to catch him. 'Whoops, sorry. Didn't mean to look in your car.'" Emma's voice rose in a falsetto as she mimicked Hailey's neighbor and the resident busybody, although everyone on the street poked their noses where they didn't belong and needed to have them smacked.

Hailey giggled though, picturing Loretta in her velour track suit chasing her dog onto the property. "My dad would have been furious. No wonder he wanted me to bring everything in after dark."

"Of course. So no one would see. Although, if you did it

in broad daylight, your mother would have something to complain about to all the other mothers in town. It's a win-win."

"Not for me." Hailey frowned.

Emma sobered. "No, not for you. How long are you staying?"

She grimaced. "My firm closed last spring, after tax season. I found a new job, but Mom had her stroke and I thought it might be easier to be closer to them. They're not getting any younger and I want A.J. to know his grandparents."

"That's good. Your mom will be happy to have you close by. And you're a CPA, right? That shouldn't be so hard to find a job. Everyone needs their taxes done."

"In Granite Junction? The original small town?" Hailey rolled her eyes. "Not so much. But taxes only come around once a year, and I'm more than a CPA. I consult with small businesses and help them grow. However, I didn't quite expect it to be so difficult to find a job here or have to live at home for so long."

Emma shuddered. "I love my mom, but I couldn't go back there. I'd rather eat ramen noodles for a month. Hence the glorious life of a waitress." Emma paused. "Wait, are you only looking to work for a firm or would you be interested in working on your own for someone?"

Hailey shrugged. "I guess it depends on what they need. I did a lot of accounting for businesses of all sizes, and not just taxes. Eventually, I want to work on my own, for myself, like a consultant or something. I want to work with small businesses. Family-run places. Service or retail shops.

Tradespeople. Internet businesses, things like that. I like helping them find better ways to do business."

Emma bit her lower lip and looked out the window to the street and the cars driving by. Suddenly, she snapped her fingers. "I have a brilliant idea. Can you hang out a little while? There's someone I'd you to meet. It's Wednesday so I know she'll be in. Her fiancé comes in every Wednesday to pick up feed and stuff, and she comes with him for lunch here. They're opening a guest ranch on the old Robertson Ranch, the one that combined with Rawlings Ranch to be the Double R? Anyway, Tara Rawlings is back and she's opening the place and has been looking for a business manager. You'd be perfect!"

Just thinking of Rawlings Ranch brought back too many memories—memories of her husband Adam and his best friend, Chase Summers. Hanging out by the watering hole. Flirting with fire when it came to Chase, running to the safety of Adam when Chase's grin became too mocking.

Memories of her husband had faded from painful to soft and regretful now. More sadness than pain. But Chase? She had followed his career on the circuit, even as she worried about him, dreaded hearing news about him as she had heard about her husband. She had not caught up on recent news, with the slower cycle of events over the summer and her own move to Granite Junction, so she had no way of knowing if he'd be home or on the road somewhere, practicing, or taking part in some of the events to increase his points. She couldn't resist thinking about Chase, even through this distant connection. While she may have some regrets with her husband and their marriage, Chase was the one she always had questions about, the one man she wondered what-if about.

Before her mind could wander too far down that path, Hailey stuffed those memories deep into the box in her head and slammed the lid shut. Being back in Granite Junction sucked. It pulled out all these memories that she didn't want, resurrected ghosts that needed to stay buried.

She had a son to raise, a job to find, and she needed somewhere to live because damned if she was going keep living with her parents.

Emma was chattering on about the new venture, oblivious to the fact that Hailey had checked out and wasn't even paying attention. The door to the diner opened and a blonde woman walked in, escorted by West Morgan. His hand was riding low on her back, his eyes fixed firmly on her. This must be the prodigal Rawlings's daughter, someone Hailey could relate to. Only Tara seemed to have come home in triumph while Hailey had her tail tucked between her legs. Damn it.

Before she could stop Emma, the other woman had waved the couple over and stood, gesturing them into the booth. West nodded at Hailey soberly and gave Tara a kiss, mumbling something about talking with one of the ranchers about bulls or something. Tara just waved him away, laughing.

"Thank God you're here. The last thing I needed was another conversation about feed, grazing rights, and the price of beef. Do you have any idea how freaking boring that is? Tell me you know how to talk about anything other than cows or horses." Tara grabbed her arm as if she were a lifesaver and Tara was drowning.

Hailey blinked a few times, unsure how to respond. Emma plunked a Coke down in front of Tara, breaking the moment. "Not sure if you remember Hailey Barnes Spencer. She used to live here and has just moved back with her son. She's looking for a job, and I thought of the ranch. She's a CPA and consults with small businesses. Your usual, Tara?"

Tara cocked her eyebrow at Hailey, her expression cooling a little, assessing Hailey. "Thanks, Emma. That would be great." Emma nodded and left them to talk alone. "Are you related to Tom Barnes at the bank?"

Hailey nodded, completely understanding the almost glacial expression. Her father often distanced himself from business owners in town, and if Tara had gone to him for a loan, Hailey could only imagine how difficult that conversation had been. "He's my father. I'm a CPA, certified in Montana. Worked for a couple of firms and did some small-business consulting up in Billings with some ranches, a couple of feed stores, and retail shops around there. I moved back to town because my mom got sick and I wanted to be closer to her and have my son get to know his grandparents. My son is going into first grade in the fall so I'll be free most days, but I have to warn you, he comes first with me. I don't want to work for someone who says they're family friendly then docks you when you need to take time for your son."

Hailey got the words out in a rush, the last of them more forceful than she normally would, but she wanted to be clear.

Tara studied her carefully, almost as if seeing through her words to the motivation beneath them. "Well, you should know that your father's bank holds a loan on Redemption

Ranch, the new name for the guest ranch, and I don't think he was overly thrilled about us doing this. He had an investor to buy the ranch before we decided to go this route. As to your son, I wouldn't expect anything less than a commitment to him. Family is important to us too. We'd never get in your way of family obligations. Tell me a little about your experience."

Emma took that moment to place a burger in front of Tara, who started to eat while listening to Hailey. She walked through her education and her work history with a minimal amount of questions from the other woman. Finally, Tara finished eating and wiped her fingers carefully on her napkin. She placed it on the table and went back to her perusal of Hailey, who squirmed under the scrutiny.

"I used to be a partner in an interior design business in San Francisco, so I'm no stranger to running a business. However, design and hospitality are two very different businesses. I need someone to help me plan this business and get it off the ground. We want to be ready to take reservations for next season, so we have a lot to do. What I want is a partner in this, someone who plans to stick around and wants to learn, not just doing a job and taking off next year for something else. We're pretty casual, more like a family than a business, and your son would be welcome. There may also be flexibility if you decide to branch out and help other businesses because, frankly, once we get moving and growing, I may not need you as much unless you want to switch to more of the day-to-day operations. Does this sound like something you'd be interested in?"

Hailey heard the words *partner*, *family*, and *growth*. This was more than doing taxes or the occasional consultation. Here, she had a chance to really work on her small-business consultation skills and make a difference. Her CPA had been born of necessity, not out of a desire for accounting. She much preferred to use her business degree and expand, but she'd never seemed to find the right fit. Now she had the opportunity to try it. And, like Emma said, at least she would have tried.

A slow grin crossed her face. "I'd love it. Sounds great."

Tara clapped her hands. "Fabulous. When can you start?"

HAILEY RESISTED THE urge to smile throughout dinner with her parents that night, knowing they would want to know the reason and she wasn't quite ready to share yet. She wanted to see the ranch, get a better feel for Tara and the work to be done, and, most of all, ensure she wouldn't have to face Chase while working there. Only then would she accept the position. Although, honestly, what other choices did she have? The town wasn't big enough to have more than one accountant, and he was middle-aged and not going anywhere and wouldn't hire her without permission from her father. Opening her own business wouldn't work either since there wasn't enough business in town for a business consultant, so she was stuck, really.

"Why are you so happy tonight, Hailey? Did something happen today?" her mother asked from the foot of the table.

Apparently, she hadn't been good enough at hiding her

feelings. "No, I just caught up with some old friends at the diner."

Her father frowned. "Well, you won't have much time to fritter away your day starting next week. I found you a position at my bank as a teller. You can start Monday."

Her mother gave a bright smile. "That's wonderful, dear. I didn't know you had any openings."

He frowned, one of his default facial expressions. "Well, I had to create it, but we'll figure it out."

Her mother, oblivious to the undercurrents as always, nodded as if everything had worked out. "There you go. Everything is all set, Hailey."

Hailey paused, anger a slow boil in her blood, and tried to find a way to express her feelings without starting a fight she would never win.

"Dad, I never asked to be a teller. In fact, I'm a CPA. Working as a teller is an insult to me and my education, don't you think?"

He shot her an irritated look. "I can't just give you a position in the bank because you're my daughter, can I? You have to earn it, like everyone else."

She stared at him, shocked. But when had he ever done anything to help his children in any way besides set high expectations and unrealistic demands? Instead, he believed in Darwinism in terms of childrearing and business. No wonder her brother fled as far as he could from Granite Junction.

"But you just stated you created a teller position for me. Besides, plenty of people start in a higher position due to their educational background. Instead, this is a slap in the face."

"You should be grateful for the job, something you seem to have trouble finding elsewhere."

"A.J., if you're done eating, please go play in your room. I'll be up shortly. Now," she said firmly as he started to protest. A.J. slipped from the table and scurried up the stairs while Hailey kept her eyes fixed on her father. When she heard the door close upstairs, she laid her fork on the table and folded her napkin deliberately.

"I won't have these discussions in front of my son, is that clear? Now, I could find work, but I came home to help after Mom had her stroke. I'll find my own job."

Her mother paled more than she already was from her illness. "I'm so sorry, Hailey. I didn't want to be a burden to you. If you need to move back to Billings, I understand. Although, I've loved having you and A.J. nearby."

Hailey reached across the table and gripped her mother's hand, feeling the frailty under her fingers. "Mom, I wanted to come home. It was my choice."

Hailey shot her father a look and took a deep breath. "For your information, I've found a position better suited to my skills. I'll be working at Redemption Ranch as the business manager. Since it comes with room and board, A.J. and I will be moving in a few days."

Now, she only hoped she wasn't making a rash decision and jumping from the frying pan into the fire. Was Chase Summers still chasing the elusive bull-riding belt and buckle bunnies? Had he completely forgotten about her and Granite Junction? And how would she react after all these years if she saw him? The hidden, feminine part of her wondered.

Chapter Four

HAILEY DROVE DOWN the winding, hard-packed dirt road toward the old Robertson Ranch. Or, rather, Redemption Ranch, as the fancy new sign by the road reminded her. Maybe using the new name would help banish the ghosts that had haunted her dreams last night and any night she thought about the ranch. About halfway down the drive, she stopped the car and looked out across what had been the front pasture when it had been a ranch.

Beyond the low hill was a place as familiar to her as the diner had been when she was growing up. She was tempted to get out and walk over to the small pond where she and Adam and Chase swam and relaxed as a way to hide from their parents—Hailey from the demands and pressure of her father, Adam from his absentminded father, and Chase because it was his foster father's property and he had few other true friends, besides his foster brothers.

She sighed and put the car in gear. Today wasn't the day for ghosts. She had the future to plan, not the past to lament. Within a few minutes, a beautiful white farmhouse appeared at the end of the road. It didn't look anything like the rundown, ramshackle place Hailey's dad had described when he'd ranted at her the night before. No, this place looked positively charming, freshly painted in a bright white with hunter-green shutters. The porch had a set of rocking chairs just waiting for someone to sit and visit, and a beautiful porch swing hung from one end, creaking gently in the late-summer breeze. Flowers were a riot of color along the front of the house and in the flower boxes at each window, with no perceivable structure or order. No rigidly planned garden. No, this was chaos and Hailey loved it. Her son could be a little boy here, not stuffed into a box and stifled by grief.

The front door opened and Tara stood there, a sheepish grin on her face. "I hope you don't judge my planting. I went a little overboard, but I couldn't resist. Next year, we might want to lay it out a little better. Make it a little more organized."

Hailey grinned. "Well, if you asked my mother, there's a certain way to place flowers including size, color, type, when they bloom, and all sorts of things that I never really paid attention to. If you ask me, I like the way this looks better. Less formal, more comfortable."

Tara nodded as if Hailey had just passed some sort of test. "Perfect. I think we'll get along just fine. I thought we'd start out here on the porch, talking a bit, then we'd go on a tour so I can show you my plans for the whole ranch. We'll end up in the office and talk about how we can work together to get this guest ranch up and running and look at the living space. Does that sound like a plan?"

Hailey nodded. "I think I should tell you. I've already decided to accept."

"That's good because you're my only candidate. I guess we both suck at negotiating. Now, iced tea or something stronger?" They exchanged glances and laughed.

"Something stronger."

HAILEY WAS ENCHANTED by Redemption Ranch. Tara was less of a boss and more of a hands-on kind of manager, looking for a partner to work with her, speak her own mind, and offer balance to the business side of things, particularly with the numbers and accounting Hailey loved to do, leaving Tara to focus on the creative side, designing the themes and vision for the ranch. Yet when Hailey hesitantly offered a few suggestions she had gleaned from previous clients, Tara gobbled them up as eagerly as the horses in the corral had eaten the apple slices from their hands.

Yes, Hailey could see herself living and working at the ranch. Only one question remained, and Hailey wasn't sure how to bring it up, or if she even wanted to know the answer.

As Tara led her back to the house from the stables, she said, "I have one small change in what I told you, and I'm really sorry about this. I hope it doesn't make you change your mind."

Tara looked so uncomfortable, biting her lower lip and studying the ground. Hailey gave a small laugh. "I doubt there's anything you could say that could make me change my mind. To lay it on the line, my other job options were waitressing at the diner or being a teller at the bank. And I love my dad, but I can't live with him, much less work for him. Honestly, this is a dream come true. This is what I've always wanted to do, help a business really grow and develop, so it would have to be really bad for me to walk away."

Tara sucked in a deep breath. "Hold that thought."

The front screen door to the house opened and a man stepped out on the porch. At first, Hailey thought it was West, Tara's fiancé. But judging by the way Tara tensed next to her and shot her a glance, it was someone else. The sun blinded Hailey for a moment as she continued walking with Tara toward the house until the light was blocked by the house and the trees behind it. She froze as soon as she could make out his features.

"Hello, Hailey. I didn't expect to see you here."

Hailey's breath caught in her throat and she swallowed hard.

Chase Summers.

Her heart pounded in her chest and the world felt like it tilted under her feet. She had expected to run into him at some point. She had only hoped to have some time to settle in, time to prepare herself before being confronted with the reality of him.

She drank in the sight of him eagerly, despite the pit in her stomach. It'd been three, no four years since she'd last seen him, since Adam's funeral. Chase had been a rock for her, solid as the granite the town had been named for. He stood by her side, making sure she had everything she needed while she slept-walked through those horrifying days when she'd tried to figure out what went wrong and how to move on with her life and raise a two-year-old on her own. He had offered to stay on in Billings and help, but what was there for him to do? So, she'd sent him on his way and tried to get on with finding her new normal.

He'd called a couple of times after Adam died, but she had always responded with a text saying she was busy or something. He'd seemed as relieved as she was, and she had no trouble staying away from Grand Junction in the Professional Bull Rider's off-season, effectively avoiding him, even as a part of her wanted to be near him. But she had to make her own way, and Chase was too much of a loner for her to rely on.

Tara's head was bopping back and forth between the two of them like a tennis match. Chase was standing at the top of the porch steps, patiently waiting while Hailey processed this new information. She took another step to see him more clearly in the shadows of the porch and gasped.

"Oh my God, Chase. What happened to you?"

He was leaning on a cane and his face had a few yellowed bruises to match bruises on his arms. The fitted T-shirt normally would have outlined the six-pack stomach she knew he had, but instead it showed a smooth area where bandages were wrapped tightly around his ribs. Her gaze fixed on the subtle tightening of his jaw and the muscles around his eyes, revealing the tension and pain he must have been feeling. Damn that move that had kept her from staying current with the circuit, damn this fucking sport that had injured him, and most of all damn his adrenaline need to risk his life for the sport that had killed her husband.

He quirked a grin at her. "Not a pretty sight, is it? Oleander took offense at me riding him for eight seconds and got his revenge. I'll be all right in a few weeks."

"But for now, he's staying here in the apartment I promised you. I'm so sorry, Hailey," Tara finished in a rush. "I completely forgot yesterday. I was so excited that you were interested. But the whole house is empty and the rest of the place is planned for a B&B, so the other rooms are all finished but not rented until next season. You and A.J. can have the run of the place until then."

Tara's words slowly sank in, and Hailey pivoted and stared at her. "You mean, have me and A.J. live here with Chase? For how long?"

Chase, too, stared at Tara. "Wait a minute. You never said anything about having a roommate."

"It's perfect. Chase, someone needs to make sure you're okay, especially after your lung injury, and Hailey needs a place to stay."

Chase's jaw clenched, but he only aimed a questioning look at her, and she flushed. "I have a place to stay. I just prefer to find somewhere else."

Tara waved her hand and arched a brow. "Come on, Hailey. Do you really want to stay with your parents when you can live here?"

Chase started down the steps and both women stopped him immediately. He glared at them. "I can walk down the damned stairs. It's just a sprain. I was at the barn earlier today. Tara, can you give Hailey and me a few minutes? I think we need to talk before we agree to being roommates."

Tara's gaze shot between them, full of questions, but she nodded. "I'll go hang with Ty at the barn and be back soon. Don't run her off. She's the second-best thing to happen to Redemption Ranch, and we need her."

Chase grinned. "And you're the first?"

Tara shot him a saucy grin over her shoulder. "And don't

you forget it."

CHASE LEANED AGAINST the post and studied Hailey. It had been a few years since he had last seen her, at the funeral for his best friend and her husband, Adam. Shock had rendered her almost catatonic, and she had a toddler to manage at the same time. Her parents hadn't exactly been the rock she could rely on, still nursing their anger over her decision to marry a rodeo cowboy instead of a businessman, as they had insisted.

Adam must have had some inkling of his own future because one night, on the road, he had made Chase promise to look after Hailey and A.J. if anything should happen to him. Chase had chalked it up to too much tequila and time on the road. But the next morning, he'd woken up to an oddly solemn Adam, perched on the edge of his bed, staring at Chase and making him reiterate his promise. He did everything but make Chase swear a blood oath. Chase promised but forgot the intensity of that moment in the heart-pounding world of bull riding.

Fast-forward a few weeks and there he was, standing by his buddy's wife at his friend's graveside, trying to figure out where it all went wrong even as his heart beat a little faster at the thought of being close to Hailey without the buffer of his best friend.

Chase stood by her side, fulfilling Adam's request, yet he couldn't get past the look in her eyes when she'd finally look at him. Her eyes bore into him, a heavy, steady gaze filled with accusation. As if she knew what was really in his heart.

Chase Summers desired his best friend's wife.

He was ashamed to admit that he'd walked away as she clearly had wanted, not been there for her, even as he had promised Adam he would be. But how could he when she would barely take his calls and had become quite the expert at finding excuses for avoiding him whenever he did get a hold of her? Not to mention his own culpability in Adam's death and his feelings toward Hailey that he now knew were still present, no matter how she felt about him. He had failed Adam. Had failed Hailey. But most of all, Chase had failed A.J. He owed them now. He wasn't the guy who stuck around, but he had to make things right. He only hoped it wouldn't be too little, too late.

Hailey stood at the base of the steps, awkwardly clasping her hands in front of her. She wore a pair of dress slacks and a nice blouse, as if she were going on a job interview. He could have told her that Tara didn't a give a damn about that and Hailey would be wearing jeans or shorts around the ranch soon enough, but Hailey liked to do things properly.

Her deep auburn hair was pulled back in a fancy braid, not the ponytail he remembered from back in high school, but a few strands had escaped and danced around her face in the summer breeze, easing the image of the tough business-woman. A few sprinklings of freckles remained on her face, but they would deepen in the sun from what he recalled when he, Adam, and Hailey used to hang out at the swimming hole. Her body had rounded out nicely from her lanky youth, and lust kicked in right away, an unwelcome remind-er that he'd be spending the next couple of weeks under the same roof with her.

Her eyes darted around as if unsure of her reception. It killed him that they were so awkward around each other when they had once been friends. But maybe it was for the best, especially if they had to share space together.

"You don't need to stand down there, Hailey. I won't bite. Unless you want me to."

He couldn't resist poking the bear a little, hoping to get a rise out of her. Her deep blue eyes flashed fire at him, and he grinned. *Gotcha.*

He limped over to the one of the rocking chairs on the porch and sat down heavily in it, not opposed to playing on her sympathy if needed. Her face softened immediately, and he knew he had her. "I hope you don't mind, but I need to sit down. The leg bothers me a bit if I stand too long. I'd offer you some tea, but I think Tara has already offered you some with a little extra kick. Mine doesn't have the extra since I'm still on some of the fancy meds from the hospital."

She narrowed her gaze at him but slowly walked up the stairs and sat in the other rocker. She folded her hands in her lap then cocked her head. "I don't think I need anything special in mine for this conversation. How are you feeling?"

He shrugged with a wince as the motion tugged the ribs a little. Okay, so maybe he exaggerated the wince, but he needed her to stay. "Like I've been kicked around like a soccer ball. I'm on the mend but will be off the circuit for a few weeks. I'm stuck here for a while. And you'll be working here now. What happened to your job in Billings?"

She shrugged. "My mom got sick and I decided to move back here to help out."

"Because they were so supportive when you needed them."

She held up a hand and shoved it in his face. "Not going there, Chase. They're my family and they need me. Besides, I want A.J. to know his grandparents."

Chase snorted. "You could have done that from Billings with a few well-placed vacations."

She rocked back on her chair and drawled, "I'm beginning to think you don't want me here, Chase."

"It has nothing to do with that. I'm glad to see you, Hailey. Truly. But is Granite Junction the right place for you? There aren't a lot of opportunities here."

She looked around the old ranch yard, seeing the updates Tara had made. The upgrades to the outbuildings. The plantings and yardwork. The fresh coat of paint on the house. "There seems to be a big one right here. And a lot of potential. Does it bother you that I'm working for your sister-in-law?"

He laughed, a full-on belly laugh, the first one he'd had in months. It made his ribs hurt, but it was worth it. "First off, she's not my sister-in-law, not yet. Though, I think that's just a formality. Second, technically, the guest ranch is all of ours so you really work for all of us, including me." He shifted in the chair so he could lean over the arm and peer into her blue eyes. "Can you work for me?"

Without even pausing, she met him halfway, facing him squarely. "It won't be a problem, since you probably won't stick around for more than a few days."

Instead of being offended, he settled back in his chair and took a long swallow of his nonalcoholic iced tea. "Touché, darlin'. But, unfortunately, you'll be stuck with me for a little longer than that. Like I said, these injuries will keep me here for a little longer than I expected, since a bull took exception to me riding him. So, I thought I'd sit on this porch and make a general nuisance of myself." He raised his eyebrows at her, waiting for her response.

She only shrugged. "I'm raising a six-year-old. You can't be much worse." She ran her eyes down him. "Although, on second thought, maybe you could be. But that's easily remedied with a few simple rules."

He shook his head. Hailey and her rules. He had forgotten how much she needed to control everything. He struggled to his feet, ignored the sharp pain in his knee. He limped to the railing and turned, leaning back on it and quirking a grin at her. "Sure, honey. But I can't promise anything. You know me. I'm the original rulebreaker."

"More like heartbreaker," she muttered under her breath and stood to face him, folding her arms under her breasts. "First, and most important, no women prancing in and out of here on a daily basis."

He ran a hand down the post of the porch. Women were certainly not going to be a problem since none of them had shown up since he'd been home. And if they had, well, he hadn't been interested in the weeks leading up to his injury and he'd have no problem showing them the exit now. "No problem. I'm not in any shape to be entertaining, and rumors of my ways have been exaggerated."

She cocked her head, her lips pursed as if not buying what he was selling. "You forget, I grew up with you. You can't bullshit me, Summers. Second, no telling my son stories of the glory days of bull riding and going on the road. He doesn't need to hear how great being a bull rider is. That's not the life I want for him, and he's easily impressed."

Chase sobered immediately. "Trust me, I don't want A.J. following in his daddy's footsteps either, but I do think he should know about his father if he asks."

She nodded. "Fair point. And he knows about his father. I haven't hidden anything from him. You can tell him, but no exaggeration and carefully edit the story."

"Deal. Next?"

"Clothes to be worn at all times. I remember your exhibitionist ways, and I have enough trouble keeping my son dressed on some days."

Chase threw his head back and laughed out loud. "Honey, I only stripped my shirt when there were women present. And I seem to recall your husband being the same way, as most teenage boys were. But I find it interesting that your son is following in that tendency."

She pursed her lips and rolled her eyes. "Young boys like to run around without their clothes, although most outgrow it by his age. We thought he had outgrown it, but he still sometimes takes his shirt or pants off when he's home."

"So do I. It's comfortable that way. Anything else?" He waggled his eyebrows, trying to lighten the moment, and she laughed with him then stared at his mouth a beat too long, making him wonder if maybe she had feelings for him beyond friendship.

She shook her head quickly. "No, I think that's it. So, we're good?" She wiped her hands on her slacks, straightening them automatically even though they were perfectly pressed, with a seam and everything.

He remained leaning against the post. "Not quite. I have a few rules too." She froze and narrowed her gaze at him suspiciously. He grinned innocently. "You think I didn't have any?"

She folded her arms under her chest, which only served to push out her breasts a little, something he really didn't need to notice. "What game are you playing?"

"No game. Just setting the ground rules, like you did." He winked. "Where to begin. Ah, clothing. It's always optional for you. And my clothes stay on as long as you want them to."

She burst out with a laugh, stared at him, then laughed again. "You must be joking."

He waggled his eyebrows. "Hailey, I never joke about clothes. Two, I don't need a nursemaid or someone checking up on me. You never go in my room unless you want to spend the night."

She smirked at him, clearly not taking him seriously. "What if I want to do your laundry?"

He leaned back and considered the topic. "Well, I do hate to do laundry. I guess that would be okay. Would you wear a cute little maid's outfit too?"

She slapped his arm, laughing harder now. "You're insane." Finally, her laughter slowed and she sighed. "Thanks, Chase. I needed that. It's been far too long since I've had this much fun. I guess I hadn't realized how stressed I've been."

This time, he felt comfortable enough to reach out and draw her close. "This is why you came home, to have people around you to help you. Come work here. You'll love it. And

A.J. will have a blast."

For a moment, she rested against him, letting her head lay on his shoulder, a warm, comforting weight that felt so right when so many other women only felt cloying. Finally, she straightened, moving out of his arms and leaving him feeling oddly bereft.

"Thank you, Chase. I'm looking forward to working here. But I think you need some looking after too, so I can't promise that I won't be doing a little of that while you're here."

He sighed, sounding completely put upon. "If I must. I'll take a sponge bath if you're offering."

She pushed him away, laughing the whole time.

Chapter Five

A COUPLE OF days into his enforced recuperation and Chase was already going crazy. Tara had spent each day at the house, supposedly working—preparing for the guest ranch operations, setting up hunting and fishing tours—but the reality was she spent more time nursing him, babying him, and, worst of all, bullying him. Now, she'd hired someone to ostensibly help her with the guest ranch, but she'd also made it clear that Hailey was to keep an eye on him, babysit him like he was a child. To avoid taking out his bad temper on her, he'd fled the house for the security of the barn—although, judging by the gleam in her eyes, that had been her plan all along.

He didn't want to snap at either one of them, but it was bound to happen if he stayed in the house. He knew he was a downright cranky bastard when he was injured. And he'd never been hurt this bad before and had never been out for this long.

He'd taken the cane, even though it galled his pride to use it, but he suspected that he'd need it for the walk back from the barn, and the last thing he'd want was to ask someone to help him, whether with an ATV or a helping hand. Then they'd be all over him, wrapping him in cotton and hiring a nursemaid, and not some pretty young thing but that evil bitch from *Misery* or, worse yet, a male nurse.

He made his way down the groomed dirt path toward the barn, admiring the upgrades to the old ranch. Tara and West had certainly done a lot of work in the month or so he'd been on the road. This old ranch had been her grandparents' property, merged with her father's place when her parents had married. Once they passed on, it had been rented out to ranch foremen and workers but slowly fell into disuse. Now, it was coming back to life, with landscaping and flowers added to enhance the place. The barns had been repaired and painted a deep red with white accents, and the corrals had been upgraded with strong, white fencing to be safer for horses and more appealing to guests. It was looking more and more like a fancy lodge than a working ranch, though. Not all the buildings had been renovated, but he could see scaffolding and people working on those sites. It was a good start, even if they weren't getting any official lodgers until the next spring.

A couple of horses walked over to the fence as he drew closer, nickering to him, curious about the stranger in their domain. He rubbed their noses gently and grinned when they nuzzled his pockets, looking for treats. Someone had already been spoiling them, getting them used to people and teaching them to be friendly to guests. Fortunately, Chase always had a little something in his pocket just for these occasions.

He pulled out two peppermints and held one in each hand. Both horses lipped them gently. An unusual treat, but one he'd found horses loved, so he bought the candy for just these occasions. He rubbed the spot between their eyes, and both horses leaned into him, enjoying the scratches as much as the treat.

"I see you're already making friends with our newest additions," Ty said from the open barn door on Chase's right. He stepped up to the corral and rubbed one horse's neck. "What do you think?"

Chase ran a hand down the neck of the chestnut, feeling the solid muscle and ease with which the horse let him touch her. He leaned over and eyed the rest of her as best he could, then did the same with the bay Ty was patting. "They appear to have good lines and conformation. The temperament is solid, and they're friendly enough and don't seem to startle easy. I can take a closer look in a few days when I'm more mobile. Where did you get them?"

Ty gave the bay a gentle push and folded his hands on the top of the fence. "We found them at a trail horse auction. I was surprised at how many ranches were there. These seemed pretty solid and good for trail riding."

Chase snorted. "How did you assess them beyond looking at them? Trail riding horses are different than working horses, you know."

Ty took his hat off, rubbed the dark hair off his forehead and put on his best hayseed look. "Gee, I had no idea. I read a few articles on the computer at the library and thought these horses looked mighty fine." He slapped Chase, almost knocking him over. "I'm not an idiot, asshole. I know what to look for. It would have been easier if you had been here, but you were busy getting your ass handed to you by a bull, so we made do."

Chase grimaced. "That wasn't exactly the plan. I had

won the round and would have taken the purse if I could have ridden in the final round."

Ty slapped his hat on his head. "Yeah, well, you know what Douglas used to say. 'If wishes were horses.' Now, come see some of the other horses we've added. I'd love your take on them."

Chase followed him into the barn, noting how open the barn appeared, bright and cheery, not exactly like the working barn on the ranches he was used to. A couple of horses popped their heads out of their stalls, nosy beasts all of them, which boded well for their duties. Guests liked horses who showed an interest in them, had personality and spirit. But they needed them to be safe and steady on the trail, because it was likely that most of their guests had rarely been on a horse or had varying degrees of experience, and there were a lot of distractions and obstacles on a trail, like branches, critters, or running water. Even if they bought proven trail horses, they'd need to be trained on their trails. But more often, horses were sold as trail horses when they didn't make the cut in another area such as the show ring or rodeo circuit or even as a cattle horse, which was a damned shame because a good trail horse was a skilled ride in their own right. So, he was skeptical about the horses bought even at the trail horse auction.

But after checking out the dozen or so horses in the barn, he was cautiously optimistic. They seemed to be solid working horses, with good conformation, quiet, laid-back dispositions, and what appeared to be positive attitudes. But he wouldn't really know that until he got them under the saddle. And right now, he needed about a week before he could ride with his knee and ribs.

All of this he told Ty, who nodded thoughtfully.

"Well, we expected that, which is why we didn't buy too many. I thought maybe West and I could try to work these out until you got back from the circuit and could train them properly. But maybe your injury comes at a good time if you'll be able to ride while you're recovering." Ty shot a pointed look at Chase's leg.

"My leg isn't the problem; it's my ribs. I probably can't work cows, but I can ride as long as the horses are easygoing, which these should be. Are you taking over this part of the operation?" Chase hiked his butt up on a tall stool to rest his knee while Ty leaned against one of the stall doors.

"We were hoping you'd take it over, little brother. Horses were always more your specialty," West said from the doorway, where he stood framed with Tara by his side.

Tara beamed at Chase as if she were a proud mama watching her baby take his first steps into the wide world. She raced forward and gave him a hug, careful of his ribs. "I'm so glad you left your room. What do you think of the barn? We're not quite done yet, but we wanted it to be more open than your other barns so the guests would feel comfortable walking in and out to see the horses and maybe even help out."

Chase couldn't help but laugh. "You expect the guests to pay to shovel shit? I'd love to see that." West scowled at him and Chase sobered. "But the barn is real nice, Tara. As is the whole place. You've done some great work here."

Her smile grew even bigger and then her attention was caught by another horse at the end of the row of stalls, a somewhat gaunt, dull chestnut who peered at them, the whites of her eyes flashing. Tara's expression softened and she walked slowly down the aisle, crooning nonsensical words under her breath designed to ease the horse. The horse's head jerked up and down but didn't retreat from Tara even as she crept closer until she stood a few feet away. She held out her hand with an apple in the flat of her hand. The horse sniffed it and jerked away. They repeated this cycle a couple of times, and then the horse took the apple, retreating into the stall to eat the treat.

Tara backed away slowly and turned, beaming at them. "That was quicker than yesterday. She's beginning to trust me."

West slowly let out a breath Chase hadn't realized he had been holding and smiled too. "Sure, baby. She's getting used to you. Why don't you check on the other horses?"

Tara went to pet the other horses while West met Chase's gaze. "You bought her an abused horse? Are you crazy?"

"Well, we basically rescued the beast. She wouldn't let anyone else have her and felt she deserved a good home. I couldn't say no." West shrugged.

"You're so whipped. You know that horse will probably never be a trail horse or cow horse. You may never be able to do anything with her," Chase stated flatly.

"You could help her," Tara called over from one of the stalls. "It's what you do best. I'll bet you have her eating out of your hand in no time. She wouldn't bite you like she bit Lew."

"Lew?"

A lanky young kid sauntered around the corner in that moment, pushing an empty wheelbarrow. He nodded at everyone standing by the tack room then froze when he caught sight of Chase, his jaw gaping open for a moment. The kid dropped the wheelbarrow with a clank and almost ran over. Chase gave an internal sigh. Well, at least most of the horses barely twitched, except for that crazy mare of Tara's. Maybe the others would do for the trail.

"You're Chase Summers. Holy shit . . . I mean cow. Wow."

The kid's eyes couldn't get any bigger if they tried. Hero worship always made Chase uncomfortable—well, unless it was a woman and he was looking to get laid for the night, but even then, he hated it. Hell, it wasn't like he was a hero or anything. He just rode a fucking bull for eight seconds, and many times he never made it that far. It's not like he ran into flaming buildings or faced bullets or bad guys to save the world. He held a rope and tried not to get killed by a big-ass beast.

He shifted on the stool. "You must be Lew. Nice to meet you."

"I saw you ride once, you know. In Missoula. You were awesome! Last year." The kid tried to be casual but couldn't hide the awe in his voice while Ty and West looked on with broad grins on their faces. They were going to be all over his ass later for this.

Chase racked his brain, trying to remember the event. "Oh yeah, I drew Quick Draw in the finals. Biggest bastard, next to Oleander. He dumped me in three seconds."

"At least he didn't kick your ass too," Ty drawled. Chase

shot him a glare. Like he needed the constant reminders.

Lew looked at Chase's ribs then knee. "I heard about your injury. How are you doing? Are you here for a while or going back on the circuit?"

Ty clapped a hand on the kid's shoulder. "We'll talk more about that later. For now, Chase will be giving us a hand around here with the horses. Lew Kirby is our stable hand for the guest ranch. We're training him to be the head stable hand, once he finishes school. We'll hire more staff when we bring in more horses. Right now, we only need horses for the hunting and fishing tours."

Lew nodded. "I mainly clean the stables and groom and exercise the horses right now, but I want to train them too. My dad trained horses mainly for the rodeo, but he got sick a few years ago and had to stop. I need more experience, but I'm eager to learn. I've heard that you have the touch with horses. My dad talked about you all the time."

West and Ty's faces were expressionless, but Chase still felt the weight of their expectations on him. They hoped he would stay and work this side of the business, help Lew settle in and be Chase's assistant. They probably were slowly setting all of this up and hoped to present it as a done deal when he came home at the end of the season. No one expected he'd be home this soon or with an injury.

"Your dad is Chuck Kirby?"

Lew nodded eagerly.

"He's a good trainer. I heard about his heart. He taught me a lot about horses when I was growing up here. You listened to everything he told you?"

The kid blushed. "I tried."

Chase grinned. "You wouldn't be a kid if you listened to everything. Well, at least you didn't go on the rodeo circuit. That was the smartest thing you could do."

Lew's head jerked up. "Dad would kill me. Besides, my parents need my help. And I have to finish school." The last was said with a sideways glance at West who nodded once.

Ty stepped in. "Finish cleaning the stalls and then we'll talk about the next tasks. Chase will be here for a few weeks. You can pump him for stories later."

Chase nodded and the kid ran back to his wheelbarrow, heading into a stall at the far end of the barn. "How old is he? Sixteen? And you want to put him in charge?"

"Just of the stalls and shit. We really want to put you in charge, but you're not here. So, we wait until you're ready. In the meantime, we need contingencies. And Ty isn't the contingency. He's stepping up, but it's not his thing."

Chase winced. "I've been stepping up, West. For years. I've sent home my winnings as often as I can to help keep the ranch going. We both know settling down isn't for me."

"What happens the next time? Or when you're too old to ride the bulls? What will you do then? Just think about it, okay? That's all we're asking." West gripped his good shoulder and peered into his eyes. "We appreciate all your sacrifices you made for us and this ranch, brother. We're telling you that you don't have to do it anymore. We want you to come home."

Well, fuck. What was he supposed to say to that?

Chapter Six

CHASE MADE SURE he was at the barn the day Hailey moved in. He had told her that he was okay with her moving in, encouraged it even, and he was, but having her in the same house with him every night for the next few weeks was going to be torture. Time hadn't lessened the attraction he felt for her and reminding himself that she was his best friend's wife didn't help matters either. But it was only for a few weeks, and he had to keep telling himself that he was headed back on the road and had nothing to offer her and her son but a vagabond life. He was not the settling down kind of guy. Hailey was a white picket fence, fancy house, and respect job kind of woman all rolled up in one neat package.

Chase had never known his parents. He'd been abandoned within a few months of birth on a church's doorstep, which was the closest he'd come to God in his whole life. From then on, he'd been condemned to be bounced from foster home to foster home in a downward spiral of despair, totally belying the belief that babies got adopted quicker than older children. Probably everyone back then sensed something about him, sensed that he was tainted and didn't deserve anything better.

He'd resolved years ago that he'd never marry or have a

family, never condemn a child to carry his DNA, and consoled himself with good-time buckle bunnies who knew the score. He also learned quickly who would stay and who wouldn't, and since most people didn't stick around he contented himself with the ones who wanted the same things. When he was done with the rodeo, he was lucky enough to have a place to come home to, thanks to a generous foster father who'd saved him and two other men who were brothers by everything but blood. He'd satisfy himself working the ranch and being an uncle to West and Tara's kids.

A pair of gloves smacked him on the side of the head. "Are you going to pull your head out of your ass and help us or stand there mooning like a calf all day?"

Chase bent over and picked up the work gloves and glared at Ty. "Just what are you expecting me to do with these? Climb into the hayloft and toss down bales? Don't think I'm cleared for that."

Ty snorted from inside the tack room. "No shit. Why don't you take Lola out to the corral for some exercise? Work her on the lead. Or is standing in a circle too much for your delicate constitution?"

Chase shot Ty a hand signal but took the offered lead and headed for the pretty chestnut mare's stall to check out her paces, which is what Ty really wanted him to do. At least he'd feel useful for once instead of standing around as helpful as teats on a bull, watching the work get done. Hell, this injury thing was for the birds. He was past ready to get on with life. At least he was out of bed and moving around per the doctor's orders. Apparently, hanging around in bed or lazing around the house was actually worse for his lungs. Fortunately, he had been able to ditch the damned cane most of the time.

Unfortunately, the corral was in full view of the house, and he had a clear shot of Hailey in her tight shorts and T-shirt, bringing boxes in and out of the house, stuff he should be helping her with, only it had been deemed "too much lifting" for his condition. Like he was a fucking pussy. So, he was relegated to the barn to walk a horse around with Ty to monitor him while West and a couple of ranch hands helped her out. Story of his life. Other people helped Hailey while he walked away.

Lola reared, pulling his attention rather forcibly back to her, and he drew her in carefully, rubbing her nose as she calmed.

"Why did she do that?"

A little voice spoke from somewhere toward the bottom of the fence and Chase peered through the railings to see a strawberry-blond kid peeking back at him. As he got a closer look, it was like a sucker punch to the gut. This had to be A.J., Adam's son. God, he looked so much like his best friend that it hurt. This little guy had Adam's eyes and face, but the freckles that dusted his nose and cheeks were all his mother's. The main difference was the eyes. Adam's eyes always had a hint of mischief in them, laughing as if he enjoyed everything about the world. This little boy's eyes were big and solemn as if he'd already seen too much and been forced to be too serious.

Chase swallowed hard past the sudden lump in his throat. "Well, like any lady, she doesn't like me paying attention to another woman while I'm with her."

The boy carefully climbed the lower rung of the fence so he could see a little better. "What other woman?"

Chase smothered a smile. "Well, I was looking at the woman moving into the house over there, and Lola here got a little jealous and decided to remind me that I was with her right now."

A.J.'s head cocked to the side as if he were thinking over Chase's words. "There's only my mom over there. Well, and this other lady I don't really know. But you can tell your horse not to be jealous of my mom. She's my mom."

He said the last two words as if somehow being a mom meant she was gender neutral or not attractive. Although, to a six-year-old son, she probably was. That didn't mean Chase didn't want her any less.

Lola snorted and tossed her head, still not happy. Chase drew her close and rested his hand on her neck, soothing her with soft words. She settled quickly, confirming his thoughts that she needed work but was a gentle horse. Perfect for trail rides and maybe for a boy's first introduction.

He eyed the boy perched on the corral railings. There it was, that hint of mischief that had resided in Adam's eyes. Chase knew a boy couldn't be so serious all the time. "Do you want to meet Lola?" A.J. nodded vigorously and made as if to climb over the fence, but Chase shook his head. "No, you stay right where you are and be quiet and still. Remember, horses are big creatures and spook easily."

A.J. was almost bouncing on the fence. "Mom took me to a rodeo once, and I rode a pony."

Chase resisted the urge to roll his eyes. Those damned

ponies at fairs were saints to deal with kids all day. "Well, that pony was pretty docile, but most horses are more high-strung and will spook at the slightest things, or nothing at all. You see how big Lola is? You don't want her to get all nervous, do you? She could hurt someone. Always be quiet and calm when you approach a horse, or, better yet, let them approach you."

When he was satisfied that A.J. was calm, Chase led Lola to the fence. He had a good hold on the lead, keeping it short, making sure she knew he was in charge. She followed him docilely to the little boy, who seemed to be trying hard not to jump out of his pants.

"Now, let her check you out and decide if she wants you to pet her. Hold your hand out flat so she doesn't nibble your fingers and stay still."

Lola lipped at his hand and A.J. giggled, pulling his hand back. Lola snorted, lifting her head, but immediately lowered it for more attention. Chase dug in his pocket with his other hand and found a peppermint. He was saving this for after their training session, but this was just as important.

"Hold out your hand again, flat." When A.J. complied, he laid the treat in his palm. "Now, offer it to Lola. Don't close your hand."

A.J.'s eyes were wide as Lola gently took the treat from him with her lips and crunched the peppermint. He turned to Chase, a broad grin creasing his face. "She ate a candy like my grandma has. I thought horses only like sugar and apples and carrots."

Chase rubbed Lola's neck. "They do, but peppermints are extra special treats. Only given when I say they can have them." He sensed he'd better add that or the boy would be doling out the peppermints constantly.

A.J. nodded solemnly. "Kind of like ice cream. Only when Momma says I can."

"Exactly."

A.J. followed Chase's motions on Lola's nose, and soon the horse was in ecstasy at being the center of attention. Chase's knee ached a bit and he leaned on the fence, letting the silence grow between them. He had no idea how to talk to a kid, hadn't spent much time around them since he had been one, and when he had been one, well, no one really wanted to talk to him.

"My dad rode horses. He was a rodeo star." A.J. finally said the words quietly, as if afraid to spook Lola.

Chase swallowed again. "I know. Your dad loved to ride."

"I wish I could ride, but we lived in a city and there's no place for horses there." The words were matter-of-fact, practiced, like something he'd heard his mother say multiple times.

Panic rose inside of Chase. What the hell was he supposed to say now? When a woman said things like that, she was fishing for Chase to buy her something or do something with her, although they rarely asked for him to take them on a horseback ride. Another kind of ride, maybe, but not with horses.

A.J. didn't seem to be hinting around for Chase to do anything, but what did Chase know about kids? He glanced around, looking for someone, anyone who could maybe run interference in the conversation.

A shadow moved in the barn doorway. Ty flashed a grin and ducked back inside. Asshole. Running from the kid. He'd get him back later. But for now, what the hell to do with Adam's son?

HAILEY TOOK A deep breath and thanked the hands who had offered their help unloading her Ford Explorer. Now the real work began, unpacking and settling herself and A.J. in the house. Chase had been absent; he wasn't able to move the boxes easily yet and so he was down at the barn with the horses. Hailey had tossed and turned all night at the potential of seeing him again, but the band that had wrapped tightly around Hailey's chest eased when Tara told her that Chase was going to be at the barn during her move. Only she wasn't sure if she was nervous or excited.

She glanced around now. A.J. wasn't sitting in the living room playing games on her tablet anymore. The tablet lay discarded on the end table, but the boy was nowhere to be found. Her heart raced as she ran through the house calling his name, but the house was empty. Everyone had scattered to their own jobs once they had unloaded her car, and Tara said she was going to grab some lunch.

Hailey stood on the porch, her pulse pounding in her throat. A.J. had never wandered off in the city. She had always been so clear to him about staying close and telling her where he was going. But out here, where it all appeared safe and no one was around, he might think he was alone. He wouldn't even know the hidden dangers that lurked, like animals or getting lost. God, what if he had gotten into a pasture where the bulls were? What had Tara told her about the summer pasturing for the cows and bulls? Had A.J. followed someone? Maybe to the barn?

She shaded her eyes and looked toward the barn, seeing a tall man she knew instantly was Chase, standing at the fence with a horse. A smaller figure had clambered onto the rails and stretched precariously to reach the horse. She let out a shaky breath and pressed a hand to her chest. God, A.J.'s obsession with horses and his father was going to give her a heart attack.

She used the walk to the barn to slow her breathing and pray that her hands would stop shaking. Fortunately, by the time she got to the corral, she had mastered the urge to grab A.J. and hug him close. Now she wanted only to shake him and impress on him the fear he had put her through. But neither were great responses to the situation. Instead, she pasted on a smile and slowly approached the fence.

"So, this is where you'd gotten off to. I've been looking everywhere for you, young man." She was proud that her voice wasn't shaking, and she seemed almost calm.

But Chase seem to sense her tension and flashed that charming, sexy smile that had gotten him out of a lot of trouble—and into a lot of beds—in the past. "He was well within sight of the house, just a short distance away. He was fine, Hailey."

She barely avoided rolling her eyes but only because her son was watching and she had to be careful. "That's not the point, Chase. I didn't know where he was. He's not used to the ranch and he could have gone anywhere, gotten into trouble, and no one would have known."

Chase leaned against the fence. "Come on, Hailey. Adam and I spent years roaming both this ranch and his. No one checked on us or anything."

"You weren't six years old and you grew up here."

"I didn't, but you're right; I was older. But he was in sight of the house. What could have happened?"

"A rattler could bite him. A horse could hurt him. He could wander somewhere and face off with a bull. He could get lost. Any number of things."

Chase sighed and sidled closer to her, lowering his voice so only she could hear, while A.J. continued to lavish attention on the horse. "Hailey, rattlers around here are rare. They're mostly in the mountains, near the rocky areas, although it can happen. We tend to keep our mice population under control with barn cats so they find other places for food and shelter. The bulls are in the summer meadow, a long distance away. Has he ever wandered out of sight?"

She bit her lower lip. Some of her scenarios were a bit out there, but she wasn't wrong. "No, but that's not the point. He's my son and needs to know that he should tell me where he's going. He's too little to be exploring alone. And yes, I know the barn is not that far, but what if no one had been here?" She planted her hands on her hips. "Chase, you're not his father, but I am his mother. This is a nonnegotiable rule. Understand?"

Chase flinched but nodded. "As you wish, Hailey."

He stepped back, moving the horse away too. A.J.'s head lifted and he protested the move. Hailey smoothly stepped into the breach, holding out her hand. "Chase has work to do and so do we. Let's leave him to it and get to ours. If we don't unpack your room, you won't have a bed to sleep in tonight and you'll have to sleep on the floor."

"Like camping?"

His voice sounded way too excited. Hailey shot Chase a glare that promised retribution for any glorified stories he may have been sharing with her son about his wild adventures with A.J.'s father. Chase only shrugged and turned his attention back to the horse. She force-marched A.J. back to the house.

A firm outline of the rules was in order for both the men in her life.

Chapter Seven

H AILEY WAS ABLE to avoid Chase for the rest of the day
and keep A.J. occupied in the house, settling into his
new room. Her son had an obsession with cleaning things,
which she admitted was odd for a six-year-old, but she wasn't
going to argue with it, especially when she needed to keep his
attention diverted for a while. But she wasn't going to be
able to keep him inside every day, nor would she want to.
That would defeat the purpose of moving out of the city and
to the country. She wanted him to have the freedom to play
outside and have more fun than he would in an apartment.
He had too much of her husband in him; A.J. longed for
something more.

Fortunately, she had prepared for this eventuality and
had enrolled A.J. in the last few weeks of a summer camp.
She'd had to beg, cajole, and plead her case to the director,
and basically promise to help find ways to improve his
program for next year and increase enrollment until he'd
reluctantly made an exception for her son. Her mother
wasn't thrilled, since she had hoped to spend time with A.J.,
but she was still recovering and didn't need an active boy
wreaking havoc in her house. Besides, Dad had made it plain
they weren't babysitters, although he had bent enough to
being open to watching him occasionally.

After the long, tiring day of moving, they had joined the Redemption Ranch family for a welcome to the family dinner at the main house, driving over with Chase, who wasn't quite in shape to walk the distance yet. He hadn't said much to them, only waited in what was designated to be the registration area of the guesthouse until they were ready and escorted them to his truck. She mentioned that she could drive in her car, but he only gave her a hard stare until she capitulated. She told herself she only agreed because she was tired and it made sense to save gas since they were going to the same place, but she kind of liked having someone else drive. It felt like someone was taking care of her.

She had expected dinner to be awkward, but she enjoyed the casual conversation, the joking between the brothers and the easy way they accepted A.J. at the table. No one even minded when he knocked over his glass of milk or asked a bunch of questions. The guys talked about bulls and breeding at one point while Hailey and Tara talked a little about their plans, though Tara kept swearing she didn't want to talk shop that night. Chase's eyes kept straying to her during the dinner, but she couldn't read anything in his expression.

By the time they got back, the sun was setting and A.J. was drooping in the seat between her and Chase. He parked the truck near the house and she slid out. She unbuckled A.J. but, before she could lift him, Chase was reaching across her to grab her son.

"He's too heavy. You'll hurt yourself," she protested but only to Chase's back as he walked steadily into the house with only a slight limp.

He paused at the bottom of the stairs that led to their

rooms, as if daunted by them. She lifted a hand to touch his back and hesitated, the heat from his back radiating to her palm, even though they weren't touching. Just an inch or so remained between them, but it may as well have been miles. It had been so long since she'd been this close to Chase. Too much had come between them—time, circumstances, memories.

She shifted to rest her hand on A.J.'s head. "He's awake enough to make the stairs. We'll be fine."

Chase nodded and gently set A.J. on the floor. He rubbed his eyes and yawned, holding his hand up for his mother. She led him upstairs, feeling Chase's eyes on her the whole way.

Less than an hour later, A.J. was sleeping soundly with his stuffed horse, Randall, and Hailey debated between going downstairs or collapsing in bed. But she had things to say to Chase and she doubted he'd be in bed yet. The real question was if he were still at the ranch or if he had gone into town to pick up a lady for the evening.

She bypassed her room and headed downstairs, where she heard the gentle creaking of a rocking chair on the porch. Through the window, she saw the back of Chase's head, resting against the top of the chair, his sandy-brown hair messy as if he'd been running his hands through it. She paused for only a second then headed out, unable to resist the call of the quiet Montana summer night and the lonely man sitting on the porch.

The wood screen door banged against the doorframe, but Chase never jumped. Instead, he gestured to the table to his right.

"I wasn't sure if you prefer wine now, but I only have beer in the fridge."

She walked past him and grabbed the beer as she sat in the other rocking chair. "Fortunately for you, I haven't lost the taste, not that I've had a lot of chances to drink in the past few years." She studied the label. "Ivan the Terrible stout? This is an upgrade from our cheap Pabst or whatever we could afford back then."

He grunted and tilted the bottle, taking a long swallow. "What can I say? I guess I've refined my taste over the past few years."

She took her own drink and coughed. "That's definitely darker than I've had, but I like it. Might take some getting used to though." She paused for a moment. "How did you know I'd be coming out here?"

He took another long drink of the beer. "Just hopeful, I guess. Or maybe I knew you wanted to talk about earlier."

She rested her head against the back of the old rocker and let it move gently on the porch, ignoring his words for a moment. The summer breeze coasted over her, cooling her after the heat of the day. The evening sounds of the birds and insects created a symphony of sounds much more soothing than the cars and people that she was accustomed to back in Billings. In the distance, the sound of horses in the barn, a dog barking, and even farther out, a coyote howling, added to the music of the night. For the first time since she had come home, her muscles relaxed and she closed her eyes, letting everything soak into her soul, easing her spirit and soothing her.

"I missed this," she said quietly. "The city has nothing

COMING HOME TO THE COWBOY

on the country. I don't know how you ever left."

"I had to go. The ranch needed the money and I was good at riding bulls. It was the only thing I was ever really good at. Yeah, I could punch cows, but so could anyone else. Besides, I had an urge to see the world, see what existed beyond Granite Junction and Montana."

"You're an adrenaline junkie, Chase. Working the ranch is a little slow for you, not enough action." She smiled at him. "I should know. Adam was the same way. Why do you think he followed you on the circuit?"

For the first time since she'd sat down, he looked at her. "I thought you would blame me for his death."

She blinked, surprised. Chase studied her carefully in the twilight, his dark eyes unwavering and solemn, not the laughing, carefree man she remembered from her youth. What had happened to him? Finally, she exhaled. "Maybe at one time I blamed you, only because it was easy."

He started to turn away, his eyes reflecting pain, but she reached across the small table and grabbed his hand, forcing his attention back to her. "But that was wrong. Adam was his own man, and he was a lot like you in many ways. He was addicted to the excitement, the danger. He loved taking risks and, when the ranch started struggling, the last thing he wanted was to put in the time to make it work. He saw the circuit as a way to make some money, have some fun, and maybe help us out. But the reality was, he wanted the fun of the road rather than the responsibility of a ranch or, maybe, being a father. I loved Adam, but he just wasn't ready for what his father needed, what I needed."

Chase turned away, tilting the bottle again to drain it,

staring out into the night. "You're wrong. I am exactly as selfish as Adam was. And he loved you and A.J. He was on the road for you both."

"Was he?" The words bubbled up from somewhere deep inside, words she had never given voice to before now, words she had not wanted to acknowledge ever but somehow had accepted over the past four years. "Is that why I was a single mother even before my husband died? Adam stayed on the road longer than he needed, avoiding coming home when he could. Oh, he said it was to save money, but I have to wonder if he had other reasons. Maybe women? Fun times? I know screaming babies, diapers, and late-night feedings aren't fun."

Chase steadfastly avoided her and stared at the barn as if the answers to all of her questions were somewhere written on the red wooden sides or the white trim.

She snorted. "You don't need to answer. I already know."

Chase sighed heavily. "It wasn't like that. Adam wasn't like that. He loved you."

She smiled a little ruefully. "I know he did. We were probably too young or too naive to make it work. Or maybe we were looking for an escape and found it in each other."

"Why did you leave Granite Junction? You could have settled on his daddy's ranch. Maybe Adam would have come home and worked it once you had A.J.," Chase said.

She scoffed. "You know Adam had no interest in the land, and those two fought like two cornered wolverines. Besides, the ranch needed so much more than either Adam or his father could do to resurrect it. Whatever happened to it?"

"Cam Miller bought out the herd that remained and the land too. He's got the second-largest ranch in the county now."

She smiled. "I always liked Cam. His sister was a couple of years behind me in school, but I knew her pretty well. And the girls all had crushes on him."

She cast a sideways glance at Chase, who scowled at the corral but only grunted. "He's too busy for any of that now. The life of a rancher. But you're right; that never suited Adam. Neither did city life, so why Billings?"

Hailey shrugged and took a long sip of her beer. "I went to school there and had a better shot of finding a job that could support us there. Besides, you know how my dad felt about Adam. It would have been different if the ranch had been successful, or maybe not. Who knows? He's not a big fan of the ranching way of life. And cowboys? Even less. So, when I got pregnant so soon after we got married, we decided to settle in Billings where I could find work to support us. Adam could come in and out quickly with the airport. Who knows what would have happened next, after his rodeo days were over. We never got that far."

Chase stood and walked to the railing, clenching the wood tightly. After a minute, he turned to look at her, his eyes intent like laser beams focused on her. "He showed pictures of A.J. everywhere, you know. He loved you both. He may have done some things he may not have been especially proud of, but that was near the end. He got a little lost, I think. But he loved you both, Hailey. You have to know that."

His words were a soothing balm on the wound she didn't

think she still had, the small aching part of her heart that still wondered what had happened between her and Adam and what would have happened if he hadn't had the bad luck to get bucked off that bull and stomped on in that arena so far from home. Would they have made it, or would they have continued to drift apart, allowing distance and time to create the divide that was already between them until they were no more than polite strangers, meeting up when the bull-riding season was over or on hiatus? At least she had some comfort in knowing he did care and wasn't cheating the whole time he was gone. They did have something real most of the time. Chase wouldn't lie to her, not about this.

Chase started to head down the stairs, and she remembered what she had come outside for. "Hang on, mister. We have something else to discuss."

He froze, then half-pivoted as if facing a firing squad. She gestured to the seat next to her, but he shook his head. "I think I've had enough deep conversations for one night. Hell, for one year. You may have forgotten, but I'm not big on the soul-searching, touchy-feely kind of conversations. If you want to have those, talk to West. He's got a girl now, so he's gotten soft. Or better yet, talk to Tara. She'd love to have another girl to bond with."

"Nope, this is between you and me and won't take long. It's about A.J."

He groaned. "Let me guess. I'm not a fit role model for the boy and you want me to stay away from him."

She rolled her eyes. "God, why do you have to be such a drama queen? It's just a conversation. I have rules, rules I'd appreciate you follow for my son. Mine. I'd appreciate it if you didn't counter me in front of him."

Chase's whole body relaxed and he came back up the steps to lean his lanky body on the railing. "Hailey, he was a couple hundred feet from the house, in full sight of you. And I could see him. When I was his age—"

She arched her brow. "Yes, Chase. Please tell me what you were doing at his age."

His whole face shut down and went blank. "No, I don't think that's a good idea. My past is nothing you'd want your son to live. But this is Granite Junction and the ranch. What could happen here?"

She stood and walked over to the railing next to him, facing the corral. "Maybe it seems safe to you because you know the place so well. A.J. has lived in Billings his whole life, and believe me, I would never let him wander alone there. He's not used to the outdoors. He doesn't know the land, the animals, or how to interact here. He's just a little boy."

"And he'll stay that way as long as you coddle him." Chase sighed. "But you're right. I don't know anything about kids. Hell, the way I grew up, no one gave a hairy rat's ass about where I was or what I was doing unless it came time for the support checks. I ran wild and got into more trouble than I can tell you."

She laughed. "Now, why doesn't that surprise me? Even when Douglas cared, you got into trouble. Please don't share any of those stories with A.J. He'll get ideas."

Chase quirked that adorable smile that got women to drop their panties and hop into bed faster than they could say "yes, please." "I'll do my best, honey. My point is, you can't tie him to you. He's going to want to explore."

She shifted to her side, hiking her hip on the top rung. "And my point is, he needs to tell me where he's going every time so I know where he is. And you need to back me. Every time."

"Is this another one of those rules?"

"Nonnegotiable." She made sure her voice was firm.

He nodded. "I understand. I'll make sure he checks in with you before he takes off. Anything else?"

She cocked her head. "No, I think that's it."

The twilight had deepened, leaving them in shadow, the only light coming from the lamp that had been left on inside the house spilling out from the windows. With sundown, the air had grown chilly and the breeze wafted over her skin, bared by her shorts and T-shirt, and she shivered. Chase's eyes darkened, and he tucked a strand of her auburn hair that had come loose from her braid behind her ear. Her skin prickled under the brief caress that had nothing to do with the cool breeze and everything to do with the heat left by his touch.

She stood close enough to feel the warmth radiating from his body and, for the first time since Adam had died, she wanted a man. Oh, she'd been on dates, dipping her toes into the small dating pool that existed in Billings. The occasional blind date or friend of a friend. But none of them drew her like a moth to a flame. Like Chase. This had been her real fear when she found out he was living on the ranch. She could pretend otherwise, but even back when they were friends, she couldn't deny the attraction she had felt for him even though it never went beyond the friend zone. It couldn't because it would have hurt Adam and neither of them wanted that.

She had hoped those feelings had died.

But she hadn't buried her libido four years ago. It only seemed like she had, and it was back and it wanted Chase Summers. And he was the absolute worst man for her and her son.

Chase cursed under his breath. "Adam was a goddamned fool."

And he stormed off the porch toward the barn, leaving Hailey behind, sucking in the cool night air, struggling to control her raging hormones that had just woken up after hibernation.

CHASE STORMED INTO the barn as fast as his knee would let him, the pain welcome after his stupidity on the porch. What the hell was he thinking? Adam may have been dead four years now, but that was his wife in the house and Chase had no right getting close to her. This was definitely not what Adam had meant when he asked Chase to look out for Hailey and A.J. Adam would beat his ass if he knew what was on Chase's mind.

A gentle guitar strumming caught his attention, and he strode farther into the barn to find his brother in the empty stall across from the abused horse. He was sitting on a stool, leaning against the wall and playing a soft tune on the guitar, singing in a low voice. The chestnut horse's nose peeked over the stall door just enough to showed that she was interested in the sound—real progress for the abused horse, who had mainly been standing in the back of the stall with her back pressed to the corner so no one could sneak up on her. Poor beast.

Chase slowed his walk and crossed to the other side of the barn across from her so she could see him coming and not get spooked. He wasn't going to try his peppermints with her. They were too small and he worried she would take his hand off getting those treats. Instead, he had a couple of carrot strips. Anything to save his fingers from an accidental bite. Or intentional. With this horse, you never knew.

Once she saw him, he slowly advanced with the treat in his outstretched hand. She snorted and backed away, then advanced. They played the dance a few times, while he stayed steady until she took the treat. Ty continued playing without pause. Chase backed away slowly and into the stall to find a second stool, as if Ty had been waiting. Two beers sat on the barn floor, condensation still collecting on the outside of the bottles.

"Expecting someone?"

"You, dumbass. Took your time." Ty ended the song and laid the guitar in a case behind him. Then he opened one bottle and took a long swallow. "Unless this interferes with your meds."

Chase snorted and opened his own bottle. "I stopped the painkillers a few days ago. I may not be able to punch cattle or haul hay, but I can ride lightly and work with the horses."

Ty nodded. "So, you and Hailey?"

Chase choked on his beer and wiped his mouth on his T-shirt. "Jesus, Ty. Wait until a guy finishes, won't you? And I don't know what you're talking about."

Ty shrugged. "You seemed awfully close on the porch."

"You spying on me now? We're roommates. We're bound to talk once in a while."

Ty only nodded, but a little smirk played about his lips. Chase shoved him, but Ty had braced himself solidly. "Seriously, nothing happened. Besides, her husband was my best friend. I don't poach."

"Was. He died four years ago. That's not poaching. It's called moving on," Ty pointed out.

Chase gave a mirthless laugh. "It's a bad idea. I'm the last thing she needs in her life. Another bull rider who won't be staying around."

"You don't have to go back."

Chase stared at him. "Is that your game? Show me an abused horse, a woman I could like, and hope I decide to stay?"

Ty shrugged again and leaned against the wall, his eyes grave. "You scared us. How long can you keep going on the circuit before a bull kills you? There are other ways to get the adrenaline rush. Hell, use that rush to build an attraction here for the guests. Tara would love it. You don't need to leave."

"I'm tired of hearing the same old, same old. I like riding bulls. I'm good at it, and I have a shot at the championship. Why do you all want to keep pulling me down? What if we told you to stop playing music? How would you feel?"

Ty froze, his face going blank. "Fuck. Man, I'm sorry. Look, I'll shut up about this. You have to know, everyone was freaked out about your injury. But you're right. We're

75

trying to force you into a life you don't want."

Chase ran a hand through his hair. "I'm sorry. I know it wasn't easy to get that call, but bull riding is who I am. I love it and I'm good at it."

Ty clapped a hand on his shoulder. "I get it. I'm sorry. I'll back off. But what are you going to do about Hailey?"

Chase stared at him. "Nothing. I can't pull her into this since I'm leaving in a couple of weeks. I have nothing to offer her. If Adam had been less selfish, he would have left her alone. I need to man up and leave her alone too."

Ty nodded. "It's the right thing to do."

So why did the thought gut him every time?

Chapter Eight

HAILEY WAS UP early to start her first day on the job and make a good first impression with Tara. She had wrestled A.J. to summer camp, even though he hadn't been as thrilled as she had been for his first day, and she was back cleaning the kitchen and brewing a fresh pot of coffee before the start of the day. She had no idea where Chase was, but she assumed he had gotten up early and left since the coffee-pot had been on and half empty. There was a noise on the front porch—Chase may have forgotten something—and she opened the front door to a couple kissing passionately.

Tara pulled her lips from West and gave Hailey a dazed smile. "Sorry for the PDA, but he's headed to the far pasture and staying overnight so I wanted to give him something to remember me by."

West gave her a lazy grin. "It's not like there's going to be any competition for you out there, darlin'. Just cows, cows, and more cows. Trust me. They're not my type."

She punched him in the arm. "Keep it that way, mister. I know it can get mighty lonely on those drives."

West smashed his hat on his head. "Not that lonely." He faced Hailey. "How has it been going with Chase?"

Hailey felt her face flush. "It's fine, not that I've really seen him. I think he's been spending most of his time at the barn."

An oddly satisfied grin crossed West's face and he nodded as if he were happy about something. "Good. If you have any problems, you let us know."

"I can take care of myself," Hailey retorted. Why did people think she wasn't capable of handling Chase or anyone else for that matter?

He tipped his hat, gave Tara one last kiss that threatened to linger, then stomped off the porch toward the black pickup that waited in the driveway.

Tara gave a sigh. "I'm crazy about that man. God knows why."

"Because he's sexy as hell and is head over heels for you?"

Tara laughed. "That'll do it. I take it you're ready to dive right in?"

Within ten minutes they were seated in the office with fresh cups of coffee and two computers booting up.

Tara was clearly a visual person, and they quickly filled the whiteboards on the walls with plans and tasks that needed to be done for the guest ranch. They had so many things to do in a relatively short time that Hailey could easily see how Tara had gotten overwhelmed. Once they had the majority of tasks identified, they began breaking them down to assignments and dividing them between the two of them. But there were still a lot of tasks remaining in the middle that neither one had a lot of experience doing, including the marketing plan, website design, and reservations.

For the first time since accepting the job, Hailey began to have second thoughts about being able to handle it. As if sensing her mood, Tara closed her laptop.

"I think that's enough for one day. We have plenty to get started and a good plan for the future." Tara reached across the desk and took Hailey's hand in hers. "You had some great ideas and some thoughts I hadn't considered to get us going. The layout for the website and the pictures were brilliant. Do you think you'll be able to work on that soon? I don't expect you to do everything yourself. We're going to outsource some of this work, although it would be good if we could learn it so we could do maintenance and anything not major, like for the website. I know you'll want to dive into the financials first and get a good structure set up for that, but I'd really like to get this other stuff going too."

Hailey heaved a sigh of relief. This was her first real shot at doing more than accounting. She had advised other small businesses, but in a smaller capacity, with suggestions and ideas, not a full-blown business plan and start-up ideas. "The financial records won't be a problem. You have a good start here already. We'll start with getting a storyboard in place, a layout so we can see what we'll need, then build the information from there. I might be able to take some of the pictures myself. I dabbled in photography in school, but it's been a while."

"Awesome. I know a web designer from my interior design days. I'm going to use her for my Granite Junction design business, in fact, so we'll use her for this, especially since the e-commerce side might be tricky. The reservations and all that." At Hailey's look of surprise, Tara laughed. "Yeah, I never expected to be doing design work here, but somehow I got roped into doing some renovations and I kind of like it. I get to pick and choose my projects and keep up my skills. I'll be working out of the house until the ranch is up and running. Then I'll probably find an office somewhere if the business gets bigger. I might need an accountant for that, too, if you're free."

"I think I have room for another client, if my current client doesn't mind," Hailey teased, but inside she was dancing. Maybe her dreams of her own business weren't too far off.

"Good. Today, for the next few days, work on your stuff and get a feel for the land. Start marking trail rides and potential walking paths as well. You can grab pictures that way, too, for the website. Chase can help you with that. He has to test some of the new horses for their suitability for riding anyway. West and I are taking a little vacation."

Hailey grinned. "That sounds like fun. Where are you going?"

Tara grimaced and rolled her eyes. "The glamorous life of a rancher. We're headed to Wyoming to see a prize bull to add to our breeding stock. Not exactly Cabo or the Caribbean, but hey, I knew what I was getting into. Bull semen, calving, and breeding. Can't wait."

Hailey laughed. "Well, I spent my honeymoon at a rodeo, so I totally understand."

Tara stared for a long moment. "West had better come up with something way better than that or I'll castrate him. And I know how, sort of."

Both women laughed, then Tara's words sank in. Hailey bit her lower lip. "Maybe I could talk with Ty or one of the hands about showing me around? I don't want to bother Chase when he's still recovering."

Tara looked up from her notebook where she had been scribbling ideas, her eyebrows furrowed. "Well, West was going to ask Ty to head out to the south pasture while we're gone. But if you're not comfortable with Chase, I could have West talk to him."

A flare of alarm raced through Hailey. "Oh no, it's not that. Chase is fine. I just didn't want him to get hurt any more than he already is."

Tara waved her hand. "According to Chase and West, he's supposed to be somewhat active. Not calf-roping, cattle-driving active, but riding is okay. He needs to keep moving to heal, believe it or not. And, honestly, we could use his help assessing the horses for trail rides. The more riding, the better. How're you at riding?"

Hailey shrugged. "It's been years. I haven't exactly had the time or money."

"Perfect. You'll be one of our test subjects. I assume A.J. hasn't done any riding either? We don't have any ponies and will need to add them at some point." Tara glanced at the clock. "Speaking of A.J., it's almost lunchtime. I know you've been wondering what to do with him in the fall after school. Emma knows everything for kids in town. Why don't we head to the diner, grab lunch, and you can check out a few places for him? And we get decent food. Bonus."

Hailey grinned. Sounded like a win to her.

THE BARN WAS quiet when Chase made his way down to the last stall, holding a lead rope in one hand. Lew had groomed all of the horses and turned them out to the pasture for some grazing, all except the chestnut mare who resided by herself at the end of the stable. Lew poked his head out of one of the stalls to see who was walking around but only nodded at Chase and resumed shoveling shit. The mare poked her head out of the stall and rolled her eyes when she saw him coming but didn't retreat. Progress. He held out his hands with some oats in them and she lipped them eagerly without using her teeth. He took a handful more from the bag at his side and held it out to her, this time stroking her gently. Her ears flickered, but she allowed it. The reports appeared true that she wasn't bad tempered, just nervous. He could work with that.

He clipped the lead rope to her halter and waited, talking quietly to her. She froze for a moment then began jerking her head, up and down in a panic. He kept up the slow, one-sided conversation until she settled, and he resumed stroking her, moving to between the eyes. When she was calm, he opened the door and led her out the door and through the stables to the corral.

He spent about an hour with her, walking her around, leading her, and seeing how she responded to him. By the time he'd finished, she was nuzzling him, looking for treats and, more importantly, affection, which he was happy to give. A noise by the fence roused him from his focus with the mare; it was Hailey leaning on the top railing. Her auburn hair was again in a solitary braid down her back, but wisps of hair escaped and glinted in the sunlight. Her dark green T-shirt and worn jeans molded to her slight frame and accentuated the womanly curves she'd gained since the years they had known each other, years she had spent raising her son and married to his best friend. Facts he needed to remember, but right now all he could think about was how sexy she looked leaning on that fence and how right it was to see her there, how he had longed to see her waiting for him and only him after working all day on the ranch.

A strand of hair came loose from her braid and whipped across her face; she tossed it aside and laughed. "I'm not used to being outside so much. I think I need industrial-strength hair spray."

He walked over to the fence, the clopping of the horse's hooves proving she followed him after their short training session. The mare trusted him already. He hitched his bad leg on the lower rung of the fence and tilted his hat to see Hailey better. "Maybe you should just forget the braid and let it loose. And you need a hat, honey. You're going to get sunburned out here."

Her hand flew to her nose and she crinkled it a little. "The bane of all redheads. Pale skin. I should have picked one up in town today. I'll get one tomorrow. And if I left my hair loose, it would be a mess in a few minutes. Impossible to untangle."

He had a momentary vision of her hair mussed and loose on his pillow, and he stifled a groan. *Not the time, Chase.* "A hat will help," he muttered. "What can I do for you?"

"Tara said that they're headed away for a few days, a rancher's vacation or something. I'm going to start looking at the trails for riding and would also like to get some pictures for the website. Tara thought you could help me with that. I'll understand if you can't ride or anything." She stepped away from the fence as if to leave.

"Hang on. I never said I couldn't help you." He frowned, pissed that she was quick to walk away. "Give a guy a chance to respond, Hailey. I'll need to check on the places they want to use. I haven't been back in a while, and I'd like to see the updates for myself. Besides, West asked me to check out the horses for riding, to see if they're suitable. No better way than to actually ride them on the trail. Did you have any specific places in mind?"

Hailey nodded. "Tara has a list and a map. She said you'd know where these places are."

"Perfect. We can start tomorrow, do a few a day maybe. What about A.J.? We don't have any ponies and the horses are too big for him. I don't want to take him double yet until I know how the horses will react."

A big grin crossed her face "Thank you for thinking of him. He'll be at summer camp every day so he can meet a few kids from town before school starts. But he's never ridden before, so he'll need to start slow with riding."

A horse head shoved between them; the mare was tired of being ignored. Instead of being scared, Hailey reached out to the horse, holding her hand flat. "Oh, you're so pretty, aren't you?"

The mare stretched her head and sniffed Hailey's hand then snorted as if disgusted that there was nothing there to eat. Chase handed Hailey an apple slice. "Try this. Flat hand only. We're still not sure how she'll do taking treats."

Hailey held it out and the horse lipped it from her hand gently, crunching the treat and nosing for more. Hailey ran her hand down the center of her face, and the mare leaned into the stroke. "What happened to her?"

"I guess West and Tara found her when they were getting some of the trail horses. Tara couldn't resist her and they brought her back here. Although I have my suspicions about it all."

She spoke quietly to the horse, soft, nonsensical words. The mare pricked her ears but didn't pull back. Hailey held out her hand with another large wedge on it. The mare sniffed it then delicately lipped it from her hand, crunching the treat. Then she looked at Hailey as if expecting more.

Chase relaxed as the mare leaned into Hailey and said quietly, "I think she likes you."

Hailey tried another and she took it just as gently, not showing as much fear. With Hailey's presence, the mare seemed more at ease now even with him. Maybe he should consider having her around for the horse's training sessions. "Maybe she is more afraid of men than women. Interesting."

Hailey slowly ran her hands down the horse's neck. "What's her name?"

Chase paused. Well damn, he hadn't thought about that yet. Naming a horse created more ties, something he hadn't really wanted to create. But if Hailey named her, that wouldn't be so bad.

"She doesn't have one yet. Besides, not sure we'll keep her. She's just eating her weight in feed every day and not giving back. Doubt she'll ever be a good trail horse. We can't afford to keep taking in strays all the time." A tiny voice whispered in the back of his mind, *Douglas took you in and didn't know if you'd contribute.*

"That's awful. She needs a name. Then she'll know she's

welcome here and wanted." Hailey glared at him for a moment, then resumed stroking the mare's neck and crooning musically to her.

God, she had to stop stroking the horse. He was getting jealous of the beast, wanting her hands on him, running over his skin, talking to him just like that. "Hey, I'm just saying this is a business and we can't keep taking on animals who can't pull their weight. Literally, in her case. I mean, we have bills and feed isn't cheap."

"Then you should help her, make her a contributing member of the ranch. Haven't I heard that you're one of the best trainers around?" He could feel the ropes tightening around him, especially when Hailey gave him her most disappointed look.

He held up his hands in surrender. "Okay, okay. I give up. We'll name her and I'll work with her, see what I can do. Since she seems to like you, why don't you name her?"

Hailey ran her gaze over the beautiful chestnut, considering her options. "She's gorgeous, or will be once she fills out. Her coat and lines are really nice. She carries herself like a queen and deserves a royal name. Cleopatra."

Chase eyed the horse, trying to see what Hailey saw. "She's a looker, or will be, that's for sure. Cleopatra? That's a mouthful."

"Cleo for short. But she's a queen, taken advantage of by men, but she knows her mind."

He considered the horse, who met his gaze as if challenging him then sighed dramatically. "Fine, Cleo it is. But if anyone gives me any shit over it, I'm sending them to you."

She laughed, the sound wrapping around him like music,

and he felt lighter immediately, happy. "Your family isn't so bad. Will you be training her?"

Hailey sent him a sideways glance, and he shrugged. "West wants me to come home and work with the horses. He thinks by dangling an abused horse, along with a stable full of other horses, he might get me to reconsider going back on the circuit. Doesn't help that they're constantly telling me how scared they were with that call."

"Can you blame them?" Her words were soft, and she was focused on the horse, but he froze at the underlying pain in her voice. "I remember getting that call, Chase. It was the middle of the night. Nothing good ever comes of a call in the middle of the night. And you guys are always riding late, it seems."

She stopped stroking the horse and stared off in the distance, but she wasn't seeing the mountains or the fields, only the past. Chase pushed the horse away and wanted to pull her in his arms, but the fence and years of distance separated them, not to mention the ghost of his best friend. So he endured the silence and pulled at the string of the denim fraying at the seam of the pocket on his jeans.

Finally, she started up again. "I had just gotten A.J. down. He was in that terrible two phase, stubborn and determined to do things his own way. Much like his father." She said the last with a quick sideways glance and rueful smile at Chase, who quirked a grin. She heaved a deep breath and exhaled. "He hated going to bed, fought me every time. But, after four stories and songs, he finally fell asleep. I was exhausted. I had to be up early the next day because, of course, he's a morning kid and I had work, so I had just tumbled into bed myself when the phone rang. I couldn't believe the words, made them repeat it a few times. By the time I realized it was true, I didn't know what to do next. I was alone with a toddler, and my husband was already gone."

Every word hit Chase like a bull's kick in the gut, sending him straight back in time to the night when everything had gone dead silent except for the sounds of the emergency crews working on his friend. He hadn't been there. He'd had a successful ride and was in the media room being interviewed. He hadn't been there for Adam until word filtered back of the accident. He had gotten there in time to see the ambulance crew carry him off in a stretcher. He crowded by the fence with the other riders as they watched in horrified silence while the emergency crew failed to save his friend. And he'd been giving a goddamned interview.

Hailey focused her gaze on him, her blue eyes watery yet steady. "I know what it's like to be on the receiving end of one of those calls, so I understand what they're saying, how they're feeling. I just can't understand why you want to give all of this up to ride a couple of cranky bulls intent on killing you. If you want to kill yourself, that's your business. But you have a helluva lot of people who care about you and you're pissing it away, Chase Summers."

And she walked away, back ramrod straight, without looking back at him once, leaving him feeling like a pile of horse shit.

Chapter Nine

H AILEY DIDN'T SEE Chase after their scene at the barn. Dinner was again at the main house, though she had protested because she couldn't keep eating off the family. Marie Baxter, the family's cook, seemed to take offense that Hailey didn't want to eat her cooking, so Hailey and A.J. dutifully headed over there for dinner. But Chase was nowhere to be found. No one said much of anything or even asked where he was, though West and Tara exchanged worried glances when Hailey came in without him. She gave A.J. his bath and put him to bed, only half listening to how excited he was to be going to camp the next day. She kept waiting for headlights to flash on the wall and the sound of a truck coming down the lane. But it didn't happen.

She took her notebook and headed out onto the porch with a glass of iced tea and a plate of gingersnap cookies Marie had sent over, hoping to get some work done. She wasn't waiting for Chase, or so she told herself, but she owed him an apology and she hated to go to bed with this hanging over her head. Finally, when full dark had fallen and she had just about given up, a flash of headlights down the lane caught her attention. She stayed in the rocking chair until he parked the truck and came up the walkway.

He made it up the steps then frowned at her waiting in

the shadows on the porch. "I didn't expect to see you still up. This is becoming a habit. Well, good night." He paused for a moment then headed for the door, ducking his head and avoiding her gaze.

She untucked her legs from under her and lifted a hand. "Chase, wait. Please. I think we need to talk."

He froze, fingers grasping the door handle, and, for a minute, she thought he'd continue into the house without acknowledging her words. After a long moment, he let out a breath and dropped his hand, shoulders slumping.

"If it's all the same to you, I'd prefer not to go another round about how selfish I am and how I'm making everyone miserable with my life's choices, okay?"

His words drew blood, even as he said them in a quiet, almost sad voice. Damn, she'd really hurt him and she hadn't meant to even though his words had brought back the nightmare call about her husband, the night she knew she would be alone for the rest of her life. But Adam hadn't cared when he had a wife and son who wanted him home. She just didn't want Chase's family, the people who loved him, to get that same call. And maybe, if she could give Chase a sense of how hard his life was on the people around him, maybe he would reconsider his decision. For their sake, if not his own. But that wasn't her call to make.

She slowly stood and stumbled, her legs numb from being cramped into one position for a couple of hours waiting for him to come home. Before she could hit the wooden floor, Chase was there, catching her in his arms and pulling her close to his muscled chest. He hauled her close, bracing her while the blood pounded through her body and adrenaline sang. She lifted her head and stared into his eyes and her breath caught in her throat.

The feel of being in a man's arms again, even if he was only saving her from her own klutziness, was enough to make her body burn. She missed a man in bed with her, holding her, being with her. The fact that it was Chase made it even more thrilling, the one man whose arms she had always wanted to feel.

He held her effortlessly, as if he could shield her from the stresses of daily life, protect her and give her the strength to go on another day. His hands rode low on her waist, fingers spread to gently hold her in place. The warmth of his touch burned through her cotton T-shirt, heating her blood and reminding her that she was more than a mother, more than a daughter. She was a woman who'd gone too damned long without touch.

"Are you okay?"

His words slowly penetrated the haze that fogged her brain, and she blinked at him. Reality intruded. He had done the gentlemanly thing, helping her because he didn't want to see her hurt, nothing more. He'd set her on her feet and she'd be alone again, facing the world as a strong, single woman. As usual.

She nodded and made a move to step away, but his hands didn't let her go, not right away. They softened around her waist, not holding her in place but caging her loosely, giving her the opportunity to move if she wanted but keeping her close if she chose. She was frozen in place, the warmth of his body thawing that place deep inside her that had been frozen for so long, dormant and on ice for years but quickly melting under the heated gaze inches from her face.

He lifted a hand and cupped her cheek, rubbing a thumb across her lips, gathering the stray pieces of sugar there. "You've been eating Marie's gingersnaps."

"She sent them over after dinner." She smiled under his touch, her voice sounding breathless even to her.

His gaze sharpened. "They're my favorite. Did she send them for me?"

Hailey cocked her head and smirked at him. "If you had joined us for dinner, you could have had some. Since you weren't there, I commandeered them. You snooze, you lose, Summers."

"She usually sends some without sugar for the horses. Judging by your lips, you ate the right ones. Because if you ate the ones for the horses, they might get a bit peeved if you don't have any treats for them for your ride tomorrow."

"She labeled the boxes. The horses clearly got the bigger box, by the way." She knew she sounded disgruntled and didn't care. Those cookies were awesome. Her mother never made cookies that good. Well, considering her mother rarely baked without burning something—or allowed the cook to make cookies or cakes because they were fattening—well, any cookies would probably be as good. She licked her lips to gather some of the remaining sugar and watched Chase's eyes darken to a deep espresso. Nope, these cookies rocked.

He groaned. "I hope you saved me some. Those cookies are all that get me through the day on the road, you know. And the horses love them."

She snorted. "I've never heard of horses eating ginger-snaps. I think you're conning me, Chase Summers."

He wrapped an arm around her waist, bent around her, and snagged a gingersnap off the plate on the table and bit into it, closing his eyes in pure bliss. "Nope, these are pure heaven."

"Hey, get your own damned cookies. That was my last one." She tried to pull away, but his arm locked her to his chest.

He held out the other half of the cookie to her mouth. "I'll share."

She went still in his arm, hands braced on his chest, eyes locked with his. She went for it with her hand, but he pulled it out of reach, shaking his head. She narrowed her eyes and lowered her hand to his chest again. This time, he put the cookie near her mouth and lifted an eyebrow. He should never dare her. She took the remaining cookie in her mouth, giving his fingers one lick to get the sugar off the tips.

He threw back his head and laughed. "Well, I didn't expect that, honey. But now I need to get myself a little sugar."

He leaned down, keeping his eyes on her the whole time. He settled his lips on hers, gently, almost tentatively, not the kiss she expected from Chase, a known womanizer and man-about-town. No, this kiss seduced, coaxed, enticed her into playing along with him, opening her lips under his. His tongue swept along her lips, gathering the grains of sugar that had previously dusted the cookie and now coated her mouth, then made a foray into her mouth, sharing the sweetness with her. She tasted ginger, sugar, and a faint hint of beer.

He pulled her closer to him, if that was possible, so she was pressed against him, both of his hands now firmly clasping her lower back and holding her against his warm body, heating her while the cool night air drifted around them. Her hands were trapped between them, but she spread her fingers, feeling his muscles and . . . the bandage still wrapped around his ribs.

She pulled back, turning her head, her breath coming fast as she tried to gain her bearings. He let her go, holding her loosely to ensure she was okay to stand but not keeping her too close, giving her the freedom to walk away if she wanted.

"Why did you do that?" Her words were a whisper in the night.

"I've always wanted to. Will it be a problem?" He spoke low and carefully, as if afraid to spook her, like she was one of his horses he was working with.

She had no idea. Would it? She felt dazed, like she was just waking up from a dream and wasn't sure where she was or what was going on. Only, was the kiss the dream or was it her real life that had been the dream?

She shook her head. "No, we're both adults. It's not a problem."

He dropped his hands and took a step back. "What does that mean, Hailey? Does that mean that you're ready for more?"

She stared at him, not sure what to say to that, her mouth gaping like a trout gasping for air. Why not just go for it?

"What if I am? Are you, Chase? You've made a life out of running from any kind of commitment. Can there be anything more between us?"

He scrubbed a hand over his face. "Ah hell, Hailey. I like you. I always have. But you're Adam's wife."

She nodded, her throat tight and dry. "Of course, Chase. But Adam's dead. Four years now. And he told you to look out for me and A.J."

He gave a hoarse laugh that had no humor in it. "I don't think this is what he had in mind."

She cocked her head and studied him. "He knew you had a thing for me. In fact, right before he went out on the last season, he said something to me that I never really thought about until now. He said, if anything happens to me, you would be the right guy for me. Almost as if he were giving me to you."

She had been so angry with him, handing her off to someone else because, she assumed, he was tired of being a husband, a father. They had fought bitterly that night over his return to the circuit, his traveling so much, and, most of all, his voicing her own secret of what might have been with Chase Summers. If only she'd known it was the last time she'd be with Adam. But she'd forgiven herself and her husband for that night. They'd talked after that and all had seemed right in the world. She understood now it was his way of taking care of her.

Chase was staring at her, a mix of shock and longing she knew was mirrored in her own eyes. Then he shook his head. "Whatever. You wanted to talk to me about something?"

She blinked at the sudden change in conversation. What had she wanted to talk to him about? Oh, yeah. "I was out of line earlier today with what I said at the corral. About Adam. I had no right to use my experiences to influence you."

He just looked at her, an inscrutable expression on his face. "You said nothing different than what everyone else has been saying."

She took a step forward and laid a hand on his arm, feeling the tightly corded muscles and desperately wanting to smooth away the tension wrapped around him. "But they're your family. They have a right to say their piece. I'm not family."

He jerked under her arm, an incredulous look on his face. "Are you kidding me? Adam was almost like a brother to me, as close to me as West and Ty are. You were his wife. You are family and have as much a right to talk to me as they do."

She yanked her hand back and planted it on her hip. "Then why the hell have you stayed so far away from me and A.J. for years, Chase? The most contact we've had is awkward phone calls, if that. I thought we were friends. You clearly think we were family. And yet, somehow, we haven't spoken. Can you explain that?"

He whirled and took a couple of steps, hands fisted at his side, body rigid. Finally, he turned, his face tired. "Because it was too damned hard, Hailey. Just too fucking hard to be near you. I'm no good for you, for A.J. Look what Adam did for you and I'm no better. Just a broken-down bull rider with nothing to offer. I know what Adam asked me to do, but you deserve so much more. I had hoped you had found it."

What was he saying? Was he confessing what she thought he was? She sank down in the rocking chair and stared out over the front yard, not seeing anything. Chase came and stood next to her, his boots just in her line of sight. Finally, he too sat in the other chair, his hands clasped between his legs.

"I'm sorry, Hailey. I never meant to say anything. I was never going to tell you. At the funeral, I did what I could, stood by your side, but all I wanted to do was take you in my arms. What kind of an asshole does that to his best friend's wife when her husband has just died? But, fuck, you were so goddamned angry. And I was just another reminder of what you'd lost."

She didn't even look at him. That day had been sunny. No days for a funeral should be sunny and bright. But the day reflected Adam and his personality, always cheerful, laughing. It was like he was there, telling them he was okay. Only she wasn't okay. She was numb, in shock, and so fucking angry. She wanted to curse Adam and his god-damned need for adrenaline. She wanted to pummel Chase for encouraging Adam to follow him on the bull-riding circuit and making it seem so glamorous. Wouldn't that have been a sight at the funeral?

Instead of screaming to the world, crying and bellowing about how unfair it all was, she'd wrapped up her anger deep inside, buried it deeply under layers of ice so she could get through the day, until one day it had withered and died.

But she had spoken some of her truths. Privately. To Chase. When he had done nothing but stand by her, she had been vicious to him, chasing him away because the reality was, she needed her space and needed to be on her own so she could grieve.

She buried her head in her hands and moaned. "I said

awful things."

Awkwardly, he patted her shoulder. "You were right. He followed me on the circuit. I'm the reason Adam is dead. If I hadn't gone, he would have stayed and worked his father's ranch."

She lifted her head and glared at him. "That's so not true. He would have died on that ranch. It was going under faster than the *Titanic*, Chase. His father had mortgaged the hell out of it. There was no saving their business. And Adam would have found another way to get his rush. He may have gone regular rodeo, but he always liked the bulls. I blamed you because you were there. It wasn't your fault."

She studied him, seeing for the first time the guilt that weighed on him. She put her hand on his cheek and turned him to face her. "You had nothing to do with it. In fact, you probably kept him alive as long as he was. You were so serious about training and being smart. Adam was reckless and wanted the big pot. You gave him focus, and I thank God you were with him on the circuit."

Without thinking, she leaned forward and brushed a kiss across his lips. He didn't respond so she tried again, this time lingering longer until he responded, his lips softening, opening under hers, his tongue coming out to stroke against hers. She pulled back.

"I should have said this a long time ago, but thank you, Chase Summers, for being a good friend."

And she got up and went inside, with a lingering touch on his back.

Chapter Ten

THE NEXT MORNING, Chase had hoped to avoid Hailey by heading to the barn early, but he forgot about the shared kitchen. After the initial morning chores were done, he headed inside to grab breakfast only to be confronted by an unexpected domestic scene. A.J. sat at the scarred wooden kitchen table, his feet banging against the chair as he stirred cereal around his bowl. Hailey pleaded with him to finish his Cheerios, but A.J. was having none of it. As soon as he saw Chase though, his whole expression brightened and he started to get off the chair.

"Don't even think about it, mister. Not until you finish your breakfast. And hurry because we have to get you to camp or we'll be late," Hailey threatened, looking thoroughly frazzled. "Did you need something?"

Chase grimaced. Too late to escape now. "Just grabbing some breakfast and coffee before heading back out to work."

Her eyes closed for a moment, as if praying for patience, although he had no idea why his presence would irritate her—until A.J. started peppering him with questions.

"Why don't you get what you need for the day, and I'll handle this little guy?"

She arched her brow, clearly unsure, then glanced at the cowboy clock ticking on the wall and yelped. That seemed to decide it for her, and with one last doubtful glance at him, she raced upstairs.

Now that he was left alone with the boy, Chase had no idea what to do. A.J. stared at him, slouched in his chair, sneakers banging against the table and chair legs, now suddenly mute. But there was still a bowl of cereal in front of him that had to be finished. How hard could it be? Although that kicking was really starting to get annoying.

So, Chase did the only thing he could think of. He pulled the chair out and sat down, fixing a stern gaze on A.J. "Not hungry?"

"I want eggs."

Shit. How was he going to handle that? He was pretty sure Hailey didn't have time to wait for them to make eggs and then eat them. He glanced at the cereal box on the counter then shrugged. "I prefer cereal myself, especially my favorite. Cheerios."

The boy eyed him suspiciously and didn't make a single move toward his spoon. Chase stifled a sigh. Looks like he was eating cereal for breakfast. He got up, grabbed a bowl, the box of cereal, and milk, then sat back down and started eating. A.J. watched him for a long moment, brow furrowed.

"You like cereal?"

"I'm hungry. This is breakfast. I was taught there are two things for breakfast: take it or leave it. You eat what's in front of you, or you don't eat. I don't like to be hungry. Besides, I like Cheerios. It's how I got strong."

A.J. cocked his head, his lips pursed as if he didn't believe anything Chase said. Chase barely spared him a glance until he was done with his bowl. He then reached over for

A.J.'s bowl. A.J. made a sound and blocked Chase's move.

"That's my bowl."

Chase shrugged. "You weren't eating it. I figure I may as well."

A.J. scowled and started eating, glowering at him the whole time. Chase poured himself another bowl because he truly was hungry and plowed through the second bowl in the time it took A.J. to finish his. Hailey came running downstairs at that moment, clearly prepared to fight with her son about finishing breakfast but found A.J. done and ready to go. She stopped dead at the bottom of the stairs and stared at Chase.

He gave her a grin and shrugged.

A.J. smiled. "Chase said there were two choices. Take it or eat it."

Chase flushed. "Leave it. Take it or leave it."

Hailey closed her eyes and took a deep breath, then opened her eyes. "That's great. You'll need a good breakfast before your big day at camp. Are you ready?"

Good. She'd decided an argument wasn't worth it.

A.J. turned excited eyes on Chase. "I'm going to a camp and play with my new friends today."

He nodded, not really knowing what to do or how to respond. "That's great. Have fun today."

"I'll meet you out front, baby." Hailey gave him a slight push out the door. As she walked past Chase, she said, "Take it or leave it?"

He shrugged. "Hey, that's how I was raised. You ate what was in front of you or you didn't eat. He wanted eggs. I didn't think you had time for that."

She sighed. "He doesn't really like eggs, but he asks for them all the time. When I make them, he whines and refuses to eat them. I have no idea why he keeps asking for them."

Chase frowned. "Why make them? He won't starve if he misses a meal. I missed plenty of meals. Taught me not to refuse food."

She glared at him. "And do you really think that's the best way to raise a child?"

He held up his hands. "Whoa, I didn't mean anything by it. I just meant that maybe if he knew you wouldn't cater to him, he'd eat better."

"He eats just fine. He's not a big breakfast kid and he's nervous about going to camp so he does this to let me know he's scared. You saw how he ate dinner." She sighed. "I'm sorry. Thank you for helping this morning. I'm a little tense about leaving him at camp."

Chase rubbed her shoulder. "No, you're right. I had no business telling you how to raise your son. He'll be fine today. He's a good kid."

She smiled. "Thanks. Oh crap, we have to go. Have a good day!"

She raced out of the house, leaving Chase standing in the kitchen. Was this how regular families felt every day? A slow grin crossed his face. It was nice not being alone for breakfast.

CHASE SPENT MOST of the day working with the various horses they'd bought for trail riding. He'd mostly been working on them in the corral, putting them through their paces to see how they reacted to distractions and took commands. He used the lead and rode them too, testing his leg and body, not just the horses. The worst thing that could happen would be to go out riding and get into trouble, either with his own body or with a horse acting unexpectedly. Ty showed up as he was turning out the last of them to the field.

"How did we do?" Ty fell into step beside Chase and the sorrel as they headed toward the field where the remaining trail horses were relaxing and grazing.

Chases patted the sorrel on the base of its neck. "Overall, pretty good so far. They seem even-tempered and didn't seem too disturbed with the distractions Lew and I used."

Ty nodded. "Thanks for including the kid. He's eager to learn and was hoping to do more than muck stalls." He hurried in front to open the pasture gate, and Chase released the horse into the field. Ty closed the gate and they both leaned on it to watch the horses for a few minutes.

"We don't have enough horses to keep Lew busy enough with cleaning, mucking, and grooming right now. Besides, he learned a few things from his dad about training. He picked up a few things quickly. I'll probably have him ride out with me to test the horses. But I promised Tara I'd take Hailey out every day and show her the land to get her used to the guest ranch layout."

Ty nodded. "Is she okay on these horses?"

"I don't think I want to chance it. She hasn't ridden in years, and I don't know these horses well enough. Think Tara would part with Trixie for a few days?"

"Tara isn't here, and I don't think she'd mind anyway.

She's been riding Ghost, believe it or not. She's been the only one who can ride him. It's like that horse senses she's Douglas's daughter."

Ty referred to their foster father and Tara's father who'd died a few months prior, leaving them equal partners in the ranch.

"Well, horses aren't stupid animals, no matter what we might think. But I'd appreciate bringing Trixie over here for a few days. Could she be stabled here for a while?"

"Sure. I'll bring her over after dinner. You going to be okay riding out?"

They turned and headed back to the stables. Chase stretched his body, wincing slightly at the motion. "I'm still a little sore with the ribs and lungs, but the knee is doing ok. No cane anymore and almost no limp unless I overdo it. I think I can handle it. Going to try to work with the new mare."

"She needs a name."

"Hailey named her. Cleopatra. Cleo for short."

Ty's mouth twisted in a grin. "Really? And you said you were going to get rid of her. Liar. You never get rid of abused animals. You're like a mother hen with those creatures."

"Whatever. I'm just worried about what we're going to do with her. Can we really afford to take on her feed?"

"She may surprise you. She might turn out to be a great horse that could be a trail horse, or a cutting horse, or someone might even buy her someday. You never know. You've sold others in the past." Ty shrugged, seeming unconcerned about the horse.

"None of them had the history of this horse, or the

abuse. Not that we know her history since you just plucked her out of an auction and dumped her here." Chase grumbled.

Ty clapped a hand on his shoulder. "Whatever. The key is you and what you can do with her. I'm just worried what will happen when you leave. Who can work with her while you're gone?"

Chase shoved him. "We'll figure that out. Get your ass back on the range. Those cows won't move themselves."

Ty's laugh echoed behind him all the way into the stable. Chase tried to ignore how good it felt to be home again, the camaraderie with his brothers, the stability that came from being home every day, and the peace and quiet of the ranch. He took a deep breath and let the scent of sweet hay, horse, and, yes, even manure fill his lungs. It all smelled like home. His soul was at peace here more than anywhere else.

Yet a part of him itched to get back on the road, to get back in the arena and complete the task he'd assigned himself years ago. He'd been so close this time, closer than he'd ever been. When he had been a boy growing up in foster care, his world had been so small, trapped and controlled by everyone else. He had no options, no way of expanding his world. On the first day of school every year there was always that stupid report everyone had to do—what I did on my summer vacation. God, he hated that assignment. He was the only kid who did nothing but avoid being sent to a new home. And more often than not, he had been moved to a new home, so he was the new kid in the class. Every other kid talked about their vacations, the places they went.

He'd vowed then and there that one day he would travel,

somehow. He would never be tied to one place.

He loved owning a piece of the ranch. Having a home, a place where he always belonged, was so important. He'd never give that up. But it also gave him the freedom to roam. And West, being the one who loved his roots, was his anchor, allowing him that rope to travel as he needed, even if he didn't understand his need to do it.

For the first time, he was surprised to find himself reluctant to leave, liking the peace and quiet of the ranch and the routine of working with the horses. He enjoyed his nights on the porch, his conversations with Hailey, and spending time with his brothers. And he feared that he would lose himself if he got locked down at the ranch.

CHASE FOCUSED COMPLETELY on the chestnut mare at the end of the lead rope. She had been frisky, nervous, and even on edge during most of the training session that day. He had put a saddle on her and laid a sack of sand on her to see how she'd handle weight and she was clearly uncomfortable with it. Her head tossed and eyes rolled, and she danced from side to side, bucking occasionally, trying to dislodge the weight. But he had been patient with her, letting her work through her fears and nerves, letting her see no one would hurt her. Slowly, she had settled down and was now, after about an hour's work, trotting at the end of the lead with only the occasional snort and head toss. She'd look back at the sack, especially as she went around a curve and the sack shifted, but she was settling nicely.

Chase's muscles were screaming at him, shoulders and arms getting dangerously tired, and his ribs were aching like a bitch, especially after working the other horses this morning. But it had been a good day's work and he was ready for a hot shower, a cold beer, and some rest for his beat-up body. He slowly reeled the mare toward him until she was a couple of paces away from him, staring at him suspiciously, still not sure of him. He stretched his hand out with one of the gingersnap treats in it for her to sniff.

"Chase! Chase! I had the best day today at camp. I met new friends and there was a dog there and we went on a hike and we saw a deer or something. It was awesome!"

The loud, excited voice of the young boy shattered the calm of the training session and startled the horse. She reared, eyes rolling and front hooves pawing the air and flailing at Chase. He dove to the ground, his elbow digging into his injured ribs, sending shock waves of pain throughout his barely healed body, and he swore he saw stars. Instinctively, he dropped the lead and rolled, trying to get away from the bucking horse who was out of control in her fear. Once he had rolled far enough from the mare, he got to his feet to see A.J.'s shocked face staring at him from the fence, Lew and Ty running out from the barn to check the commotion, and the mare on the other side of the corral, sides heaving, and head still tossing.

Ignoring the renewal of pain spreading through his body, Chase leapt over the fence and grabbed the boy by the arms. "Do have any idea how dangerous that was? You never run up and yell around horses. You or someone else could have been hurt. Where is your mother?"

"A.J.? Oh my God. What happened?" Hailey came running from the house, panic in her voice.

"Goddamn it, Hailey. He came running down here, yelling, and could have been seriously hurt. You need to teach your boy how to act on a ranch." Chase's hands shook as he glared at her.

She grabbed A.J. and pulled him close, wrapping her arms around the sobbing boy. "Did you have to yell at him? He's just a small boy and didn't know."

"Well, maybe he should have. Come on, Hailey. It's dangerous to run around yelling like that anywhere."

"He's six. That's what they do. You might want to try to be a little nicer." Her face was getting red as she yelled right back at him like a momma grizzly protecting her cub.

He pointed at the horse, which was limping at the other side of the corral, avoiding Ty and Lew's efforts to get close. "And he could have hurt me and the horse. Not to mention himself. That's not okay."

"Forgive me if I think my son is more important than a horse."

"Not on a ranch. You need to explain the rules or he can't come down to the barn again." Chase turned his back and limped into the corral, adrenaline still spiking high in his body, yet his muscles were already screaming at him to stop moving.

He heard her huff of frustration and then she murmured, "Come on, baby. Let's go back to the house and you can tell me all about your day at camp. Ignore the grumpy man."

The little boy sniffled but didn't say anything. Chase refused to turn and apologize, even as Ty and Lew shot him disapproving looks.

As he got closer to the two men and the horse, they continued to stare. "What?" he snapped.

"Don't you think you were a little hard on the kid? He's only six," Ty remarked mildly.

"As Hailey has reminded me repeatedly. He needs to learn." Chase wouldn't be swayed. He couldn't afford to be. "Dammit, he could have run into the barn like that and one of the horses could have been in the ties or something. Better he gets his feelings hurt now and learns not to do it again rather than getting physically hurt later."

"My daddy believed that. Boy, you tiptoed around the horses all the time. No matter what," Lew commented as he slowly circled the mare. "We learned that from the time we could walk. He'd switch us if we didn't." He started murmuring nonsense words to her in a low, soothing tone. She pricked her ears.

"I don't think Hailey would let you do that to A.J. But you could have explained that you were afraid he could have gotten hurt rather than yelling at him." Ty continued to gently manipulate Chase, slow walking him to some sort of epiphany like he was the goddamn shy horse, and Chase was fucking tired of it.

"Fine, you're right, okay? I'll apologize to the kid later, when everyone has calmed down. If I went up to the house now, I think Hailey would skin me alive."

"And roast you for dinner. You'd be a bit stringy. Not a good meal." Ty grinned then sobered. "Seriously, you hurt, man?"

Chase took a deep breath, and, fuck, did that hurt.

Seemed like his injuries blossomed all over again. His knee, his ribs, his lungs, and even his shoulder. He groaned. "Damn. I did not need this."

"We got this, brother. Head back to the house and a shower, then ice. Take those painkillers tonight. Don't be a goddamned hero. You need them. Get some rest. We've got this."

Chase glanced at the house. A confrontation awaited him. "Nah, I think I'll stay here, make sure she's all settled before I tackle the house. Moving will make sure the muscles don't tighten up. Let's bed her down and settle her first. She needs to know she's safe with me."

Then he'd have to grovel like he's never groveled before. How the hell did you apologize to a six-year-old?

Chapter Eleven

HAILEY HALF-LISTENED TO A.J. telling her about his day at camp. At first, he had been silent, still in tears over Chase's almost abusive treatment of him, but he had quickly overcome that with a special snack and chocolate milk. He chattered through their dinner and his bath, seeming to have forgotten about the whole incident by the corral.

As she tucked him into bed, he got quiet. "Momma? Chase was real mad at me, wasn't he?"

She sighed, her anger having faded a bit in the couple of hours since the altercation, although she intended to have a serious discussion with Chase Summers about how he spoke to her son. She smoothed A.J.'s hair back from his forehead. "Yes, baby. He was."

"I didn't mean to make him mad. I wanted to tell him about my day." A.J. sounded confused and so young.

"I know, honey. He didn't mean it."

"I did mean it," Chase said from the doorway, his deep voice filling the room. Hailey jumped and turned, about to tell him, but Chase stepped in the room, his eyes firmly fixed on A.J. "But I was wrong to yell at you like I did. I was scared, and I shouldn't have done that."

A.J. struggled to a sitting position and cocked his head. "You were scared?"

Chase nodded, twisting his hat in his hand. "When you come running like that around horses, they get nervous, even the calmest ones. Cows too. And don't get me started on bulls. Anyway, we were in a corral, but we could have been in a barn or somewhere where an animal could have hurt you."

A.J.'s lower lip jutted out. "But I didn't mean anything."

Chase limped to the bed and sat gingerly on the edge. "Horses are dangerous and easily spooked. They could hurt you very quickly. You need to be careful around them. When you want to come to the barn or the corral or any-where there's animals, you need to walk slowly, be aware of where any animal is, and be quiet and calm. Can you do that for me?"

A.J. studied Chase solemnly for a long moment then nodded. "Yes, sir."

Hailey blinked, shocked by her son's response and by Chase. She started to speak, but Chase glanced over, a bit stiffly now that she noticed, and gave her a warning look. She closed her mouth. She'd let them have their moment.

"Good. Then you can come back to the barn. However," he held up a hand, "you have to always tell your mom where you're going and get her permission. And if I say it's not a good time to be down there, no argument. You go back to the house. Is that understood? We have rules on the ranch, and they're to keep everyone safe."

He gave A.J. a stern look and her son nodded. Chase turned to her. "Mom? Do you have any rules you'd like to add?"

Now he was just teasing her. Damn him, taking all the

wind out of her sails just as she had worked up a good mad at him. Just . . . damn him. But she definitely needed rules in place. She folded her hands in her lap to keep from planting her fist in his face and nodded.

"One more rule, at least for now. No going to the barn without me." A.J. opened his mouth to protest, but she shot him a glare. "That's your punishment for scaring Chase and the horse today and causing trouble."

"But I didn't know the rules."

His lower lip stuck out and started to tremble and her heart melted, but she couldn't weaken, not this time. Chase was right, damn it. Now that she looked back on the incident, A.J. could have been hurt. Chase arched his brow at her out of A.J.'s line of sight. How dare he doubt her backbone to handle this situation. *Watch and learn, Chase.*

"No can do, mister. You know your manners better than that. You wouldn't run into Grandma and Grandpa's house like that. No running and yelling in the barn either. Besides, I want to check out the barn for myself before I give you the freedom to roam around by yourself."

A.J. flopped back on the bed and sighed, a dramatic sound designed to make her give in. But not this time. Chase slowly stood and held out his hand to the boy. "Are we good?"

A.J. stared at the hand. Then he took it and shook it like a little man, and he nodded solemnly. Her heart clenched a little. "Yup."

Chase nodded. "Be good for your momma." He limped out of the room slowly.

Hailey watched him. He was moving slower than usual, a

113

bit more gingerly. Could he have gotten hurt today because of her son's actions?

She read one story instead of the usual two or three. A.J.'s eyes were drooping by the end of one. The day's activities tired him out, for which she was grateful because she wanted to check on Chase before he shut her out for the night. She kissed him good night and turned off the light. A.J. was already asleep before she closed the door.

Now to tackle the other man in her life.

HAILEY WENT DOWNSTAIRS with a quick detour by the bathroom for some ointment. She headed to the back of the house to the suite for the guest ranch manager. The bedroom door was closed, but a light came from under the door, proving he was in there and still up. She took a deep breath and knocked.

She was about to knock again when a grumpy voice replied, "Go away, Hailey. I'm not decent."

She sniffed. "Well, I'm sure it's nothing I haven't seen before."

She turned the knob and walked in, expecting to see Chase with his shirt off. She froze halfway in the room, and for the first time in her life, she understood what women meant when they said their mouths watered when they saw a hot man. Her husband had certainly been handsome and many women, including herself, found him sexy, but Chase was on a whole other level.

He was standing next to the bed, shirtless, displaying

every inch of his incredibly defined chest and abdominal muscles. He didn't need steroids to get that body, which wasn't muscle bound. It was lean and ripped, defined as only a working man could be, with an eight-pack rippling down his stomach to the towel that hung loose around his hips and threatened to fall to the floor with the slightest breeze. Was it wrong of her to hope for a movement, a flutter, anything to make that plain white towel reveal what it was barely covering?

She swallowed then focused on the fresh scrapes and bruises that decorated his back and shoulder, along with the healing ones along his ribs. His movement, and the wince he made as he tried to stretch and reach the injuries on his back, woke her out of her sexually aroused trance.

She cleared her throat.

"It's a good thing I came down. Sit down and I'll help you with that." If her voice sounded a bit rough and hoarse, he didn't seem to notice beyond being irritated by her presence.

He scowled. "I can handle it. Who do you think takes care of my injuries on the road?"

She snorted. "You have a full medical staff on hand at the arena for every event. And I know you have a whole host of buckle bunnies dying to service you."

"They're not interested in or particularly skilled at nursing injuries," he muttered under his breath.

"I'm sure they're more interested in other parts of your anatomy. But at least you have the medical staff to help you." She bustled into the room, trying desperately to ignore the buffet of male flesh laid out for her when all she wanted to do was run her fingers over her body. What the hell was coming over her? She hadn't felt this way in years, hadn't been interested in anyone like this in forever.

He stared at her. "You don't know men at all, do you? I only went to medical when I absolutely had to. For stuff like this, I handled it. Just like on the ranch."

"You never let anyone in, do you?" She ran her fingers lightly down his side, unable to resist touching the yellow and green faint bruising that remained from his tangle with the bull. "Chase, how did you get this? You never told me."

He was barely breathing under her touch, standing very still while her fingers lightly traced the bruises and the healing red incision from the surgery. He shifted and grabbed the towel to cover himself a little more.

"Well, me and a bull had a disagreement about who won the round. I clearly stayed on for the eight seconds. He took exception and went after me after the bell. Kind of rude of him, if you ask me. He should be penalized, actually."

"He should be made into steaks, but the meat would be too tough to eat," she growled.

He grinned, clearly enjoying her anger. "Bloodthirsty. How did I not know this about you?"

She glared at him. "Sit down so I can clean these cuts. Why didn't you tell me you were hurt this afternoon? You've been walking around this whole time with these cuts? Did they aggravate your other injuries?"

She went into the adjacent bathroom and dampened a washcloth, finding the hydrogen peroxide and some gauze, along with the liniment kept there for bruises. She brought all of her supplies into the bedroom to find him in the same position she left him, although he had pulled a pillow onto his lap and hugged it to him.

She laid out the supplies on the bedside table and first cleaned the scrapes on the back of his shoulder with the washcloth, then soaked the gauze with peroxide and dabbed the area. He flinched and yelled.

"Baby. Even A.J. doesn't whine like you do."

"You're probably a lot gentler with him."

She arched her brow at him, but her voice was prim and scolding. "He wouldn't wait so long to have me take care of him. You should have come in right away and cleaned these."

"We had to take care of the horse first. She needed to be calmed, cooled, and then checked for any injuries. I had to be the one to do it because she needs to know she could trust me. If I left it to Ty or Lew, I'd have to earn her trust again," Chase explained patiently, his voice deceptively relaxed while his body remained rigid under her hands.

Hailey softened her hands, resisting the urge to stroke his skin. The repercussions of the incident in the corral just continued to snowball. Just great. "Was she injured?"

Chase shrugged. "One of her legs felt a little inflamed and swollen. She was limping a bit so we'll keep an eye on her for a few days and see how she does."

"I'm sorry for A.J.'s actions. I should have kept him at the house. I didn't know he had run down there, and I should have told him not to go there." She discarded the washcloth and gauze on the side table but left a hand on his shoulder, maintaining a connection to him. "I never thought he'd run off like that. He never has before. Of course, we've lived in apartments so he never really had the opportunity. Regardless, I shouldn't have yelled at you either. I should have waited and listened to you."

Chase shifted under her hands, turning to face her so that her hands now rested on his chest. "Honey, you were absolutely correct to yell at me. I was way out of line to act that way to a kid. Doesn't matter why. There were better ways to handle it, and I should have known better. Although, you're right about the other stuff." His teasing tone made her smile.

"Beast." She smiled back, her eyes caught in his heated gaze. She cleared her throat, breaking the moment. "Turn back around and let me work on these muscles. You don't want them tightening up further."

Obediently, he shifted on the bed so his side was to her again. She grabbed the liniment she had brought from the bathroom and squeezed some of it into her hand. She smoothed it over his shoulder and upper back, working it into the tight muscles she found there, kneading the knots, avoiding the scraped areas and focusing on the shoulder, upper arm, and neck areas that were balls of tension.

He moaned, low and deep, and his head fell forward, clutching the pillow to his lap tighter. "God, Hailey. Don't stop."

She grinned. As if she would, now that she had her hands on him. She spent the next several minutes working the liniment deep, releasing the tension until he relaxed under her fingers. She headed for the bathroom and washed her hands. When she came out, Chase was watching her, a heated look in his eyes.

She swallowed, resisting the urge to brush back the lock of hair that had fallen over his eyes. She'd had her hands all over him and only wanted more. Her body burned with the need to touch him, to be touched, but she had to remember one thing. He was leaving. He was going back to bull riding, just like her husband, a very dangerous job, and she couldn't afford to get close to someone who put his life on the line every day and had no intention of stopping. She'd gone through that once and she couldn't do it again. But, like a bee to honey, she couldn't resist the attraction that burned between them, a feeling that she hadn't felt in so damned long, no matter how scared she was.

She gave in to temptation and touched that piece of hair, brushing it away, smoothing back his shaggy hair. "You need a haircut." She stroked down his neck to rest on his shoulder, the heat from his skin burning her, igniting the fire deep inside, awakening her from a long dead sleep. But she couldn't step away.

He lifted his uninjured arm and cupped her cheek, rubbing a thumb across her lower lip. "Hailey. This isn't a good idea."

The air seemed sucked out of the room as she remained ensnared in his trap. The sensual stroke of his callused thumb across her soft lower lip sent shock waves through her body, awakening urges she thought had died with her husband. She had enjoyed her time with her husband and had what she always thought was a healthy sex life, albeit short since he was on the road for much of it, but she didn't remember feeling this hungry before. Maybe it was the enforced abstinence or the fact they had both grown up and knew more about life and love now. Or maybe Chase was just smokin' hot and she was ready to end her sexual drought. Whatever it was, he was fanning the flames dressed in nothing more than a towel and with nothing more than a simple touch.

Her hands curved around his shoulders, stroking the hot, smooth skin, coming across the occasional ridge or pucker. She frowned and continued her exploration, seeing more scars and injuries littering his body—nothing major, just enough to remind her that he put his body on the line every day, that he wasn't in a safe line of work. Meanwhile, his thumb traced a path of fire on her lips, and she opened her mouth to suck in oxygen with a deep shuddering breath, her eyes fixed on his.

His hand slid around her neck and slowly, inexorably, pulled her closer to him until only a few inches remained between their mouths. He waited, giving her a chance to back away, letting her make her choice, as if she were a skittish horse. Hailey had seen him with horses and animals who had been abused, lost their trust and faith in people. Chase had endless patience, something few people ever saw beneath the humor, jokes, and flirtation. Chase was watchful, saw more than most people ever knew, and now he waited to see if she was ready for this next step, waited for her to make the decision to stay as she was or take a chance.

The question was, what did she want?

CHASE'S MUSCLES SCREAMED with tension that had nothing

to do with the fall he'd taken earlier that day and everything to do with the woman standing in front of him with indecision in her eyes. Hailey had followed him to his room and he had steeled himself for a fight—a fight he totally deserved. He wouldn't have blamed her one damned bit if she had told him to stay away from A.J. and from her, along with several other choice things. It didn't matter why he had been upset; he had handled it poorly and, after a lifetime of being treated like shit by a host of people in his own life, he definitely knew better.

Yet another reason why he wasn't a good role model for the kid and should be careful to stay away. He didn't know how to act like a father or anything remotely like that. But Hailey showed up, demanding to take care of his injuries with her soft hands and gentle techniques, and he was a goner. Thank God for the pillow or he would have shocked the hell out of her with his involuntary reactions to her touch. Then she'd apologized to him, taking the blame for the afternoon and her son's behavior. He hadn't expected that and wasn't sure where to go from here, although his body had very definite plans.

If she had been one of the women on the road, they'd be halfway to paradise by now, no hesitation. Of course, if she'd been one of those women, he would still be practicing contortionist moves getting ointment on his scrapes too. She was right about that. He rarely went to the medical tent and none of the buckle bunnies were too concerned about nursing him through any injuries. It was more about getting in, getting off, and getting out.

But Hailey was different, as he'd always known she was,

which is why he'd backed off years ago. Adam was a better bet for her, had a better future for her, would be a better husband. None of them could have known what the future would bring.

Now, they stood on the precipice of something that could change their future, alter their relationship forever. She was too important and he had to make sure it was her decision. He put a stranglehold on his lust, reined in his body's desperate need to touch her, the years of pent-up need for her, to give her this chance to decide what she wanted. If she walked away, he'd respect her and nothing more would ever be said. But if she closed the gap . . .

Her soft lips brushed his, tentatively, quickly, as if unsure about her welcome. He closed his eyes at the pure pleasure of her touch, then opened them to see her staring, her blue eyes darkened to the color of the sky just before the sun rose. He flexed his fingers, burying them deeper into her auburn hair, and pulled her close.

"You're mine," he growled and took her lips in a deep, drugging kiss the way he'd always wanted to kiss her but had refrained out of deference to his best friend.

Unleashed, he teased her lips with his tongue until she opened for him, her tongue tentatively dancing with his, a light flirting touch as if unsure of her welcome or her appeal. He wanted to be sure she never had to doubt her impact on his senses.

He tossed the pillow aside, pulling her into the space between his thighs so she could feel how strongly she affected him. He absorbed her gasp against his lips and pressed his advantage, taking possession of her mouth, his tongue sweeping inside as he pulled her closer, his other hand curling around her waist to haul her against his chest.

Instead of pushing him away, as he half expected, she wrapped her hands around him, sinking her hands into his hair. Her nails were a pinprick against his skull, lighting up sensations against his skin. He groaned against her mouth.

"Baby, you don't know what you do to me."

She wiggled against his lap. "I think I do."

"Minx."

Before he could pull her back again, she put her hands on his chest, a subtle pressure. He paused, attuned to her emotions. She blinked at him as if waking from a dream. "Chase, I'm not ready for this."

He frowned, not even pretending to not understand. "What do you mean?"

"This is all happening too fast. I just got here and we've just moved in. Things are all so unsettled right now."

He dropped his hands to his thighs, letting her take a step back, feeling the loss of her heat like a kick. "I understand that, Hailey, but it's been four years since Adam. Are you telling me you've never dated? Not once?"

She shook her head. "I've had a date here and there with friends of coworkers and stuff but nothing really. I've been raising my son. Alone, I might add. I haven't had time for dating. And, honestly, I don't really have time now for whatever this is. I mean, you're not exactly a dating kind of guy."

Her smile was a little forced, meant to be teasing, but it came out a bit awkward and, for this first time in his life, he resented the way his life had turned out, the way it was forced to be. She couldn't understand why he could never be that family man, the guy who did the dad thing with his kids. That was why he never made promises to women he could never keep, never gave them an inkling he would ever be the ring and a wedding man. But with Hailey, he wanted to be that man. He wanted to be someone else.

Instead, he nodded curtly. "Yeah, right. Well, I guess that's it then. Thanks for helping me with the cuts."

He stood and brushed past her, tightening the towel around his waist to hide his erection that hadn't gotten the message there wasn't going to be a happy ending tonight—or any other night for a very long time, not as long as Hailey was in his system. He could feel the weight of her stare on his back and steeled himself against turning around and gathering her in his arms and soothing her hurt feelings. Because he was just as wounded as she, only his wounds would never heal.

"Chase, I didn't mean anything. I just don't think this is a good idea. A.J. might get too attached and you're going back on the road."

He turned at those words. "Yeah, I get it. You don't want me around your son. Message received. I'll back off, okay?" He closed the bathroom door and turned on the faucet, effectively cutting off any more conversation.

Finally, after several long minutes, he heard his bedroom door open and close. He stared at himself in the bathroom mirror. "You're a damned bastard, you know that?"

And he couldn't argue with that statement. It was true on too many levels.

Chapter Twelve

CHASE STOMPED AROUND the barn the next day, his irritation plain for everyone to see. Even the horses eyed him warily and Lew made himself scarce. It was hardly the best day to be working with a skittish mare, so Chase decided to take one of the more settled horses on a trail ride to see if that could settle him down. The dun gelding was a handful, a bit spirited, and the perfect mount for Chase. He needed to pay attention to the horse and lose himself in the enjoyment of the ride. At one point, he crossed paths with one of the herds and his brothers. So, he joined them for lunch.

"What crawled up your ass and died?" West asked.

"What makes you say that?"

"You looked like you're ready to flay anyone who talks to you funny and then wear their skin as a coat. What gives?" West's voice was calm and even as he studied the herd in the little valley below from their position sitting on a small hill.

Chase ripped a few pieces of grass from the ground and shredded it, throwing it into the wind. Ty sat at his other side not saying anything, just resting. The peace of the late-summer day slowly seeped into Chase's body, providing the soothing calm he had been looking for. Being with his brothers provided the other piece to the puzzle, the other part of his soul. He sighed, and the tension started to leech out of his muscles.

"Hailey is making me crazy," he finally admitted.

To their credit, neither brother said anything, although they did exchange knowing looks. He decided not to pound on them, being too relaxed finally to get up and take them on. And his ribs still hurt like a bitch.

West cleared his throat and Chase just shot him a warning glance. "I know you and Tara were hoping for something like this so tread lightly, brother."

West held up a hand. "I never get involved in her plots. This is all on her." Then West paused and cocked his head. "Would it be so bad?"

Chase snorted, startling the horses who grazed nearby. "You would say that, Mr. Happily-Handed-Over-His-Balls."

Ty cracked up on West's other side, and West grabbed him in a headlock and gave him a noogie. He released him and gave Chase a smug smile. "You're just jealous because I get quality sex all the time. And trust me, it's better when you love them."

Chase made a vomiting sound. "I'm so not ready for the feelings talk, man. You really need to get your man card back."

West shrugged. "You brought it up, acting like a sad sack and moping around. What's going on?"

He couldn't see any way around it. He'd brought it up, just like West said, seeking out his brothers, even if it was unintentional, then acting like a whiny man-baby. What was his problem anyway? Just because she wasn't sure she wanted to kiss him anymore. That was her right, her choice. Chase never had to go running after a woman a day in his life; they came to him.

But she might be worth it, a tiny voice inside whispered.

Hell, she was totally worth it, and that was the part that scared the hell out of him. But was he ready for her? Could Chase change? Could he be the man she needed, even if that meant giving up the rodeo?

Did he want to be that man?

West leaned over to Ty and said in a loud whisper, "He looks like he's filling an adult diaper when he thinks. Ever notice that?"

Ty laughed. "He's always been a big baby."

Chase shot him the middle finger as he got up. "I've got this, thanks."

West grabbed his arm. "Whatever you're thinking, know this. You're a good man, better than you ever give yourself credit for. She's worth it, whatever you think you may have to give up. Because you'll get so much more."

Chase paused, unsure how to say what was on his mind. "What if she thinks I'm not worth it?"

"Then you show her you can be the man for her, that you want to be that man. Because, Chase? You are one of the best men I know. You hide so much behind your laughter and jokes, but if she's anything, she'll see beneath that."

"Yeah, that's what I'm afraid of."

CHASE AND TY headed into town to pick up some supplies and get something to eat other than his own cooking. The

Rock had a lot to recommend it, especially in his current state. Alcohol and women were top of his list right about now, and he hoped both of those would help him forget about a certain auburn-haired beauty who taunted him in his dreams. Hailey mentioned she was going to her parents' home for dinner so he and Ty decided to give Marie a break and eat in town.

They stopped by the feed store to get the usual order for West. While Ty was shooting the breeze with a couple of guys, Chase wandered into the used bookstore next door. He had never been the best student in school, but as a kid in foster care, he had found books to be a great way to avoid his home life when he had no other escape. Now, in the downtime between rides, he was known for pulling out a book and reading to keep tension at bay. He needed to stock up before his next time on the road.

He greeted Nell Willig, the owner of the shop, who had been instrumental in helping him find books when he first came to Granite Junction. A broad grin crossed the older woman's face and she hopped up from her cozy easy chair in the little reading nook in the front of the shop, depositing her cat, who had been snoozing in her lap, onto the floor.

"Chase Summers! I had heard you were back but I hadn't seen you. I wondered when you'd be by for a new stash." She hugged him, careful of his ribs, because of course she would have heard about his injuries. Articles about his rides were posted on her wall behind the cash register, including a more recent one about his near miss just a couple weeks ago.

"Aww, Miss Nell. You could have left that article off your wall. I thought it was only a brag board, not a wall of shame," he teased her.

She huffed. "You survived that damned bull. That's a brag, boy. Now, I have a few books I thought you might like, including one of those fantasy novels. Let me get them for you."

She bustled behind the counter and pulled up a stack of books for him to look through, an eclectic mix of fantasy, science fiction, and a couple of nonfiction books about horses. She watched his face as he read the backs of the books and picked through what he liked. "I have a few new thrillers and mysteries."

He shook his head. He'd had enough of police and violence in his young life. He didn't like reading about them. Although he didn't mind the odd western or Native American mystery. "Where are the kids' books?"

She blinked. "Well, I think you're a little old for those kinds of books."

He shifted his feet. "We have a kid staying out at the ranch, and I thought maybe a few books might be interesting for him. He's six, not yet in first grade, so I don't know if he can read. But his mother reads to him."

A light of understanding came into her eyes. "Ah, Hailey Spencer's son. Cute kid. Right over here."

She hovered for a moment, but a noise from the front pulled her attention and she left him to browse. He picked out a few books about animals that might interest A.J. and maybe teach him about horses, then he saw another section he'd never realized existed.

Parenting and childcare.

Parenting: Do's and Don'ts. Basic Parenting. Positive Par-

enting. Damn, these were books that should be given to parents when they walked out of the hospital, maybe foster parents too. He glanced around him and heard voices at the front of the store, but no one nearby so he flipped through the books. How the hell was he supposed to know if they were good or not?

"You find anything?" Nell said at his elbow, and Chase jumped nearly a foot.

She looked at the books in his hands, understanding dawning. "Those are good choices. I can pack them up for you." And she whisked them out of his hands and merged them in with the kids' books he'd picked up. By the time he got to the front where Ty waited, the books were in a bag, not visible to anyone.

"Ready to go?"

"Yup." Chase paid and gave a nod to Nell, who patted his hand with a wink.

Chapter Thirteen

HAILEY SOFTLY CLOSED the door, breathing a sigh of relief. A.J. had been cranky all night at her parents' house, talking out of turn, being louder than usual, and acting up. Granted, he was six so no one could expect him to be a perfect little angel, but even for A.J., the behavior was extreme. As a result, Hailey got treated to a healthy dose of parental advice on raising children, a lecture on her choice of work, the bad influence of cowboys and rodeo jocks, and last but certainly not least, how she was disappointing them. Not exactly a banner day for either Hailey or A.J.

In A.J.'s case, the situation was easily resolved. He fell asleep almost before she had driven down the street, over-tired from the day at camp, which was exactly what she had suspected, and she had some peace and quiet for the ride home which was fortunate because a headache pounded behind her eyes. He barely protested when she bundled him off to bed, asleep again before the door closed behind her. She sighed at the never-ending pile of laundry in her arms, now covered in dirt from his adventures at camp, and decided to throw a load on before bed. She grabbed her own clothes and headed for the first-floor laundry room near the kitchen. She paused at the hallway to Chase's room. His truck was back, but she had seen lights down at the barn, so she assumed he had headed down there to make one last check on the horses. When she had been in his room a few nights ago, she couldn't miss the pile of clothes in the corner. It wouldn't hurt to include his clothes with hers.

After a moment's indecision, she headed down the hall and knocked. When she didn't receive a reply, she opened the door cautiously to find no one in the room. His bed was haphazardly made, if you could call it that, and she wondered when the sheets had been changed. She'd leave that for the weekend. In the corner, by the hamper, clothes had piled up, mainly T-shirts and socks, with a couple of pairs of jeans on the pile. She sighed. Men were the same no matter what age. She set her pile on the bed so she could sort through to find the dark clothes, and a brown, paper bag slid to the floor.

The sack was from the used bookstore in town, and several books had slid out across the floor, a couple under the bed. She began picking them up . . . science fiction and fantasy titles. Chase still liked to read. She remembered he used to hide his books whenever they'd catch him reading, but Adam never cared that Chase read. Hailey had tried to give him other genres like mystery or suspense, but he'd get really quiet and say he already knew the world was a dark place and he didn't want to read about it anymore. He liked the escape of other places, other worlds. It looks like he hadn't changed much.

A corner of a book peeked out from under the bed. She knelt down to pick it up and froze, her heart stuttering in her chest. She sat back on her heels as she sorted through the titles.

Parenting: Do's and Don'ts. Basic Parenting. Positive Parenting. And, even more, a few early reader books.

The bedroom door opened and Chase stepped in and stared down at her, his eyes widening. "Hailey, what are you doing in here?"

She scrambled to her feet and held out the books. "Did you buy these?"

He scowled and turned a furious shade of red but made no move to take them. "I was at the store picking up some books for the road. Thought A.J. might like them. I don't even know if he likes to read, but I know you have bedtime stories."

She blinked through suddenly watery eyes. "He loves books and, even more, loves to have someone read to him. He can read a little, so maybe these might be okay, but he'd like it more if you shared it with him."

Chase swallowed. "I don't think that's a good idea."

She put the books on the bed and took a few steps forward, resting her hands on his chest, feeling the warmth of his body seeping through his T-shirt, thawing her even further from the hibernation she'd been living for the past four years. She placed one hand on his cheek and turned him to face her.

"I was wrong. Any man who bought these books for a boy he barely knows has already proven to be a good man and a good role model. Why did you do it?"

He tried to look away, but she kept pressure on his face, making sure their gazes remained locked. Finally, he gave in. "I didn't want to make another mistake."

She laughed. "You will. You'll make lots of mistakes. But

that's okay. So will I. You should have seen me tonight at my parents'. A.J. was overtired and was off the wall. Instead of leaving, I stayed and got the lecture about my parenting skills. So I yelled at my son, who then burst into tears because I was mad. Which, of course, led to another lecture on discipline. Believe me, you'll never get it right and you'll always second-guess yourself. The best you can do is try to do what you can for him. I trust you with him."

A muscle ticked in his jaw, tension radiating from every muscle in his body. He stared beyond her at the bed, but she knew he wasn't really seeing it. "I worry that I'll screw up."

She grinned. "Join the club. All parents screw up. But we do our best and hope."

He refocused on her, a teasing glint entering his eyes. "You never answered my question, honey. Remember the rules? Stay out of my room. By my calculations, you've broken those rules twice now."

Thank goodness he was finally relaxing a bit. Her own muscles eased and she cocked her head up at him. "I had only the best of intentions both times. If I recall, I was helping you with your injuries, and tonight, I thought I'd do some laundry, but first I had to clean up this mess. What are you, a twelve-year-old boy?"

He glared around the room. "What's wrong with my room? I'm barely here."

She burst out laughing. "Your clothes never make it into the hamper. Your bed's not made. And the towels are everywhere. You need a keeper. You're too used to being in hotels."

He blushed as he took in the parts of the room she identified, but he wasn't going down without a fight. "Why make a bed you're just going to get back into it? Although you might be right about the clothes."

She patted him on the chest like a little boy, although that was the last thing she felt when she touched him. "I'll take care of it for now, but going forward, sort your own damn clothes and I'll be happy to do your laundry with mine. And bring your towels and sheets to the laundry room, too. Deal?"

His gaze narrowed and he stared down at her. "That still doesn't deal with the problem of you breaking the rules. What would you do if A.J. broke a rule?"

What was his angle? She bit her lower lip as she considered his question. She needed to be careful in her response. "I suppose I would explain to him what he did was wrong and why, then ask him not to do it again."

Chase snorted, a laugh he couldn't hold back. "Maybe you need some of those books. Tell me the truth, Hailey." His voice had turned coaxing, the tone almost stroking against her skin, lighting her up, making her very aware that she was alone in his bedroom at night and no one was around. No one would know or care.

"Fine. I'd still talk to him, but he'd probably be grounded."

Chase stepped around her and sat on the bed, patting the space next to him. "Grounding, as in take away something he likes? Well, that just sounds like punishing you as much as him."

She grinned ruefully. "Yeah, when I take away television, he's such a grump and drives me crazy. Trust me, we both suffer."

He rubbed his jaw, the faint bristles from the day's growth that proved he hadn't shaved before going out that night. She longed to run her fingers against the scruff. If he had planned on scoring at The Rock, he would have shaved. It was a small thing, but something she'd always noticed about him.

"I'm not much for pain or denial myself. But I do think you owe me a forfeit or two."

She shook herself away from his fingers and focused on his words. "A forfeit? When I was helping you? That doesn't seem fair."

He quirked a grin, his eyes flashing humor. "I think it's perfect, especially since I didn't ask you to do either one. Besides, maybe you'll like this."

She eyed him suspiciously, intrigued in spite of herself. "What did you have in mind?"

He pretended to think and leaned back on the bed so his T-shirt rode up a little, exposing the abdominal muscles she had dreamed about the night before and still wanted to trace with her fingers, tongue, and anything else she could think of. He folded his arms behind his head with barely a wince for his muscles that had to still be sore, especially his right shoulder, but she wasn't as concerned about that, although she'd use that excuse if necessary to get her hands on him again. He studied the ceiling as the seconds ticked by from the clock on the bedside table.

"I think you should kiss me."

She jumped at his words in the quiet space, the same thought she had been thinking but afraid to voice out loud.

She shifted on the bed, watching him lying there as if he were laid out for her pleasure. "And why should I kiss you? Been there, done that. It was all right."

She feigned nonchalance although her mouth had gone dry and her hormones were racing through her body, trying to get her to jump on him and ride him like a bucking bronc. God, where had that thought come from? That wasn't the Hailey she'd always been. Maybe there was something to be said for rebounding after forced abstinence.

Chase smirked, clearly not buying her statement. "Liar." He propped himself up on one elbow. "But if it really wasn't that great, well, then I guess we'll need two kisses. To save my reputation, you know."

She sucked in a deep breath, feeling like the room was closing in on her. The summer night breeze drifting in from the open window did nothing for her overheated skin, and she suddenly realized how ridiculously overmatched she was with Chase. She couldn't compete with him, didn't have the experience or the raw sex appeal to be on the same level as the man who had flirted his way through all of Granite Junction and then the PBR circuit while she was a single mom who had already borne a child.

As if sensing her change in mood, he sat up and took her hand, engulfing it in his. "Hailey, it's just a kiss. Not a lifetime commitment or a night of unbridled passion, although that could be arranged if you want it."

His voice was teasing, but there was something in his eyes, something a bit more vulnerable that made her wonder what he'd say if she asked for a night in his bed. He came home alone, and she knew that was a choice on his part because Chase would have plenty of offers at The Rock. The question remained, why was he settling for a kiss from her? And why did mentioning a night in bed seem to create a different reaction in him?

Instead of responding, she leaned forward and brushed her lips lightly across his, quickly, before she could change her mind. "There you go. One kiss."

He frowned and shook his head. "Hailey, I expected so much more from you. Is that the best you can do?"

She may have left a lot of her past behind her in her quest for security for herself and her son, but one thing she had yet to stifle was her competitiveness. She may not have been the best athlete or the smartest person on the debate team, but she more than made up for it in sheer will and determination. And Chase knew how to push all of her buttons, damn him. Even knowing that he was doing it, she still fell for it.

She pushed him back on the bed and straddled his lap, finally having him where she wanted. At her mercy. Was there anything sexier than a man spread out for her delight? She slid her hands under his T-shirt to trace the muscles of his abdomen, feeling the tension in his body, but he only arched a brow and encouraged her to continue.

"Off," she ordered and he lifted up slightly to help her take off the shirt.

Now, he was stretched out on the hunter-green bedspread for her to enjoy. She sat back, feeling the thick ridge of his erection against her ass, and she wiggled to get more comfortable and not hurt him. He groaned and closed his eyes.

"Hailey, you're killing me." His jaw was clenched and his fists gripped the bedspread, but he stayed still for her perusal.

"This is my time, although it was supposed to be my punishment." She laughed softly, never knowing being in bed with a man could be so much fun. Adam had been funny and easygoing but not so much in bed. She shook her head to dispel thoughts of her deceased husband. She didn't want to bring him into the middle of this. Not now.

"Hailey, you have to do something. For the love of all that's holy. Something." He groaned and lifted his hips.

She leaned forward, letting her hands slide along his stomach toward his shoulder, careful not to snag on the healing incision or press on the bruises that marred his body. She brushed a series of tiny kisses along his jawline, rubbing her cheek against the bristle of his beard. She loved the stubble, the rasp against her skin. It felt like a real man was touching her, caressing her.

Her previous dates had all been professionals who worked in offices. None of them had calluses on their fingers and they were all were clean-shaven, would never even consider being seen with any growth. She'd never found them attractive, preferring the outdoor, rugged type, much to her parents' chagrin, who would have preferred her to marry the perfect urban professional and live a life in an office. Touching Chase, she now knew that was never going to be an option for her.

He turned his head and looked at her, his dark eyes a deep espresso. He buried a hand in her hair and reversed their positions until he was braced above her, his hard arousal notched between her thighs and his body caging her carefully onto the bed. Inches separated them. She could smell the beer and steak on his breath and the overwhelming scent of Chase all around her. But he waited for her decision, not rushing her. She licked her suddenly dry lips, and he was unleashed.

He took her lips in a deep, claiming kiss, his tongue plunging into her mouth, stroking her, learning her, until it gentled and softened, teasing her into responding. She arched her back to get closer, wrapping her arms around him and pulling him to her until no space was between them, his body a heavy weight on hers. She reveled in the feel of his body on hers, the weight a welcome comfort as he continued to kiss her like he was a starving man. But that was only fair because she felt like she hadn't eaten in forever, had been deprived of touch for so long, and she wanted to get drunk on it.

She jerked when she felt his hand slide along her torso under her blouse, a light stroke that broke her concentration. She pulled away from the kiss and stared at him, her breath coming fast and heavy. Suddenly, where she was, what she was doing . . . she wasn't sure it was a good idea.

Chase seemed to come to the same realization and rolled to the side.

"Are we square?" she asked.

"You still going to do my laundry?"

They both laughed, but Hailey knew this was just a delay. They were not done. Not even close. Not now that she had woken up and wanted. And she wanted Chase Summers.

Chapter Fourteen

HAILEY DROPPED A.J. off at camp and spent some time working with Tara. Clearly, though, Tara's mind was still in vacation mode, and Hailey wasn't much better. Her mind drifted back to the kisses with Chase, and her body clamored for her to take a casual walk down to the barn and hope he was alone for some midmorning fun. Tara finally closed her laptop and dragged Hailey into town for waffles. Tara slid into the booth, groaning a little when she sat.

Emma gave her the evil eye. "Stop rubbing it in, you lucky bitch. Yes, we know you went away with your honey and had wild, crazy sex for five days. You don't need to flaunt it."

Tara shot her a disgruntled look. "Yeah, because talking about bull semen and breeding cattle for five days is so romantic. I rode this gelding I swear had no shock absorbers. His trot broke half my teeth and possibly my tailbone. You tell me how that is a romantic getaway. Waffles. With everything." She slapped the menu on the table, glaring at Emma.

Emma just laughed while Hailey stared at the two women. They had such a comfortable relationship. Hailey hadn't had a lot of friends in Billings. Her college friends had moved on, and she hadn't been back to Granite Junction often enough to maintain any of her school friends so, for far too long, she had felt alone with A.J. She talked with his friends' parents or people at work, but those were surface relationships and would never survive distance or changes in circumstance. But this banter, she missed it, craved it almost as much as she craved Chase.

Emma only snorted. "Like you didn't jump his bones every night. Please."

Tara only laughed as Emma stalked away. Hailey cocked an eyebrow at Tara. "You enjoyed your trip?"

"Hell no." The other woman leaned back in the booth and stretched her legs out with a wince. "Seriously, I saw a glimpse of my future. Cows, cows, and more cows. There wasn't any decent shopping or food around the ranch. We were in the middle of nowhere, and you heard about the horrible horse I had to ride, right? I think the rancher was pissed I was there and gave me the worst horse in the stable, punishment for daring to come along with West. Kind of makes me miss San Francisco a bit."

Hailey had her own future in mind, the one she had been working toward since Adam died. Hell, who was she kidding? She had been just putting one foot in front of the other, trying to build a life with the goal of becoming a small-business consultant. But she'd never pulled the trigger on that dream, had been waiting until A.J. was older, the economy was better, her financial state was stronger. Coming back to Granite Junction had been a blessing for her. She'd had a few preliminary conversations with a couple of the small businesses in town—including Emma's friend, Sierra, who had opened a massage business and looking for ways to generate business, and Gene, a local woodworker and eccentric. He was a bit cantankerous and crabby on a good day, but he was looking for help expanding his business slowly and upgrading his website to accommodate more e-commerce. Hailey's business juices were flowing and she was enjoying her time, stretching her brain in a whole new way.

And there was Chase . . .

Before she could chicken out, she had to ask the question. "Do you regret it?"

Tara looked up from her phone. "Regret what? Leaving San Francisco? God no. I'd never have West if I'd stayed there. And there's no comparison. Besides, I'm still doing some design work here and more in line with what I truly like doing—homes, smaller businesses. It's more fun for me."

Hailey sank back into her thoughts. Her notebook sat open on the table in front of her where she was working on notes, but she hadn't added much since they'd sat down. Tara fiddled with her phone and Emma joined them, since it was midmorning and the diner was slow. Finally, Tara glanced over at her and put the phone down.

"Okay, I know why I'm highly unmotivated today, but what's your excuse? Is Chase keeping you up all hours of the night or something?"

Hailey's face burned and she studied the blank page even though she hadn't done much more than doodle on it all morning. Tara squealed and shut the book so Hailey had to focus on her. "Oh my God! I was thinking he snored or came in late with some of his lady friends from the bar, but that wouldn't make you blush unless he's doing it in the living room. And that's not really his style. I mean, I have a hot tub outside my room and I never caught him in there naked or with girls so I doubt he'd do that here."

Tara then paused, watching her with barely concealed glee, almost bouncing in the booth. Hailey sighed. Chase was basically Tara's brother, if not by blood, at minimum by marriage-to-be, and West definitely saw Chase as a brother. So, this whole situation was getting stickier by the minute. It was so much easier when she lived anonymously in Billings. Of course, she never had the friendships there she thought she could develop with Tara, provided she didn't screw it up by becoming one of Chase's conquests.

She opened her mouth to distance herself from the situation, but what came out surprised her. "We kissed, twice. And I liked it."

Emma sighed from her seat next to Tara, as if reliving a fond memory. "Well, I should hope so. From what I hear, he's pretty good at that; he's had plenty of practice. Not that I would know. He's avoided me like the plague, thanks to someone here who told him to back off. Thanks for that by the way, Tara. Is there a problem, Hailey?"

Hailey rolled her eyes. "It's been four years. Well, longer actually, since Adam was on the road for a few months before his death, and really, when you have a baby, there's isn't much time, you know?"

Both women stared at her, eyes wide, and Emma's jaw was open. Hailey scowled. "Stop with the damn dramatics. I am a single mom with a young son. God, you'd think it's been twenty years."

"Girl, you're in the prime of your life. You're young,

pretty, and any man would find you hot. Why did you wait?" Emma's voice rose louder than it should and Hailey winced.

One of the older guys at the counter dressed in dirty jeans that showed way more of his butt than anyone needed to see swiveled in his seat and gave her a once over. Hailey noticed his thinning brown hair was combed over the shiny bald spot on the top of his head. "You're pretty hot, little lady. I'd take you."

Hailey and Tara both shuddered and Emma glared. "You shut it, Darryl. We weren't talking to you."

Darryl snorted and turned while his buddies slapped him on the back and laughed at him. Emma frowned and took Hailey's hand. "Ignore him. He's obnoxious."

"But not wrong," Tara said. "Seriously, I get being suddenly single and taking your time to get back out there. After my divorce, I wasn't interested in anyone for a while, but eventually, it got lonely."

Hailey lifted her hands a little, waving them helplessly in the air. "I don't know what happened. I had a couple of dates, but they were boring."

The two women exchanged glances and Tara said, "Once you've dated a cowboy, well, you won't look at anyone else. Seriously, why would you?"

"Unless you're not interested in Chase." Emma whispered the words as if they were sacrilege, and they both leaned forward and stared at Hailey, eyes wide and worried looks on their faces.

Hailey couldn't stop the laugh from bursting out of her. "Oh my God, of course not. Have you seen him? Who wouldn't find him attractive? Although most of the women in town have spent time with him."

Tara leaned back in her seat and cocked her head thoughtfully, tapping a finger against her lip. "You know, I wonder about those rumors. When he was last here, he went to The Rock almost every night but never brought anyone home and was back at a reasonable hour. He flirted and danced but never spent time. Makes me wonder how much of it was exaggeration."

Hailey snorted. "You forget I grew up with him. His reputation was well earned."

Emma shrugged. "All guys are man-whores when their hormones go crazy, but Tara's right. He hasn't been as active as people might think in recent years. Be right back. Don't say anything interesting until I get back." She headed to the kitchen for their food.

Tara studied Hailey with eyes that seemed to see beneath the surface. "Is something else going on? Do you not want to spend time with him? Is he being difficult? I can have West talk to him if he's bothering you."

Hailey shook her head. "No, he's teasing but not pushing or anything. I just am so confused. I never even thought about dating anyone seriously, not for at least a few more years, until A.J.'s older."

Emma slid their food in front of them and sat back down, just catching the last part of the conversation. "We can't always choose when we find love, can we? Seriously, I'd kill to find someone who looks at me in a way other than a little sister around here. Maybe you should just go with the flow and see where it takes you."

"That's the point. This isn't love—at least I don't think so. But it sure feels like lust."

Emma sat back and gave her a disgruntled look. "Well, that settles it, you lucky bitch. You just need to cowgirl up and ride that cowboy for the good of all of us."

Tara almost spit out her waffle. "That's my almost-brother you're talking about. I did not need to have that image planted in my brain. Although, as a woman and taking the whole family angle out of it, I fully support this plan. And if you tell West I said that, I'll deny it."

Emma sighed. "Another cowboy off the market. Damn."

The girls all laughed, making the guys at the counter turn and shoot them looks, but Emma gave them a twirling motion and they grunted, turning back on their stools. Hailey felt her face burn bright red. It had been years since she'd talked about anything like this with anyone, if she had ever had these kinds of conversations to begin with. It felt good to talk with these women about life.

HAILEY AND TARA split up on their way back to the ranch and Hailey was torn on whether to give in to her body's desire to seek Chase out, or retreat and hide in her office. Despite the encouragement of her friends, she wasn't sure if she was ready for that next step. She hadn't shared her absolute fear Chase was going to leave, not because she thought it was illogical but because it was fact. He was exactly like her husband, and he was just here until his injuries healed. He was going back on the road. Nothing would change his mind. She wasn't sure she could handle a life like that again, and now she had a son who also would be affected by Chase leaving. How could she risk not only her heart but her son's?

But when she pulled into the driveway, she had no other choice but to go to the barn. Chase was waving to a pickup truck and horse trailer that was pulling out. She caught a glimpse of Cam Miller, the man who had bought Adam's ranch from his father, as he drove past with a tip of his hat. Curiosity piqued—and unable to resist seeing Chase again—she headed to the barn to see the new horse.

Chase was alone, leaning over the top of a stall, when she walked in. Her eyes adjusted to the dimmer light, and she took a minute to just watch him while he wasn't aware of her. Damn, Emma was right. He was a sexy man, with his dark blue T-shirt stretched firmly over a lean but muscular chest. His arms were crossed on the top of the stall, stretching the fabric of the shirt across his biceps. He was a poster child for arm-porn fantasies. There was a light dusting of hair across the forearms that had cradled her so gently even as he had kissed her with devastating effect. His jeans cupped an ass she wanted to grip, to see if it was as tight as she suspected, and she was so grateful he didn't subscribe to the latest trend of baggy jeans or plumber's crack. That would ruin every fantasy she might ever have for him.

Something rubbed against her leg, and she jumped with a small scream. Chase turned with a scowl that softened to a lazy smile that melted her insides. An orange tabby cat weaved its way around her leg and over to Chase, who squatted down to give it a rub along the back. The cat, like every other female around—because of course it was female—fell onto her back and shamelessly begged Chase for a belly rub, which he obliged.

"I see all women love you."

He shrugged. "I have a way with pussycats."

She rolled her eyes at his lame joke. Apparently, the cat didn't much like his joke either because she swiped half-heartedly with her claws, just missing his hand. Then she rolled back over and stood, shook herself and stalked off like a queen, tail held high. Hailey laughed at Chase's indignant expression, but a snort from the stall pulled her attention.

She peered over the stall but didn't see anything. Finally, she looked down at a short, brown and white pony with a full white mane and tail, investigating the hay, looking adorable and chubby on little legs. Her heart cracked a little bit further, damn him.

"Oh my God! What a cute little pony. Did you get him for the ranch?"

He leaned next to her, his hard body pressed up against hers, reminding her of the previous evening when they were wrapped in a much more intimate embrace.

"Not exactly. I thought he might be good for A.J. to learn how to ride."

Hailey's stomach tumbled—nerves at the potential injury and the sheer adorableness that would ensue at seeing A.J. in western gear atop the pony. "You've decided to teach A.J. how to ride?"

Chase leaned on the top of the stall. "Well, I can get him started at least, then Ty or Lew can continue the lessons. I assume you don't still think I'm a bad influence." The last was said with a teasing, sideways glance.

Her eyes burned and blurred with tears, and she stared down at the sweet little pony who was turning in the stall, exploring his space. "You got him for A.J.?"

Chase avoided looking at her. "You're not mad that I did it without talking to you first?"

She took his face in her hands and pressed a kiss to his lips, holding it for a few seconds. "No, I'm not mad, you silly man. I didn't think you could top the books but this . . . this is beyond anything I could have expected."

He held her upper arms gently, his touch searing her skin. "We need to add ponies to our stable anyway, and I heard Cam had a pony for sale. We talked last night at The Rock, and he was happy to part with him. His name is Wildfire."

Hailey sucked in a breath. "Wildfire? That was the pony Adam had as a kid, wasn't it? Could he still be alive?"

Chase nodded. "Ponies live longer than most horses, and he was young when Adam had him. He's been retired; Cam kept him when he bought out the Spencer ranch. I think he may have expected Adam to come back for him and then when Adam died, he didn't want to get rid of him. He's older but a solid pony for A.J. to learn on. Cam said some local kids have ridden him for years to keep him trained."

"A.J. is going to love this. And having you teach him will be the best thing ever. He already thinks the sun rises and sets on you," Hailey said.

"Whoa. I don't think that's a good idea, Hailey. I'm going to be leaving soon, and it might be better if Ty works with him, or even Lew. They can spend more time with A.J."

COMING HOME TO THE COWBOY

She could already feel him pulling away even as he was standing right next to her. She twisted around to glare at him. "What's this crap about you not teaching A.J. how to ride?"

He shrugged. "You said it yourself. You don't want me near him, don't want him forming attachments. I thought it best if someone else helped him."

She growled, and the pony's ears twitched at the sound. "I never said that. You assumed it. All I said is that you and I should be careful about any kind of relationship. You took that next step all on your own."

He finally turned to study her, and the look in his eyes, bleak and empty, almost gutted her. "Hailey, I know nothing about kids, which I clearly proved the other day. My entire life was spent with the absolute worst role models on the planet, whose idea of parenting at best was ignoring me and at worst a backhand and yelling. I have no idea how to work with a kid, and A.J. deserves so much better. It would be better if you find someone else, someone who isn't leaving and someone who knows how to work with him."

How little he thought of himself. She wanted to cry for the little boy she could hear in his voice, the little boy who never knew love growing up. Not that he ever said that, but she could read between the lines. But right now, he wouldn't listen to sympathy. He needed some of that tough love he was used to.

"Listen to me, Chase Summers. I was dead wrong. You were scared for my child, not thinking about yourself or anything else. Maybe you didn't handle it in quite the best way, but you know what? None of us do. No parent is perfect. But I have no doubt that you'll keep A.J. safe and protect him always. And spending time with a child is the most important thing. You'll figure the rest out. I know you. You have a good heart if you let yourself feel. No, I want him to learn from you."

Tears streaked down her face as she studied the little pony, and Chase gathered her in his arms, holding her close. She breathed in his masculine scent. It was overlaid with sweet hay and a tinge of sweat. Her heart cracked even more, breaking that shell that had encased her, protected her for years. It was now sloughing off and reminding her that she was a woman and had her own needs. And despite her head telling her that Chase might not be the right guy, that he was going to leave, her heart said he was pushing all the right buttons.

She tilted her head and kissed the notch at the base of his throat, tasting salt and Chase. He groaned, the rumble of sound against her chest soothing and exciting her at the same time. "Damn, Hailey. You picked a fine time to start something."

She pushed away and took his hand, leading him to the tack room. She pushed the door shut behind them, encasing them in the dim light. The scent of leather filled the air. Before he could say anything, she pushed him against the door, the only free wall space in the room, and kissed him.

She would take her friends' advice after all.

THE LAST THING Chase had expected when he brought a

pony to the ranch was ending up with Hailey's tongue in his mouth, although he wasn't exactly complaining. After the previous evening, he thought she'd be running scared from him and her feelings. He knew she was holding back and torn about having any kind of relationship with him, whether it was because Adam had been his best friend or because they both were bull riders or because he was leaving, he didn't know. And this morning, she'd left A.J. to finish his breakfast with Chase while she packed his camp bag then rushed A.J. out the door, all while making sure never to be alone with Chase.

Chase had hoped Hailey would miss the delivery, but when she came back early and saw the pony, he had truly expected she would rip him a new one, saying he was making decisions for her son. But she surprised him, tearing up first then dragging him into the tack room and kissing him as if he were a tasty steak and she was starving.

Was it gratitude or something more?

Her hands tugged his shirt out of his jeans and she dragged her nails up the sides of his stomach, the fine bite scoring his skin, sending electric shocks of desire straight to his cock, which hardened against the fly of his jeans. He groaned and grabbed her hands, stilling their movement. He pulled his mouth away, ignoring his body's sharp protests.

"Hailey, what are you doing?"

She blinked up at him, desire fogging her eyes, her lips swollen from their kisses. "Well, I was trying to kiss you, but you don't seem into it."

She rubbed her body against him, her hips brushing against his erection, and he groaned, pulling her against him, one hand pressing her lower back firmly against him so she couldn't move much more than a tiny wiggle, while his other hand gently grasped her wrists, pulling them behind her back, caging her neatly.

"Last night you couldn't get away fast enough, and I have to wonder what's changed."

She gave a rough sound of frustration. "Do you seriously want to have a relationship discussion right now?"

Her words flipped a switch inside him, and he remembered asking his brother almost that exact same question a couple of months ago. "Oh my God. I *am* a damned girl."

He dropped her hands and rubbed the back of his neck with his hand, staring at the far wall. Chase had sworn that would never happen to him, but this was Hailey and she *mattered*.

Finally, he looked at her again and cupped her face with his hands. "Hailey, I just want you to be sure about this. It's been a while, and I don't want you to have any regrets about this. I mean, if this is about the pony . . ."

She burst out laughing, hands on her hips. "Yeah, I hand out kisses as thank yous. This morning, I Frenched Earl for my waffles. Come on, Chase. I haven't really dated since Adam, that's true. But I haven't really wanted to. Maybe I'm ready to try again and it's not because of a damned pony. Although honestly? It helped. The pony, the books, the breakfast conversation. All sweetened the deal." She cocked her hip. "Or maybe I'm just horny and it's time I got back in the saddle and rode you like a cowgirl."

Who the hell was this and where did his sweet, shy Hailey go? And why the fuck was he hesitating when all he'd ever wanted was being served up to him on a silver platter? He studied her for a long moment, her hips cradled against the stiffness of his arousal, her hands running over his chest, igniting a fire in his blood. Her blue eyes met his without any hesitation, just steady, clear focus. She was a grown woman who knew what she wanted and right now, she wanted Chase Summers. That was a damned good thing because he was done waiting.

With a sudden movement, he reversed their positions, pinning her against the door and hiking her up so her legs wrapped around his waist, ankles hooking together at the small of his back. He kissed her deeply, pouring all of his pent-up passion into the moment. He slid a hand under her shirt, tugging it out of her jeans so he could smooth his fingers over her skin. She gasped and arched into his hand, her skin soft and delicate under his rough, callused fingers. He traced the edge of her lacey bra, pushing it up and over a fleshy mound so he could close a hand around the soft flesh of her breast.

She gasped in his mouth and pressed into him, moaning as he kneaded the soft flesh, then traced the areola with a thumb, flicking the nipple until it stiffened. Meanwhile, his tongue plunged into her mouth, tangling with hers, stroking, teasing, showing her exactly what he wanted to be doing if they weren't standing up in a tack room in the barn where anybody could walk in at a moment's notice. But he had gotten his hands on her and he sure as hell wasn't letting go yet, not when he finally had her where he wanted her. Not until he had the chance to show her how good they could be together.

MEGAN RYDER

Her hips moved restlessly against his, rubbing against his cock, and he was desperate to shove his jeans down, lift her skirt, and plunge into her. But not quite yet. He trailed kisses down her throat, tonguing her pulse point as it pounded in her neck, and sucked lightly over the sensitive spot until she jerked and moaned again, her hands buried in his hair, holding him in place. He chuckled against her skin and continued his relentless pace downward, unbuttoning her blouse to reveal the tops of her creamy mounds. His other hand made short work of the clasp and it fell away, leaving them free for his lips, his fingers, his tongue. Her breasts were round and full, a bit more than a handful and so damned pretty. He traced the tops of them with his tongue while his fingers danced around a nipple, stroking softly, then tweaking the tip sharply so she squealed a little and bucked against him. His hips kept her pinned to the wall and her legs remained tight around his waist, holding him close.

Her hips rubbed against him, running his denim-covered cock over the juncture of her thighs, her breath coming faster. He lifted his head and watched her for a moment, his fingers still plucking at her nipple. Her head was thrown back against the door of the tack room and her eyes were closed, completely lost to the passion she was feeling. She was beautiful when she let her guard down, when she opened herself up to sensation, and he considered himself a lucky bastard to be the one Hailey chose to be with.

He stroked a hand down the side of her torso, her skin soft and smooth under his callused fingers. He ran them over her skirt, over the top of her thigh, then slowly gathered the material of her skirt, pulling it up until he could slip his fingers under and smooth them over the top of her thighs once more. She sucked in a deep breath and stared at him, her blue eyes wide and dark with desire. He captured her gaze with his, kept her a prisoner as his fingers walked their way up her inner thigh until they traced the edging of her panties. She jerked under the caress and let out a sigh, her muscles going lax.

"Hang tight there, sweetheart," he murmured. "Don't want you falling too soon."

He tapped her legs, and she tightened her ankles around his lower back, opening up her core to his explorations. He ran a finger over her panties, which were soaking wet under his touch. She cried out as he found the sensitive spot at the apex of her folds, and she jerked in his arms. Quickly, he covered her mouth with his, swallowing her cries, and stroked the spot. It didn't take long until she was crying out, her legs squeezing him tight as she achieved her climax.

He eased her down, letting her head fall onto his chest. Finally, her breathing slowed and she blinked a few times. He gently lowered her legs and brushed her hair back from her face, kissing her softly. She traced her fingers over his cheek and was about to say something when voices sounded outside.

Her eyes flared open. "Oh my God! That's my parents! They picked up A.J. and must have decided to come over early. I can't go out there like this."

He looked over her, enjoying her mussed hair, swollen lips, and open blouse, exposing breasts he hadn't spent nearly enough time with. No, she couldn't go out there quite yet. But he was relatively unscathed, if a bit uncomfortable.

He placed his hands on her shoulders until she looked at him. "I've got this. Get yourself settled and come out when you're ready. We have some towels and stuff over by the sink there. I'll distract them."

He brushed a quick kiss over her lips, adjusted his cock in his jeans, willing it to go down because the last thing he wanted was to face Hailey's dad with an erection. He then slipped out the door and closed it behind him.

Chapter Fifteen

HAILEY STRAIGHTENED HER clothes and ran her fingers through her hair, knowing the effort was futile. Her father shot her a look full of condemnation even as he listened to A.J.'s excited chatter from outside the corral. Her father was wasted as a banker, really. He should have been a preacher. He would have been able to deduce people's guilt with one scan and reduce them to confession in no time flat. But she refused to feel guilty, even as she felt the pressure to do so. She was a grown woman with a son, and she deserved a life too.

She took a deep breath and stepped out of the barn and into the sunshine, her eyes blinded by the bright light. A.J. saw her in the instant and came running, throwing his arms around her in a full-bodied embrace. She caught herself just before she fell to the ground, knees still a little weak from the orgasm Chase had triggered in her. "Did you know, Momma? Did you know that Chase was getting me a pony?"

She brushed his hair back from his forehead. "I think he got the pony for the ranch, baby. But he seems to be perfect for you to learn how to ride."

A.J. grabbed her hand and dragged her to the corral, where Chase had brought out the pony for everyone to see while she had been collecting herself. Chase gestured for A.J.

to come into the corral, and Hailey's eyes widened in alarm.

"Chase, is he ready for that?"

He gave her an encouraging smile while stroking the pony. "We'll be fine. Remember the rules, A.J.?"

A.J. nodded eagerly, almost bouncing in his excitement, but under Chase's stern look, he slowly settled. "Walk slowly, talk quietly, and be careful."

Once A.J. was calm, Chase nodded and gave him a big smile. "Great job! Okay, now, come on over here."

Hailey watched as Chase slowly introduced A.J. to Wildfire. The pony was sedately standing still, patient and tolerant of the little boy who was almost jumping out of his shoes with excitement.

Meanwhile, Hailey leaned on the top railing of the fence and tried to ignore the censure radiating from her father. Her mother was standing by the gate a few feet away, completely absorbed in A.J. and the pony, snapping pictures with her phone. Finally, her father gripped her elbow and pulled her a few steps away, where they could still see everything but had a small measure of privacy. Chase glanced up, his expression darkening, but he remained focused with A.J.

"What's going on out here? Do you really think this is a good idea, encouraging your son to follow in his father's footsteps? Didn't you learn your lesson with Adam?"

Her father's words twisted like a knife in her gut, burning metal prodding at the old wounds, reopening the scars she had thought were long healed, but she refused to let him rain on A.J.'s happiness like he'd done to her for years. "Dad, it's just a pony. All of his friends ride or are learning how to ride. You can't avoid it out here. He'd stand out by not riding. Besides, A.J. is happy, far happier than he was in Billings."

"He'd be happy anywhere you chose to live. You could have found an apartment in town or someplace else to work. I wouldn't think you'd want your son getting involved in the rodeo life, especially considering his father. And don't think I didn't notice what's going on between you and Chase. Hailey, when will you learn? You're such a smart girl. How could you be led astray by him?"

She rolled her eyes. "Seriously, Dad? I'm not a little girl anymore, and I'll see who I want. He's a good man and he's good with A.J. You don't have to like it, but you don't get a say in my life. Not anymore."

She walked away with her heart pounding in her chest and blood roaring in her ears, although she wasn't sure if she was embarrassed that her father caught her in the middle of one of the best orgasms of her life, or angry that he was judging her choices. Maybe it was both. Dammit, why couldn't he just leave her alone, support her decisions, and back her? No, unless she was doing exactly as he wanted—majoring in business—he would cut her off completely, like when she'd married the man she loved and got pregnant with A.J. He'd completely shunned her after her marriage and had barely restrained himself from saying "I told you so" when she was left a widow. And now, instead of being proud of her, he was crapping all over her again.

"Momma!" A.J. called, and she smiled, waving to her little boy.

He was worth everything and his happiness with the man standing next to him was all that mattered. Even though

Chase had worried about not being good around kids, he had done everything he could to be good for A.J. He was patient with the endless questions and pestering that only a six-year-old could do. He'd gone out and bought books so he could relate better to her son. And he'd found the perfect pony for her little boy. Her father was wrong and short-sighted not to see the wonderful man who was working his way into her heart slowly but surely.

CHASE'S BODY STILL buzzed and he wanted nothing more than to pull Hailey into the darkened stable and finish what they started. But he had seen her face after her father had spoken with her. Tense, tight, closed off. He didn't need to hear the words. He had heard some version of them throughout his entire life—some of them had come from Tom Barnes, in fact. He had never figured Hailey to be a quitter, to follow her father's rules, and she clearly had grown a backbone, quietly giving her father a piece of her mind, judging by the way his face had twisted after she had walked away. She had even lightly kissed Chase in front of them before walking with them and A.J. back to the house. But she had still walked away, leaving him behind, and he wasn't sure what that meant for the two of them. Had she chosen him or not?

He led the pony back to the stall and settled him, and then helped Lew bring the other horses in since Ty was working with West out with the cattle herd. He wandered down the aisle to Cleopatra, who was waiting for him, her head outstretched as if seeking his attention. She was slowly improving and coming out of her shell, seeking attention from the humans around her, and not immediately expecting abuse. She was also filling out from regular feeding, turning into a beautiful horse, just like her namesake. Major improvements. He checked her over, noting the leg swelling had disappeared completely and she seemed healed. He gave her a treat and stroked her gently, feeling an odd sense of kinship with the horse that had gone through her own trials and abandonment before being rescued.

"Don't worry, Cleo. You're in good hands now. No one will ever hurt you again, and you'll always have a place here." She nuzzled his jeans, sniffing out the treats he kept there. He laughed and pulled out the last gingersnap. "Here you go, lady. Last one."

"She's looking good," Hailey said from the stall door.

It was a testament to his training that Cleo didn't startle with Hailey's voice. Or maybe she had sensed the woman before she spoke. Either way, he was pleased with Cleo's reaction. He kept stroking her, rewarding her for her behavior. Or maybe he was ignoring Hailey. She waited by the door, but as one minute dragged into two, she huffed and shifted her foot.

"Are you done punishing me yet?"

He finally looked over at her. "Punishing you? Why would I be doing that?"

"Look, I know my dad can be a jerk, but he means well."

"Does he? Telling me to stay away from you and A.J. because I'm no good is him meaning well?"

Her head jerked up and her eyes widened. "He told you

that? When?"

He stepped out of the stall; he was too agitated and didn't want to upset Cleo. "Before you came outside. I guess he wanted to make sure I knew that you had family to watch out for you and I needed to stay away." He shot her a sideways glance. "Do I?"

She had folded her arms across her chest and was sucking on her lower lip, staring out at the setting sun. At his question, she shook her head, and her brow furrowed. "Do you what?"

He crowded her against the wall of the barn, not quite touching her but getting as close as he could until she was forced to look up into his eyes. Her hands settled on his chest, but she didn't push him away, which he took as a good sign.

"Do I need to stay away?" His voice was low, gruff, hoarse with need.

"Do you want to?" she whispered, desire weighing every word.

"No. We have unfinished business. If you want to." He buried his hand in her hair and took her mouth in a deep claiming kiss, intent on putting his stamp of possession on her.

She broke the kiss, her breath coming heavy. "Oh, I want to. Dinner is ready. Will you have dinner with A.J. and me?"

He drew back and studied her. "Are you sure?"

She brushed her lips against his. "I am. Come up when you're ready."

She sashayed down the aisle of the stable, her hips gently swaying like a siren song calling him. Damn, he had it bad.

DINNER WITH A six-year-old was a new experience for Chase. Yes, he'd eaten with Hailey and A.J. before, but that was when they got together with the whole family, not when it was just the three of them. Hailey had made steak for the two of them and chicken nuggets for A.J., which he pushed around his plate and tried every possible way to wiggle out of eating. Chase probably would have taken it away, but he sensed Hailey wouldn't agree with his methods. Besides, he'd probably used up all of his goodwill with her after getting the pony for A.J.—a pony A.J. was now whining about going out and seeing instead of eating. Despite that, the whole situation was pleasant, almost as if they were a family.

Hailey was getting more exasperated with A.J. the longer they wrangled over dinner. He slouched in his seat, kicked the table sullenly, gnawed on the tines of his fork, and still refused to eat.

Chase pushed away from the table. "That was excellent, Hailey. If you don't mind, I need to go to the stable and bed down the horses. It might take me longer since I have to do Wildfire too."

A.J. popped up in his chair. "I'll go too."

Chase was already shaking his head. "No, you didn't finish eating. If you don't eat, you can't help me."

A.J. gave him a mulish look, his lower lip stuck out as if suspecting he was being conned. But the desire to see his pony outweighed his stubbornness and he started shoveling food in almost faster than he could chew. Hailey stepped up, laying a hand on his shoulder. "Chew your food first, A.J."

Chase folded his arms and leaned against the counter. "You heard your mother. I'll wait."

Hailey shot him a look then busied herself cleaning the table. He shoved off the counter and helped her.

"You can go sit down. I've got this," she murmured.

"Nah, I have some time and you cooked, so the least I can do is help clean. At least until A.J. is ready. Then I'll take him to the barn for a little while. What time is bedtime?"

She looked startled then stammered, "I'd like him in bed by eight. Otherwise, he's a complete bear in the morning. And he needs a bath."

Chase nodded. "That's fine. But I'd like him to start getting used to helping with the pony. He needs to know that having a pony is more than fun times like riding. Is that okay with you?"

She looked doubtful but nodded. "He's not used to chores, but he does like helping with some kitchen things like sweeping and stuff."

Chase nodded. At least she wasn't fighting him on this. Too many kids got horses and didn't want to put in the work to take care of them, leaving it in someone else's hands. He remembered Douglas making sure that he and his brothers always took care of their horses and even the cattle before they took care of themselves. It was one way to teach responsibility. Thank God Hailey was on board with that mentality.

"This won't be hard—simple tasks like helping me clean the stall, brushing Wildfire, feeding him."

She eyed her son, chewing on her lower lip as if considering, then she nodded. "As long as he's no trouble for you."

Chase tried not to let his sigh of relief be too obvious. "Done!" A.J. yelled from the table.

Hailey stepped close to him, her hand on his chest. Chase held his breath. Her hand reignited the arousal that had dampened since their time in the barn. "Are you sure you want to do this? He can be a handful."

He nodded. "We've got this. You stay here and have some alone time. Get ready for his bath or something." He leaned down, his lips tantalizingly close to her ear. "Or, get ready for me."

She shivered, her eyes darkening. "A.J. still needs a bath and a couple of stories read to him."

"He'll be too tired for stories. Trust me."

She swallowed and swayed closer to him. He brushed her lips with his and then stepped past her. "Ready, buddy?"

A.J. jumped off the chair and raced out the door. Chase followed with a lingering glance full of promise. He had to tire that kid out so he could have Hailey to himself tonight.

Chapter Sixteen

HAILEY CLEANED UP after dinner and took a quick shower, shaving and slathering on lotion. It had been so long since she'd even considered being with someone, she was grateful for the warning. Feeling like a woman, not just a mother, was amazing. Tara had snuck into her bathroom and stocked it with lavender-scented lotions and soaps sometime since their conversation earlier. There was also a box of condoms under the sink and with a note attached.

Cowgirl up.

She regretted not having anything sexy to wear, but she still had to give her son a bath and she didn't own any lingerie anyway. Chase would have to take her like she was; hopefully, she could compete with the buckle bunnies and the women throwing themselves at him. She was a mom with the body to prove it—even at twenty-eight she had a little more cellulite, a few stretch marks, and she wasn't as toned as she'd like after working in an office most of the past few years. There hadn't been time or money for gyms or tanning salons or beauty treatments.

Damn it, now she was talking herself out of tonight. Her hands shook as she slipped on the shorts and tank top she slept in, usually as a way to ensure she was dressed when A.J. woke up with a nightmare or came into her room. Not sexy, seductive sleepwear, but it would have to do.

She had just finished getting ready when she heard the clatter on the porch. Chase and A.J. burst into the house like a hurricane, A.J. chattering like a little magpie and covered with dirt. She sighed. So much for sexy times. Back to being a mom.

HAILEY RACED A.J. through bath time, helped by him being too tired to argue about anything, and he was drooping even before she tucked him into bed. A.J. struggled, but he lost the battle, going limp and falling into a deep sleep quickly. Hailey stroked a lock of his hair back from his forehead. Yes, she was procrastinating, suddenly uncertain about the situation. How could Chase want her with all of her baggage, her history, her son, everything?

But he hadn't shied away from her earlier when he stroked her to orgasm in the barn, and only seemed frustrated by the interruption. If other people hadn't shown up, they may have gone further. She was ready for it, ready for him. And she was glad she had waited all these years for the right person to come along. For Chase. He was the man she needed now, and he seemed to need her too. She wasn't going to let time and distance and thought change her mind.

With one last kiss for her son, she turned out the light, making sure the night light was on and leaving the door open a bit in case he called out for her, though he seemed down for the count. She headed downstairs and toward Chase's bedroom.

When she pushed open the door, her heart gave a small flip. There was a bottle of wine chilling in a bucket next to the bed, with a couple of glasses, and a vase with assorted wildflowers on the side table. Candles cast a warm glow in the dark room. She sank on the bed, her hands reaching out for the flowers, gently touching the petals. Their scent filled the room. The one thing that was missing was Chase, but the sound of water running in the shower in the adjacent bath clued her in that he had spent his time setting this all up instead of getting himself cleaned up from the day. The consideration brought tears to her eyes.

The water shut off and a couple of minutes later, the door opened and Chase stepped out, a towel wrapped low around his waist, showing off his chiseled abs and the notches low in the side of his torso that she decided she'd trace later with her tongue. Chase flushed when he saw her sitting on the bed.

"I didn't expect you here so early. Or maybe I took too long to get ready."

She rose and walked to him. "You did all this for me?"

He nodded. "I thought you deserved a little romance. It's been a long time since I've done anything like this." He traced her cheek with the back of a hand. "Do you like it?"

Instead of answering, she rose of her toes and pressed her lips to his, somehow feeling as if this were the first time all over again. He waited for a long moment, then he took over, his towel dropping to the floor as he curled a hand around her lower back and hauled her up against his body, his arousal pressing into the softness of her belly. She wrapped her arms around his neck and gave herself up to the passion he had inspired, surrendering to him.

With his other hand, he loosened the belt to her robe and smoothed it over her shoulders, taking a strap of her tank top with it. He tossed the robe onto the bed, leaving her in the top and shorts. She pulled back, suddenly feeling self-conscious. He eyed her beaded nipples, prominent through the cotton shirt.

"What's wrong?" His voice was low, husky with arousal.

She bit her lower lip, suddenly unsure. The candlelight was a nice touch, hiding imperfections, but maybe that's why he'd done it?

He put two fingers under her chin, tilted her head up, and took her lips in a deep, sensual kiss that threatened to leave her breathless. By the time he lifted his head, she was clinging to his arms and leaning against him, her legs boneless, all strength gone.

"I want you, and only you. Now, let's move this somewhere more comfortable where I can kiss every inch of your luscious body and prove how much I want you over and over again." He bent down and swooped her up with an arm under her knees and another under her lower back so she was forced to grab him around the neck with a squeal.

He tossed her onto the bed and followed her down, trapping her beneath him neatly, settling between her thighs, his erection brushing against the thin material that separated him from the place that ached for him to complete her. His head dipped down to kiss her, his tongue tangling with hers, coaxing her into playing with him. His hand wandered down and slipped under the tank top, pulling it up and over her head with just a quick break in the kiss, baring her to his gaze, his touch, his lips.

"Have mercy," he breathed, the appreciation in his eyes made her blush. "You're gorgeous, sweetheart. Absolutely beautiful."

His hands moved to cup her breasts, his thumbs sweeping over her nipples . . . once, twice, then again as they hardened almost painfully, begging for a harder touch. He bent down and sucked one into his mouth, licking the nub, then nipping it lightly with the barest edge of his teeth as she squealed under the onslaught. His other hand plucked and teased the other side, not to let it feel left out, then his mouth moved there to torture the tip. He pushed them together and alternated as she squirmed on the bed under his attentions. She'd never realized how sensitive her breasts were, had never known such sensations. Could she orgasm simply like this? Chase seemed determined to find out. She threaded her fingers through his sandy-brown hair and gave him the edge of her nails, massaging his scalp as he tortured her.

He laughed against her chest and gave her a final nip before laying a hand low on her belly just inside the shorts she wore. "Naughty girl. No panties?"

"Didn't think I'd need them tonight." She panted. "I could always go back upstairs and put some on."

He gave her a light slap right over her core, a little tap that sent lightning streaking through her body. She arched up. "What was that for?"

"For being a wiseass."

He placed a final kiss between her breasts and started the slow journey down her torso, stopping to kiss her stretch marks. When she tried to cover them, he simply trapped her hands and continued to tongue them until she was a shivering mess under his body. He traced his tongue under the elastic of the boy shorts and drew them down her body slowly, placing kisses down her legs until he could toss the shorts somewhere in the room. He moved to the end of the bed and stared down at her, his erection jutting out proudly. She licked her suddenly dry lips and reached for him, but he shook his head.

"I'm too close, and I'm not done with you yet." He opened the drawer in the side table, pulled out a string of condoms, tossed them on the bed, and gave her a wry smile. "Didn't want to have them out and look like I was assuming."

She arched her brow at the long strand. "You're awfully confident, aren't you?"

"I don't plan on letting you up until I've had my fill. That might take days."

He grabbed her ankles and pulled her to the end of the bed, spreading her legs in the process. He got to his knees and stroked her thighs until she relaxed. He just stared for a long moment until she shifted uncomfortably on the bed, her face burning. He settled her legs on his shoulders and lowered his head. At the first teasing swipe of his tongue, she froze, a wave of pleasure crashing over her. Her breath caught in her throat and she arched her back, locked in position. Then he did it again and she couldn't remain still, her body rocked by the sensations his tongue and fingers elicited. He locked his hands around her hips to hold her in place while he licked and nibbled and took her to the edge and backed off. Then he got his fingers involved, slowly pressing deep inside to find the spot that made her eyes roll back. First one finger, then two.

"You taste so fucking amazing, Hailey. I knew it would be like this. I've imagined this for so long; never knew this would happen. Just a little more, baby."

Damn, he was a talker during sex when all she could do was utter wordless sounds and pray her son was dead to the world and couldn't hear her. Then she didn't care if anyone heard her because Chase's mouth was fixed on her clitoris and his fingers were dancing over her happy spot deep inside and the mother of all orgasms was rushing up on her. When it finally crashed over her, her back arched and she screamed his name, her thighs clamping around his neck, and she swore she almost blacked out. When she finally came back, he was lying on top of her, his cock positioned at the entrance to her pussy, the blunt head just inside.

She lifted her hips and wrapped her arms and legs around him, inviting him in. She smiled.

"I need you, Chase."

GOD, SHE WAS fucking amazing. Watching Hailey come so hard almost made Chase lose it like a teenager for the first time. He had had to grit his teeth and grind his cock into the side of the mattress and think of anything but her to stave off his own release. She was so unencumbered, so authentic in reaching her pleasure. He was used to women who were more apt to be fake in all things, though he never had a woman have to fake her orgasm with him. But often, they were more concerned with their image, their hair, or other things to truly let loose in bed.

He found her absolutely gorgeous. Her gentle curves, her sexy body. She was amazing, so much more than he had ever imagined. While she came down from her orgasm, he rolled a condom on, groaning at his sensitivity, and slid her up on the bed to make her more comfortable.

He was so close to heaven, positioned between her thighs, just waiting for her. When she finally opened her gorgeous blue eyes and focused on him, he was lying on top of her, his cock positioned at the entrance to her pussy, the blunt head just inside. Her eyes widened at his size, then softened as she wrapped her arms and legs around him, lifting her hips so he slid a little farther inside. He felt her warmth surrounding him, thawing the cold that had fenced him in for so long, breaking through the loneliness that had encased him.

"You okay, Hailey?"

She squeezed her legs. "You're killing me, Chase. Don't stop, please."

It was the *please* that unleashed him. He flexed his hips and thrust, a steady push until he was seated to the hilt. He paused, loving the way her nails bit into the flesh of his back. He leaned down and kissed her, their tongues tangling as he started a steady, thrusting rhythm, fucking her hard. He hadn't felt this connected with another person perhaps ever. She felt like the other half of his soul, the other part of him that he'd been looking for.

The sounds of their fucking filled the room: their moans,

heavy breathing, and their bodies pressing together faster and faster as they reached for their climax. He kept his eyes firmly fixed on hers, feeling like he could see into her soul, striving for that connection that went beyond the physical. He reached between them with his hand to stroke the nub at the top of her slit, and she clenched around him, her orgasm triggering his. She tightened, crying out his name, and he followed her over.

He collapsed to the bed, shifting to his back and pulling her over him so he wouldn't crush her. He knew it would be like this, had always known. Maybe that's why he had never made a move before now. He had never been ready, had never been the right man. Was he ready now? Because no way this was a one-night affair for him. He needed more time with her, more of Hailey. He was just afraid that he'd break her heart, or she'd break his.

Chapter Seventeen

CHASE SPENT THE morning giving A.J. a lesson on how to ride Wildfire, with Hailey watching from the house, occasionally using a pair of binoculars to see better. She wanted to be by the corral, but standing by the ring would be distracting for both Chase and A.J. and they needed to focus. So, instead, she relaxed on the porch, her body pleasantly sore from last evening's activities, and spied on them from the house and admired the view.

There was something satisfying about watching a man and boy working together. She sipped her glass of iced tea and tried to focus on the present, not on how long Chase might be here or what the future would bring. For today, everything was perfect.

"Someone looks like they had a great evening. I suppose you're not up for a ride around the ranch?" Tara stood at the bottom of the porch and smirked at her.

Hailey just grinned, a hint of heat in her face. "Nope, I'm too relaxed to join the riding lesson."

Tara glanced down at the barn, where West was headed, and nodded. "He's good with kids and horses, isn't he?"

"I never knew that about him, but he's great with A.J." Hailey gestured to the pitcher and extra glass.

Tara took a seat in the other rocking chair, pouring her

own glass. "So, how was last night?" Hailey smiled but said nothing. Tara frowned. "That's not fair. I stocked your bathroom. I deserve some details."

"Isn't Chase like your brother?"

Tara wrinkled her nose. "Oh yeah. Kind of. On second thought, never mind. Just tell me this, are you up here second-guessing the whole thing or are you okay with it?"

Hailey took a deep breath. "Part of me is freaking out a bit. I mean, am I being irresponsible, getting too close to someone who is going to leave? And I'm letting my son get close too, and he may not understand why Chase has to go on the road. This could blow up in my face, and not just for me."

Tara sipped her tea and watched the action down at the barn, West giving pointers to Chase and A.J., the boy eagerly listening to both men. "It's a risk. But life—and love—is never easy. I started seeing West when I knew I was leaving. By your reasoning, I should never have started anything with him since I was headed back to San Francisco. But if I hadn't gotten to know West, I would have never found a reason to stay. Maybe that's what you're doing, giving Chase a reason to stay."

Hailey cocked her head, realization dawning. "That's what this is all about. The horses, you pushing me at Chase. You want him to stay and you're looking for any excuse to make it happen."

Tara set her glass down deliberately on the coaster and leaned forward, fixing a hard stare at Hailey. "Yeah, I want Chase off the bull-riding circuit; sue me. I would think you, of all people, would understand that. And I also expect you'd want to help him if only because of your long-standing friendship, never mind any other relationship you're having. Do you know how hard that phone call was?"

Tara jumped up and walked to the railing, gripping the wooden beam so hard her knuckles turned white. "It almost gutted West. Then to have to sit vigil by his bedside, watch them rush him into surgery not once but three times. I could only sit there, helpless. If you're asking what I'd do to keep Chase from going back, the answer is whatever it takes."

Hailey slowly set her glass down and stood, letting out a breath before joining Tara on the porch. "I know what that phone call is like because I received one too, only I never got to sit by a bedside or see Adam again. He died before they even called me. He had been on the road more than he was home, never really saw A.J. except for a few weeks here and there. A.J. was only two when Adam died. Believe me, I know how you all feel."

Tara's shoulders slumped and she laid her hand on Hailey's. "I'm sorry. I didn't mean to bring up bad memories."

Hailey tried to smile, but even she knew it was a facsimile of a real one. "It's been four years and I've accepted it. I don't want to see Chase follow the same path. But I learned something with my husband. They both love riding bulls. They say they do it for the money, but they also get something out of it. I know Adam liked the excitement, the adrenaline."

"What does Chase get out of it?"

Hailey thought for a moment. "Well, he loves adrenaline and excitement, just like Adam. That's what made them such good friends. But I think there's something more, and until we figure it out, we won't know how to counter it. He needs to decide to stay for his own reasons, not because we force him. If he feels trapped, he'll be miserable and resent everyone."

Tara rolled her eyes. "God, I don't need a whiny Chase moping around here." She eyed Hailey through the corner of her eyes. "You think you can figure out what's dragging him away?"

She sighed. "I don't know, Tara. I won't pressure him."

"And you can accept him leaving at the end of this?"

Hailey sipped her tea and watched the man she feared she was falling in love with hoist into a saddle the boy she knew was coming to idolize the man.

"I don't know."

CHASE SPENT A couple of hours learning patience as he tried to focus A.J. on Wildfire, especially when he then taught the boy how to care for the horse, including grooming and cleaning the tack. A.J. was a typical six-year-old, easily distracted and uninterested in cleaning up, whining a little about being tired, wanting something to drink, and trying to wander off. But when West came down, they worked on it together and A.J. seemed to enjoy the attention of both men. Once Wildfire was settled and they were each enjoying a bottle of water from the little refrigerator in the tack room, A.J. shifted his feet and tugged on his belt.

"Something on your mind?" Chase asked.

A.J. shuffled his feet, looking down, then said, "The kids

at camp were all talking about how they were entering events at the county fair next week. Can I enter with Wildfire?"

The boy wasn't ready, especially after one lesson, but he had to give the question its due consideration. He paused. What he remembered of the county fair events for younger kids was that they weren't much. His first fair, he was almost a teenager, but he felt left out and alone, as all the guys from school were participating and getting the attention of the girls, many of whom also competed. He hated sitting in the stands, and his foster father, Douglas, knew it. That next day, Douglas took him out to the barn and introduced him to roping.

"You and Wildfire aren't quite ready yet, but there may be an event we can get you ready for. You ever rope a calf?"

A.J.'s eyes got wide and he shook his head. "That's okay. We don't start with a real calf but with a fake one. I'll bet a lot of your friends are doing that one, right, West?"

West nodded. "That's the most popular event for kids your age. And we can get you ready for that in a week."

Chase leaned over, nudging A.J.'s shoulder with his own. "West is the king of roping. Better than I am."

"If you worked the range like I do every day, you'd be good too. But Chase is the best to teach you how to ride," West commented.

"What is this? A mutual admiration society?" Hailey drawled as she walked into the barn.

A.J. ran over and hugged his mother, getting dirt on her shorts. "Momma, Chase and West are going to teach me how to rope so I can enter the fair next week."

She lifted her head and met his gaze. "Do you have time

for this?"

Chase nodded. "It'll help him connect with his friends at school. And he can practice a lot on his own."

A brilliant smile crossed her face, lighting her up. "I think that's great, baby. And you were great on Wildfire."

A.J. dragged her outside to see the pony, which had been turned out to an adjoining corral, chattering about his ride and roping. Chase's gaze followed A.J. and Hailey outside. He tried to avoid West's intense stare, but it was only a matter of time before he spoke his piece.

"Do you know what you're getting into here? She's got a lot of baggage, including a son. And he's getting attached. What's going to happen when you leave?"

Hailey and A.J.'s laughter echoed into the barn. The sounds wove ties around his soul, pulling him closer, anchoring him to the ranch, to the people, and a part of him wanted to embrace those ties, didn't feel strangled as he expected. And that scared the hell out of him.

He stood, brushing off his jeans. "Hailey knows I'm going back out as soon as I can. She understands my life and what I do. No promises were made."

West also stood. "She's not one of your buckle bunnies, accepting a one-night stand or even a couple of nights. She was your best friend's wife. Her son is halfway to idolizing you. Hailey isn't fling material."

"You don't think I know I that? You don't think I struggle with that every day? Wonder what Adam would think about me getting involved with her?" Chase stepped closer to West, speaking in a low voice.

West put a hand on his brother's shoulder, his own tone

calm and reasonable, which only served to grate on nerves. "Adam's gone now. That shouldn't have any effect on your decisions. But you should think about whether you're going to stay or go. She deserves someone who plans on sticking around, not flitting in and out when the mood strikes."

"You don't need to worry about Chase and me. We're both adults and have gone into this with our eyes open. I'm not expecting anything more from him than a couple of weeks. And I will be responsible for A.J. There will be no awkwardness here at work, if you're worried about that." Hailey's voice coming from the entrance of the barn was stiff, formal, and filled with pain.

At least A.J. hadn't overheard the conversation, though he probably wouldn't understand what they were talking about. But Hailey's words pissed him off even as his more rational side told him he should be happy that she had no expectations.

He strode over to Hailey and grabbed her shoulders gently. "Hailey, this isn't the time."

She pulled out of his grasp, clasping her hands in front of her, a forced smile on her face. "I completely understand, Chase. You have no worries about us. Now, I'm going to make lunch for A.J. then we're headed into town for errands."

She turned on her heel and headed toward the house, calling for A.J. Chase's head dropped and he wanted to punch the wall. Goddamn it. How could he have screwed up so badly so quickly?

He avoided West's gaze and headed into the barn. "Yeah I get it. I fucked up. I don't need a postmortem."

West shrugged. "I think you should figure out what you want. Hailey is a good woman and deserves someone who can care for her and her son."

Chase whirled around and got in West's face. His brother never moved. "And you don't think I'm good for her?"

"She needs someone who will stick around. But that's not you, is it?"

Chapter Eighteen

HAILEY BARELY LISTENED to A.J. as he chattered on about his morning. Everything lately was Chase this and Chase that. Damn it, she was afraid this would happen. What would happen when he left? She'd have to deal with the fallout. What was worse, she was getting entangled with him too, falling right into the trap of looking for him, making him a part of their lives, as if they were a family. And he seemed to fit right in with them, having breakfast with A.J. every morning, sitting in at story time before bed, and making love to Hailey. That one glorious night where she was able to forget about her stress and duties as a mom and remember what it was like to be a woman—a desirable, sexy woman.

"You okay?" Tara asked from the kitchen doorway, sympathy weighing down every word.

Hailey refused to turn and look at her, couldn't bear to see the pity in her eyes. Stupid Hailey Spencer, falling for the town flirt when she, of all people, should have known better, having grown up with him and seen him in action. She cut up an apple, her vision blurring. A hand covered hers.

"Let me do that." Tara took the knife and finished slicing the apple and put the plate in front of A.J. "Your mom and I are going to be in the other room. Can you eat by yourself?"

A.J. nodded, focused on going back outside to see Chase. Tara drew Hailey to the living room just outside the kitchen where she could still see and hear A.J., but he wouldn't overhear them. Hailey sank down onto the couch and buried her head in her hands.

"God, I'm pathetic. I knew he was leaving. Said it was okay even. Told myself I could handle it. But hearing those words! Am I nothing to him?"

Tara sat next to her and hugged her. "No, I don't think so. Chase would never have gotten close to you if he didn't care. Yes, I know his reputation as a love 'em and leave 'em kind of guy. He never hides that. But he also doesn't get involved outside of the one night. He certainly doesn't spend time with his lady friends during the day. He's broken all sorts of rules with you."

Hailey sniffed. "That's because he can't avoid us and we're Adam's family. He sees me as a friend, now with some benefits, nothing more."

Tara cocked her head and studied her speculatively. "Do you really think that? Because I'm not so sure. We could test your theory though."

Hailey sat up and narrowed her gaze. When Tara got that thoughtful tone, Hailey had learned to be careful. It meant Tara was plotting. The last time she had plotted with Emma, Hailey found herself in Chase's bed. Well, hell, what else could she do? "What do you have in mind?"

Tara grinned, a twinkle of mischief in her eye that worried Hailey. "Now that you've broken your fast, so to speak, I think it's time you really got out there, see what's available in Granite Junction. And, if Chase is really leaving, he won't mind if you start exploring your options."

"I HAVE NO idea how you talked me into this. I claim workplace abuse," Hailey muttered, fiddling with the buttons on the denim button-down shirt Tara had insisted she borrow.

Tara slapped her hand. "Stop messing around with that. You can't button it without choking. I'd open the second one but the buttons are too far apart and they'd show off your boobs, although—"

"No." Hailey shot down that idea before Tara could even finish, terrified of what the other woman would even suggest. It was bad enough that she was wearing a white sequined skirt that was a few inches above the knee, a little north of what Hailey was comfortable with. Despite it being flowy, she still felt like she was flashing her goods around. The wide, brown leather braided belt was cinched tighter than a saddle on a horse, and Hailey felt like she could barely breathe. She even had to borrow the brown cowboy boots with fancy stitching, although Tara said they were too small for her feet and Hailey could keep them.

"Damn, girl. If I had known you were going to look like that, I wouldn't have bothered coming out tonight. You'll be beating them off with a whip. And many of these guys would like that." Emma grinned, wearing a pair of skintight jeans, a fancy beaded blouse, and a chunky necklace, looking just fine on her own.

"You look fabulous, too. You'll grab more attention than a single mom will," Hailey said. Hailey leaned against the high table they were standing at, easing the pressure on her feet. Damn, she had forgotten how uncomfortable real shoes could be after living in sneakers for so long. Though she couldn't deny how sexy she felt in this outfit.

Emma frowned, a ghost of sadness in her eyes. "Doubtful. I'm more like their sister than anything else in this town. But hey, I can dance and have fun, right? Has Chase seen you yet?"

Tara gave an evil grin. "Nope. West and Ty are charged with bringing him. I said this was girls' night, but West knows something's up. Ty's playing tonight, and I know they'll be here to support him."

"Like West thinks you're anywhere else but here," Emma teased.

"Hell no. He knows I'll be here—for Ty and to protect my man. Those women are shameless when they go after a man, even one who's taken. Hailey, darlin', you'd better be ready to fight for your guy tonight. The women of Granite Junction think they own him, but we all know he's yours. We got your back."

"I thought the point of tonight was for me to find someone else." Although, the thought of being with anyone else just felt wrong to her and not only because she had just slept with Chase the night before. No, she was all tangled up with him, emotions and everything, and it just didn't sit right to go looking for anyone else. The most she'd do is have fun tonight, something she'd had precious little of in the past few years. Not that she regretted anything she'd done, but she deserved a little Hailey time, and A.J. was happy to spend time with a friend from camp. Everyone won that night.

Emma shrugged. "If that's what you want, but I have a feeling once Chase sees you, he's going to be green with jealousy and no one will touch you."

Hailey eyed the crowd hanging out by the bar: women in tight jeans or short skirts and skintight tops with teased hair and lots of makeup, all looking more like the lineup for a beauty pageant than a night at The Rock. Each woman was scanning the crowd like a cowboy looking for a calf to rope, someone to cull from the crowd, reel in, and hogtie. No, she definitely wouldn't be able to tolerate seeing Chase with another woman tonight.

The only problem was, what happened once they got together? Was there a future or was it a for-now kind of thing, and could she handle it?

The Rock was filling up, ranchers, cowboys, and cowgirls all piling in for the Saturday night fun. There wasn't much else to do in Granite Junction, so this was the place to be. Live bands often played at least two to three nights a week, and everyone was ready to kick back after a long workweek. The waitress brought another round of beers before they even ordered refills gesturing to a table with a couple of cowboys, one of whom tipped his hat to them. He looked vaguely familiar and Hailey smiled.

Taking that as an invitation, he ambled over. "Hi, Hailey, Tara, Emma. I see you're all out unescorted tonight. How does West feel about that?"

Tara tossed her hair. "I'm a grown woman, Cam Miller. I can do what I want. Besides, West trusts me."

"And he'll be here soon?" Cam finished with a wry smile. She grinned and tipped her beer back. "That too."

He nodded to Emma and then turned to Hailey. "I'm sorry I missed you the other day. I had to get back for a delivery and couldn't stay. Hope your boy liked his pony."

The name finally registered and she smiled. "He loved it. I can't believe you still had Wildfire. Thank you so much for being willing to part with him. A.J. couldn't believe that was the same pony his father rode when he was a boy."

Cam gave a little smile that only partially came to his eyes, and Hailey could tell if he ever really let loose, he could be a heartbreaker. He had dark chocolate hair that was just a bit too long, with waves that curled around his ears and neck, waves that made a woman itch to run her fingers through. His eyes were serious, and he seemed to be the kind of man who would stick by you, the kind of man who thought before he acted. Too bad she preferred a bad boy with sandy-brown hair and a wild streak.

He didn't seem to smile much but was comfortable talking with the women, knew Tara well at least, and seemed to be well liked. He was built like most working ranchers, lean, muscular, and tall, filling out the jeans and button-down shirt nicely. All in all, Cam was a man Hailey should be falling all over, a man who would offer the security she had been seeking for the past few years, but she was waiting for a guy with laughter in his eyes and a teasing smile.

He gave a slow nod. "Well, James Spencer asked if I'd consider keeping Wildfire until his son moved back to town. He seemed to think he would move back here someday. I was real sorry to hear about him."

Hailey nodded. "Thanks for thinking of us. It's strange how life brings us back around again. A.J. can't wait to learn to ride on him."

"He can't have a better teacher than Chase Summers. He trains all my working horses, and he's real good with new riders too." He glanced at the table, at the three beers still unfinished, and gave Emma a vaguely annoyed look. "I seem to be interrupting your ladies' night. I'll leave you be. But, if you'd like, may I have a dance later?"

Hailey's eyes widened and the other two women stared, fascinated by the conversation. Finally, she nodded. "I'd like that, Cam. Thank you."

He nodded to all three and headed back to his table. Emma leaned in. "Don't you work fast? Boy, you come to town and get the two hottest bachelors panting over you. Maybe I'll call you the lucky bitch instead of Tara."

Emma's voice was light, but there was a hint of envy in there, maybe even jealousy. Hailey laid a hand on hers. "You don't mind, do you? Is there something between you two?"

Emma laughed. "Please. He's good friends with my brother, Nathan, and they both protect me like I'm still five years old. It's even worse because Nathan is the sheriff. Just what I need—the town cop and a rancher with an overdeveloped protective streak. No, trust me. There's nothing there."

Tara gave a small shrug as if to say, *no idea.* Hailey decided to take Emma at her word. It was just once dance. It's not like they were getting married or anything.

WEST SHOVED PAST Chase at the entrance to The Rock as if he were late and had somewhere to be. Maybe he did, since they had gotten tied up with a horse that had been injured and all three of them were needed to help settle her down. West had been antsy since then, driving faster than usual, rushing them along, all to hear Ty play.

"Shit, West. Settle down. They'll wait for Ty. Hell, he keeps this place packed when he plays. He's not late anyway."

West whirled, a look of intensity on his face, and Chase backed up a step, hands up. "Whoa, chill out man. Is something wrong?"

"I don't see Tara. Do you? Last time she was here, she almost caused a fight." He strained to look over the crowds of people, and Chase got a chill up his spine.

"Did you say Tara? I thought you said she was spending some time with Hailey and Emma."

West shot him a glare and stomped through the crowd like a bull scenting a cow in heat. As if Tara would even consider looking at someone else. She was so far gone on him. Chase followed more slowly, also scanning the crowd but not for a blonde. He was looking for a redhead who he just sensed was out looking for trouble.

He had wanted to talk to her that afternoon, but she had been gone most of the day. Tonight, the house was dark, and he didn't even have her cell number. West saved his sanity by telling him the girls were spending time together and suggesting they go support Ty at The Rock. He should have known West wouldn't let Tara out of his sight for long, or maybe she would never let him go to The Rock alone, not after the last time when she had been accosted by a couple of drunk cowboys and he'd had a couple of overly friendly women try to steal him away from Tara. Yeah, that had been a fun night, and Chase could have had his pick of women to console, only he went home alone, as he so often did now.

A hand slid down his back and cupped his ass in a familiar fashion. He whirled and a brunette took a surprised step back, almost stumbling. "Chase, honey. It's just me. I thought we could spend some time tonight. You know, like old times."

The suggestive quality in her voice, once so sexy, only grated on his nerves. Her hand came back and rested on his waist and began a slow descent over the fly of his jeans. He seized her wrist, caging it firmly but not enough to hurt her, halting her movement. "Not tonight, Shonda."

Her eyes widened and struggled for a moment but his grip was solid. He lifted her hand away and back to her side; only then did he release it. She frowned and gave him a wounded look. "I don't know what crawled up your ass, Chase Summers, but you better pull it out and soon. You're turning into a real asshole."

He quirked a grin. "From you, Shonda, that's almost a compliment."

He turned and followed his brother, ignoring the growl behind him. Maybe it was time he stopped coming to The Rock so much. His exes were becoming a real issue. They didn't seem to understand when things were over. He saw West over at one of the high tables—kissing Tara like he hadn't seen her in weeks when he'd only just left her a couple of hours ago—and wove through the crowd to get to his side. Emma Holt was on the other side of Tara, trying vainly to look anywhere but at the smooching couple. He caught her attention and rolled his eyes. She widened her eyes and blushed bright red, almost panicked, and her gaze darted away to the dance floor.

He glanced at the table and the three beers and the six shot glasses.

Wait, three glasses? Six shots? He narrowed his gaze and put his hand on his brother's shoulder, who promptly shrugged him off. "No can do, brother mine. I think I need a few words with your woman."

"Get your own, dammit. I'm busy."

"If you get any busier, you'll be arrested for public indecency. Now, Tara, sweetheart, what did you do with Hailey?"

Tara slowly peeked around West's shoulders, blinking in a dazed fashion. Nice to know his brother still had his touch with the ladies. She smiled, not a sweet, southern belle kind of smile, but the chilling, I-know-something-you-don't-and-you're-not-going-to-like-it-but-I-love-it kind of smile.

Fuck. Tara was plotting and that meant he was screwed. She was kind of evil at times. Thank God they loved her, although right now he was damned scared of her.

He focused on Emma, who squeaked and whirled around, giving him her back. He sidled around the table and draped an arm around her. "Emma, darlin'. I know you like me and I know you weren't party to whatever Tara is doing. So, in the spirit of friendship and all that, why don't you tell me what's going on?"

She wiggled out from under his arm, indignation written

on her face. "Friendship? Seriously? Is it friendship when you busted up my dancing with that new cowboy on the Triple S spread?"

Chase shifted on his feet, scowling. "He was only looking for one thing, Emma. I was looking out for you."

"Well, maybe I was looking for that too, not a forever after. I was perfectly fine and you embarrassed me. Well, you've made this easier. Hailey is dancing and having a good time. Leave her alone."

He followed her gaze to see Hailey plastered up against Cam Miller, slow dancing to a Jimmie Allen song. She tossed her hair back and laughed, gazing up at Cam with a soft smile. He saw red, but Tara placed a hand on his arm.

"Let her have fun, Chase. You said you were leaving, remember?"

"I'm not gone yet." He grabbed Emma's hand and dragged her on the dance floor, ignoring her yelp.

He pulled Emma against his body and pushed people out of his path, not even pretending to dance on his way to Cam and Hailey. Emma, on the other hand, dug in her heels and fought him every step. He glared down at her. "Don't make me pick you up."

"And my brother will arrest you for assault."

He backed off; she'd make good on her threat. "What do you want?"

"You want to make her jealous?" Emma weaved her arms around his neck and pulled him close so she could fix a stern, teacher glare in his face. "Wrap your arms around me and dance with me."

"You're mean, Ms. Holt. You must be hell in that classroom." He smiled at her, catching on to her game.

They danced slowly across the floor until they were next to Cam and Hailey. Casually, he bumped into them. Eyes wide and innocent, he said, "I'm so sorry. It's a little crowded tonight. I didn't see you there."

Hailey peered over Cam's arm and glared at him and then Emma. Cam took one look at Chase and swallowed. Chase could only imagine how pissed off he looked. The other man darted a glance between Hailey and Chase, suddenly looking like he wanted to be anywhere but in that position. "Chase, look. I was just being neighborly. Nothing happened. Want to switch?"

Before his words were even out, he fairly threw Emma at Cam and gathered Hailey in his arms. She struggled for a moment but stumbled a bit on her feet so he grasped her tightly, not letting her. "How much have you had to drink tonight?"

"A couple of beers and a few shots. Fireball is yummy. Tastes like cinnamon, but with a kick." She giggled.

"Yeah, like a fucking mule. What do you think you're doing?"

"I'm mad at you. Tara thought I needed a girls' night out. No men invited." The last was said with a glare at him. Unfortunately, she ruined the effect by stumbling to the side then giggling again. "Whoops."

He closed his eyes for a second and shook his head. Where the hell did they get Fireball? "I hate to tell you, sweetheart, but you were totally wrong." He gestured next to them where Emma was being held up by Cam and Tara was plastered up against West a little farther away.

Hailey's eyes widened. "Damn. I guess we messed up."

He wasn't so sure about that. It was kind of nice holding Hailey. She felt good in his arms, soft, warm, and smelled so sexy. His body hardened as she rubbed against him, and he shifted to the side to be unobtrusive.

Cam gave him a reproachful look and leaned over. "Took you long enough to get here. I couldn't stop them from ordering the shots. I only stopped them from ordering more." He glanced at Emma, who was pulling away from him. He locked his arms around her, holding her close.

"Thanks for looking out for them. I think we've got it from here. Will you look after Emma?"

Emma straightened. "Emma can look after herself, thank you very much. She doesn't need another big brother around here."

Cam grunted. "Thank God I'm not your brother. Let's go sit down until the band starts playing, get something to drink. No more Fireball." She pouted at his last words but followed or, more accurately, was half dragged to a table.

The music changed to a faster song and Chase sighed, reluctantly loosening his grip on Hailey, who gave him a sad look. "Why are you here? Why aren't you spending time with your other lady friends?"

"Hailey, we should talk."

She rolled her eyes. "Nothing good ever comes from that. No thanks, I'll pass. Go have fun."

He grabbed her arm before she could walk away. "Hang on. I didn't say I was done. You walked away without talking to me. Is that who you are, Hailey? The love 'em and leave 'em type?"

"Maybe I'm taking a page out of your book. One night, no ties. That way I won't get hurt. Only, you can't avoid it, can you?" Her eyes filled with tears and he crushed her to him, stroking her hair with a hand.

"Hailey, baby. I never wanted to hurt you. And I want a hell of a lot more than one night."

She sniffled against his shirt. "But it can't be more than a few weeks, can it?"

He rested his chin on her head. "I don't know, honey. Do we have to decide that right now? Or can we enjoy our time together?"

"I'd be happy to enjoy some time with you, Chase. But you already know that," a flirtatious voice piped up next to him as a hand burrowed under his shirt. It was definitely not Hailey's, judging by the length of the talons on her hand.

He stiffened under the touch, but before he could respond, Hailey let out a hiss and glared around him. "Beat it. Chase is occupied tonight. And every night."

Shonda stood there, all attitude and big hair, stroking him like she owned him, like a fucking cat, and smirked, displaying big white teeth that vaguely resembled a horse's mouth. "It sure don't seem like you want him for who he is. I'm willing to accept him for exactly who he is. And we're good together, remember?" She leaned in and blew in his ear.

He flinched but had no chance to respond before Hailey launched herself at the other woman, taking her down in a move a wrestler would have been proud of. The screeches that came out of both women made him wince and, before he could take action, he was shoved aside by Tara, who tackled one of Shonda's friends who was about to pile on and come at Hailey from the back. Within seconds, Emma had joined in and there was a major catfight in the middle of the dance floor.

He wished this were the first time he'd seen it. This was, however, the first time he wouldn't enjoy it. Damn it, Hailey could get hurt.

He bent over to break it up, but West pulled him back. "Never get in the middle of a catfight unless you want to lose your balls. You told me that once."

Cam swore next to them. "Damn it, can't you guys control your women?"

West gave him a sideways glance. "One of those women is yours, isn't she?"

Cam shook his head. "I'm just watching out for her tonight."

Chase barked a laugh. "You're doing a bang-up job, Cam."

He flinched when Shonda grabbed Hailey's hair, but then Hailey made some sort of twist and shift and Shonda was on the floor, her hair in Hailey's hands and an arm twisted behind her back.

Sirens sounded outside, and each man jumped in and grabbed their woman.

Chase ducked as Hailey came up swinging. "Hold on there, slugger. It's just me. You won, okay?"

She glared at him. "We'll see about that."

She shook off his hands and stalked to the table, followed by the other women, who high-fived when they got there. Chase shuddered. "There are three of them. We're so screwed."

Cam strode to the table, his face red. He grabbed Emma and dragged her to the back door just as her brother Nathan came in the front with one of his deputies. Chase and West exchanged glances and followed, hustling their women out the back, too, before they spent the night in the jail.

Chapter Nineteen

HAILEY TWISTED THE light fabric of her skirt in her hands, picking at the silver sequins that reflected the moonlight coming through the truck windows. She didn't get to enjoy a full night out, but she supposed they accomplished their goal of getting Chase to pay attention. He certainly acted like a man who was jealous and not like a man who had a one-night stand and was ready to move on.

Hailey hadn't quite been prepared for the haze that had come over when that hussy had all but humped Chase while he was still holding her. The brazenness appalled her, and next thing she knew, she was rolling on the floor like a farm animal, reminding this woman who Chase belonged to. It was nice to have women on her side, fighting with her, but tomorrow, she'd pay. Her father would hear about it, despite how quickly Cam had gotten them out of there. They'd managed to avoid the sheriff, but rumors traveled fast in Granite Junction, and her parents would hear before church or worse, at church. Hailey would blame the Fireball, but she couldn't say she wouldn't have done the same thing sober. At least they'd made one thing clear tonight: Chase was hers, for however long he was around, no matter what pain it brought her at the end.

Chase drove with a single-minded intensity, but she

couldn't tell if he was mad at her or the situation. Judging by his speed, she decided to stay quiet until he calmed down. He pulled into the driveway for Redemption Ranch but stopped about halfway down the lane at a small cutoff. He put the car in gear and stared out into the night without saying anything for several minutes.

Finally, he heaved a long breath. "Do you need to pick up A.J. tonight? Or is there a babysitter at the house?"

Her heart melted a little more. His first question was about her son. Whoever thought this man was all about fun, laughter, and himself didn't know him very well. She shook her head. "No, he's staying with a friend from camp. His first sleepover, but if I haven't heard from them by now, chances are, the boys are sound asleep and won't wake until morning."

A muscle in his jaw flexed as he continued to stare into the night for several more long minutes. He turned and glared at her. "What the hell were you thinking tonight? Going out, drinking like that, getting into a bar fight? Jesus, Hailey. Do you know how I felt when I saw you there tonight? Do you know what could have happened if the wrong guy paid you attention? Thank God for Cam Miller."

Anger flared, bright and hot, and she couldn't stand to be in the truck with him anymore. She fumbled for the door handle and pushed her way outside, slamming the door behind her. She sucked in the night air and wrapped her arms around herself, the chill in the air doing nothing to cool her anger. She heard the driver's door slam shut and Chase coming around the car.

"What the hell, Hailey?"

She whirled and faced him. "It's all right for you to go out and have fun, meet girls, and flirt. But I have to stay home, do laundry, and be quiet? Is that what you want me to do?"

He looked completely baffled. "Where is this coming from? I never said that. You don't belong in a place like that. Besides, you're a mom. What would have happened if you had been arrested tonight?"

"I just wanted to have fun for once. It's been so long." She turned from him and let out a shuddering breath, surprised to find herself on the verge of tears.

Chase came up behind her, placing his hands gently on her shoulders then running them down her arms. He pulled her against his front and wrapped his arms around her, letting the warmth of his body seep into hers. "Tell me, honey."

She blinked, and tears fell from her eyes. She laid her head against his chest and let the tears fall. "I love being a mom. I love A.J. But it's been hard."

"You've been alone, focused on raising him." His voice sounded gruff, with surprise and maybe a touch of anger in it, but she didn't think the anger was directed at her.

She nodded. "I'm twenty-eight years old, Chase, and tonight was the first night I've been in a bar since I turned twenty-one. My entire life until this point has been about working, raising my son, finishing school, or meeting my father's expectations. I can't remember the last time I had fun. But I've had fun with you this entire week." She shifted in his arms to look up at him.

He looked like she had punched him in the gut.

"Hailey, I wish I had known. I could have helped you. Adam was my friend, so were you. Why didn't you tell me?"

She gave a low laugh. "Come on, Chase. Do you honestly think you'd want to spend time with a woman and her baby? Doubtful. Besides, it wasn't your responsibility. I handled it."

"You shouldn't have had to do it alone. I could have helped you."

She lifted a hand to his cheek and turned it to face her. "People don't really see you, Chase Summers. They think you're just a good-time Charlie, and West is the responsible one. But you're just as responsible, just as protective. You just hide it better."

His lips curved in a small smile. "Don't tell anyone. It's been a secret. If they find out, I'll never get rid of the ladies."

She narrowed her gaze. "There better not be any more girls. Not as long as we're together."

He pulled her closer. "I don't need girls when I have a woman in my arms."

He lowered his head and kissed her softly on the lips, testing her. When she softened under him, he hauled her closer and angled her head for a deeper kiss, his tongue sweeping in to claim every part of her. When he finally lifted his head, she blinked, dazed and a little dreamy.

"Fuck. Get in the truck before I take you here on the side of the road."

THEY BARELY MADE it in the house before he was on her,

pinning her against the wall right next to the front door and kissing her as if his life depended on it. Apparently, there was something to the old adage that watching girls fight got men hot because he had never been this horny before. Or maybe it was just Hailey. Either way, he didn't think they'd make it to the bedroom, and thank God no one was home.

Hailey buried her hands in his hair and pulled him to her lips, wincing when he kissed her. He pulled away. "Tender, baby?"

She grinned a little ruefully. "Shonda packs a mean punch."

He laughed. "She didn't punch you. She slapped you. If she had punched you, you would be hurting a whole lot more." He took her hands. "Do you need some first aid?"

"Not in my hands but somewhere a little south," she said, leading him to the couch.

He spun her around, propped her on the back of the couch, and tugged her blouse right off of her. His mouth immediately watered and he cupped her breasts, sliding one hand around the back to loosen the bra.

"You're awfully slick with that move, Chase. Lots of practice?" She arched her brow.

Oh shit. Even he knew better than to answer questions about other women than the one he was dating now. She just laughed and patted his chest. "I'm just teasing. I already know all about your past. But you should see the look on your face. I'd like a turn tonight. Shirt off."

She hopped off the back of the sofa and forced him to turn so he was pinned against the back of it. She didn't wait for him to take off his shirt. She tugged it up and over his shoulder, tossing it somewhere in the living room. She spread her fingers over his chest and stroked his skin, scraping her nails lightly over his nipples. "Are you as sensitive as I am here? Let's find out."

She placed a kiss over one nub then sucked a little harder, nipping it lightly with her teeth. He groaned and plunged his fingers into her hair, tugging her hair just enough to make her gasp. But he didn't want her to move; he just needed to touch her, to be connected. He was content to let her play for a while, and then he'd take over.

She traced the lines of his muscles in his torso, finally arrowing down to his jeans where the top of his cock peeked out. She brushed the tip of her finger over it and it jerked a little but had nowhere to go. She shot him an impish look, and he gritted his teeth and moved to undo his pants.

"Nope. This is my night." She placed his hands on the high back so that his fingers curled around the frame. "Keep them there or everything stops."

He gripped the soft fabric and waited, every muscle in his body tense. Slowly, she undid the button of his jeans and unzipped them, pushing them down with his underwear, revealing his cock, which was painfully erect after all the teasing. Hell, it was always half aroused around her these days and didn't need much to be ready to go.

She took his cock in her hands, stroking it gently, torturing him with light, teasing touches. His fingers protested— the tension on the damask fabric was almost painful—but he was determined to let her have her time. Suddenly, she licked the head and sucked it into her mouth. His eyes rolled back in his head. He gave a low shout, and his knees almost buckled. She gazed up at him, a teasing glint in her eyes as she laved the head then took him as deep as she could and sucked hard.

That was all it took. He grabbed her and hauled her up. "Clothes off. Now."

He kicked his jeans away, grabbing them briefly to take out the condom he'd stashed in there earlier in the day. As she undressed, throwing her clothes on the floor, he donned the condom. He gave her a quick kiss, then spun her around and bent her over the top of the sofa, kicked her legs apart, and positioned himself at her entrance.

Before he pushed inside, he paused. "Are you okay?"

"Goddamn it, Chase. Don't you dare stop now!" she almost bellowed at him.

He grinned and thrust deep to the hilt. She lifted her hips to meet him and they both groaned at the same time; the sensation of tight, wet heat almost made Chase lose it. He bent over her, one hand braced next to her, the other going under her to find her clit.

"Get ready, sweetheart. This is going to be fast."

And he started to play with her clit. Within a few thrusts, she was clenching and coming around him, screaming his name. He wanted to make it last, but it wasn't going to happen, not this time. He followed her over with a shout. He draped himself over her, his legs weak and his breathing like he had run a marathon.

"I guess chicks fighting turns you on, huh?" she said from somewhere under him.

He just started laughing.

Chapter Twenty

THE NEXT WEEK passed in a blur of work and passion. Chase spent every day working with the horses, even enlisting her to ride out for part of every day to test the trail ride effectiveness of each of the proposed horses for the guest ranch. More often than not, these rides ended in a picnic lunch and lovemaking on a blanket in a field. Later in the day, he and Lew would give A.J. the promised riding lesson, and then he worked with A.J. on roping using a sawhorse dressed like a calf. A.J. giggled the first time he saw it, but he found out his friends would be competing in the same event so he doubled down and focused.

She spent her nights with Chase, and Hailey had to unearth her baby monitors after A.J. went looking for her one night and she wasn't where he expected. It was pure luck they had been up in the living room still, enjoying a beer and making out. A.J. didn't seem to sense anything going on between them, but he was enjoying the attention from Chase, and by extension Ty and West, who were treating him like a nephew.

As expected, Hailey received the promised lecture from her father then got the silent treatment, his usual punishment when he disapproved of something she'd done. For her part, she was busy developing ideas for the guest ranch and barely noticed, which she was sure irritated him to no end.

Finally, the day of the county fair arrived and A.J. was almost too excited to eat until Chase reminded him that he needed the energy to rope the calf or his friends would beat him. A.J. cleaned his plate in no time. Who knew it would be that easy to get her son to pay attention and eat his food quickly? They arrived at the fairgrounds a little after ten, and the fair was already in full swing. Events were going on in each of the arenas, including rodeo and demonstrations. Craft booths were set up for shopping, food booths were everywhere with all kinds of food, and music played all day from the stage where local bands would set up until the headlining band played at night.

Hailey held A.J.'s hand tightly. "I had forgotten how many people come to these events. I think all of Granite Junction has turned out."

"More than that," Chase replied. "The rodeo events are actually part of the national tour, a small part, but they do count. Some of the younger and newer rodeo guys come here to get points."

A.J. looked up at Chase. "Will you be riding today?"

Chase was gazing at the bull-riding ring, a faraway look in his eyes for a second. Then he shook his head. "No, I'm not registered here. These points wouldn't help me anyway. And I need a little more time to heal."

But he avoided looking at Hailey when he said it, and she felt a chill in her heart. It wouldn't be long now. Just last night in bed, she had traced the spot where he had been injured and noticed the bruising was gone and the incision from the surgery was pretty well healed. Not perfect, but even she knew that bull riders often rode with fresher injuries than he had. She was losing him and had no way of keeping him.

After registering A.J. for the roping event, they headed for one of the arenas. Rounding a corner, they came face-to-face with her parents, and Hailey froze. A.J. dropped her hand and hugged his grandparents, not sensing the chill in the air from her father or the disapproving glare he gave Chase. Chase, for his part, laid a hand on her lower back, a comforting, supportive warmth, but didn't say anything.

"This is where you've been hiding, young man. I've missed you," her father bent down and hugged A.J. That was one thing she could give her father. No matter how pissed he was at her, he never took it out on A.J. He truly loved his grandson. Of course, maybe that was because he was the only grandchild they had close enough to see, since her brother had moved to Seattle and rarely came home for a visit.

"I've been learning how to ride and rope cows. Chase has been teaching me. I'm going to be in the contest today," A.J. explained.

"Really?" her father said but gave her a narrow look and Hailey sighed. She was going to face the inquisition shortly.

A.J., still completely oblivious to the tension, waved excitedly to someone. "Mom, that's Michael from school. Can I go talk to him?"

Michael's mom waved to Hailey and smiled. Their sons had become fast friends already at camp. "Okay, but stay with them until I come get you, okay?"

A.J. was already gone with barely a backward glance, talking loudly with his friend. She turned to her father, who had his arms crossed in front of him. "Chase, do you mind? We have to have a family discussion for a moment."

"Nope, I don't mind at all." But he made no move to leave, only pulled Hailey closer to his side.

"Dad, Chase stays. What do you have to say?"

He frowned and let out a deep breath, stalling for time, all usual tactics designed to get her to speak first and give in. But not this time. She hadn't done anything wrong and wasn't going to be kowtowed into following into line with his ideas.

"Do you really think this is the best way to raise your son? Riding horses and roping calves? You see where it got his father. And he's getting awfully close to someone exactly like his father, someone who is just going to get back on the road, leaving you behind."

Her mother looked worried but didn't say anything. She just gave Hailey a sad look. Hailey waited a moment for the bright burn of anger, but she felt nothing. Chase, on the other hand, was tensing next to her, his arm like a rock where it lay against her back. She put her hand on his stomach and stroked him, soothing him. Her parents followed the gesture. Her father's jaw clenched as he focused on Chase's arm, while her mother's gaze kept straying to the connection, with a softer, thoughtful consideration on her face.

"There's a big difference, Dad. First, A.J. is happy doing these things. It doesn't mean anything. He's six. He could change his mind about what he wants to do with his life a hundred times before he's grown. Besides, what did you expect him to do when we moved back to Granite Junction?

All of the kids here are involved with ranching and horses in some fashion. It's unavoidable." She stepped forward, and Chase's hand dropped away, leaving her to stand on her own.

"As for Chase, that's my decision. He's been wonderful with A.J., which you would know if you came by any of the times I've invited you. He's been more involved in A.J.'s life than you have, and I'm grateful for him. Even if he's only here for a short time, that's fine."

Her father stepped forward and loomed over her. "He's going to leave you alone. I don't want you hurt."

"Tom, that's her decision." Her mom took his arm and tugged him back. "Hailey is a grown woman, has done a wonderful job with her son. If she trusts Chase, we should too. Chase, you're a bull rider, right? I never quite understood that. Maybe you could sit with me and explain it over there."

She held out her hand like a queen. Bemused, Chase took it and allowed himself to be drawn along with her to the ring where they were doing bull riding. Hailey and her father followed close behind after gathering A.J. in silence.

Hailey let out the breath she had been holding. Her father had backed down and her mother had accepted Chase. She had no doubt that the battle wasn't over, but maybe, just maybe, they could all get along.

THE DAY HAD taken on a bit of a surreal quality for Chase. First, he had been walking around the fairgrounds, holding a little boy's hand with Hailey on the other side and getting sideways glances from people staring at the picture of a family they made, an image he never thought he'd be a part of. Then, Hailey's father had berated her for all sorts of things. He wanted to step in, but this was a battle Hailey needed to fight if she ever wanted to stand on her own. And, boy, did she ever fight it, defending him in the process. Hailey's dad spent the morning glaring daggers at him while her mother treated him like a son, which was disconcerting at best.

Chase was pathetically grateful that it was time for A.J.'s event, and he escaped their clutches with A.J. in tow. Hailey and her parents would follow and watch, even though he knew it killed Hailey not to come with them. Again, he was acting like a father, and the ropes of responsibility he'd once thought would feel as constricting as a calf being hogtied weren't half as bad as he'd expected.

They were waiting outside the ring with some of the other kids and their fathers, A.J. chatting with a friend, when a couple of women approached him. Thankfully, it wasn't Shonda or her crew, but it was just as bad. Amy Jo was Cam Miller's younger sister and had once set her sights on West. When that seemed doomed, she had turned her attention to Chase. For his part, he had never reciprocated, partly out of friendship with Cam and partly because he had grown tired of the whole shebang and had put a moratorium on women. Amy Jo clearly hadn't gotten the memo.

"Hey there, Chase. Haven't seen you around The Rock lately. Where you been hiding yourself?" Amy Jo leaned against the fence and cast a flirtatious look at him, her two friends standing behind her.

"Haven't you heard? He's been shacking up with a woman on the ranch. He doesn't need to go to the bar." One of the girls leaned forward and imparted the gossip like it was a secret, her eyes wide and a sly smile on her face.

He cocked his head and ran his gaze over Amy Jo and her posse. What the hell had he ever seen in her or any of the girls she surrounded herself with? He settled on a noncommittal answer. "I'm keeping myself busy."

Amy Jo stepped forward and ran a finger down the center of his chest, one hot pink nail tracing a line along his T-shirt. "I'd be happy to keep you company sometime, Chase. Help you recover from your injuries."

He restrained the shudder that wanted to run through him and just stepped back. "Hailey has that covered quite well, Amy Jo."

She glared at him then stomped off with a toss of her hair, her crew following her reluctantly. His breath heaved, and he suddenly realized he was the center of attention for a couple of the fathers, but, fortunately, none of the kids had paid much attention.

"It's like that, is it?" One of the men quirked a grin. "Kind of surprising when a woman knocks you off your feet. Never thought I'd see the day when Chase Summers fell, but good choice."

He stared at the man, trying to place him. The other guy smiled and held out his hand. "Kyle Timmons, Michael's dad. A.J. and Michael have become good friends. I own the feed shop in town. You may not remember me. I came to town after you left for the circuit."

The name clicked, and Chase shook his hand. "Nice to meet you. I think we've talked, but West mostly handles that. Sorry."

"Don't be. Hailey seems to be a good woman and her son is a good kid. He adores you, based on what he said when he was at our house last weekend. They have a way of getting under your skin, don't they?"

"Yeah," Chase muttered, still bemused by the realization of how embedded A.J. and Hailey were in his life and how right they felt here.

Sure, watching the bull riding during the day at the county fair, he had felt that yearning inside to climb on board and pit himself against the beast, even knowing those bulls were lower ranked than any of the ones he had been riding on the PBR. But he had been content, too, sitting in the stands with his family, explaining the event, talking about horses, greeting people from the surrounding areas.

He belonged. For the first time in his life, he had a place.

Yes, Douglas Rawlings had given him a foster home, then left him shares in a ranch. He had his foster brothers, West and Ty, and eventually Tara too. He knew on some level they were a family, but he never had that complete sense of belonging until that very moment. Maybe he had never let himself completely connect with them, keeping himself apart. Moving from foster home to foster home for his whole life could do that to a man, to the point where he'd never quite believe that he was going to stay. He'd always been waiting for the next move, for the social worker to come and take him to the next home, even when Douglas swore he was going nowhere.

But with Hailey and A.J., he had a place, a purpose. He fit.

Being home the last couple of weeks, finding his place, he was starting to think that maybe they could find a way through without him going back on the road after this season. If he won the championship, or even just a few more events, that might see them with enough money to give them some breathing room and he could consider settling down. Oddly, the notion of not going back on the circuit after this season didn't cause him to feel stifled but seemed right. Maybe it was the right time. Maybe it could work.

A small hand tugged on his own and he looked down. A.J. smiled up at him, biting his lower lip like his mother often did when she was nervous. "It's time."

Chase knelt down and gave him a hug. If it was a little awkward, neither of them mentioned it. "You'll be great, buddy. Do your best. Let's go."

Chapter Twenty-One

"WE MAY HAVE been wrong about your young man, dear." Her mother took her aside. "He's not like Adam at all. He's settled and more responsible. And he seems to care a great deal for you and A.J."

It was a gift more precious to her than money.

Hailey smiled as she glanced over at A.J. showing off his trophy for Chase and her dad. "He's been surprisingly good with A.J. I think even he was shocked by it. But Adam was a good man."

"He was, just a little young and impulsive. He hadn't quite grown into the man he would have become. We worried about you getting married so young, but you both had a plan and we didn't want to interfere. Maybe we should have. Well, that's the past. Don't worry about your father. I'll talk to him. He can be a bit rigid, but it's only because he doesn't want you hurt again." Her mother patted her hand and then called to A.J.

A.J. hugged Chase, who looked surprised by the affection, and Hailey waved goodbye to her parents and A.J. They were taking him home for the night, letting her enjoy the rest of the fair.

Chase wrapped an arm around her waist and pulled her close. She snuggled into his arms, loving the warmth of his body.

"What do you want to do now? We could get something to eat and then dance by the bandstand," he murmured in her ear.

"Sounds perfect." She turned and hugged him, pressing a kiss to his lips. "In case I forget, thank you for today. You were wonderful with A.J. and patient with my parents. Thank you for letting me fight that battle."

"It was yours to fight. But that was a free pass. I won't let him insult you like that again." His words sounded like a vow and Hailey shivered. "I'll grab us something to eat. Why don't you find us a place to sit? I think West and Tara are around. Ty too. Get a table for all of us, okay?"

She nodded. He pulled her close and gave her a quick kiss, then headed for the food tent. She took her beer and wandered until she found an empty table along the outside of the picnic tables. She texted Tara and settled in to wait and people watch. She greeted a few people she knew from school and growing up in town, but no one stayed long, all looking to settle into their own meals and find places for the music to come, leaving her to her thoughts.

She wasn't alone for long, however. Shonda, the woman from the bar came up, this time alone. Hailey steeled herself for another battle of words if not fists, but the other woman held up her hands. "I'm not here to cause trouble. I created enough chaos the other night, and I'm sorry. I'd blame the alcohol but, well, that would be bullshit."

Hailey eyed her suspiciously but gestured to the seat next to her. "Would you like to sit down?"

"Only for a moment. I don't think Chase would be happy to find me here." The other woman was pretty when she wasn't wearing too much makeup and groping Hailey's man. The woman gave Hailey a shrewd look. "You and Chase Summers are not having a fling."

Hailey sipped her beer and tried to appear casual. "Why do you say that? Not that my relationship or life is any of your business."

Shonda shrugged. "He's never been possessive of another woman. He treats women well, makes everyone woman feel special, but he never makes any promises for the future, no matter what. Rarely does he commit to more than one night. If it is, he is very clear to state that it's nothing serious. He's not a forever kind of guy."

Hailey set her beer on the table and cocked her head, narrowed her gaze at the other woman for a long moment. "Some might say he hasn't found the right woman."

The woman smiled, a bittersweet look in her eyes. "Maybe. Or maybe that's a delusion of someone who thinks they can change a man." She leaned forward and took Hailey's hand in her own, gripping it tightly. "Look, I like you. You have spirit and strength. You don't fawn all over him, and you push him. He clearly is infatuated with you, maybe more. But he's not going to stay. I'm sure you've heard this from others but I'm here to tell you, it's true."

Hailey yanked her hand out. "I'm well aware of that. I won't ask him to change."

"Good. But are you strong enough to let him go and wait while he's on the road for weeks at a time doing God knows what?" Shonda studied her shrewdly. "You have a son who loves Chase. I saw them today in the ring. It's clear how your son feels, and I've never seen Chase with another kid like that. Can you handle a man who comes in and out of your life like a whirlwind? Always on his schedule, not yours, not when you need him. Is that what you want?"

Hailey stood, trying to remain calm when she wanted to scream at the other woman. When she finally spoke, she was gratified to note her tone was even, calm. "Do you expect to scare me off so you can have him? Because that won't happen."

Shonda also stood. "No, it's clear that our time is over. I just don't want to see you hurt. And I think you're in deep, deeper than I ever was. Be very careful, Hailey, if not for yourself, for your son. Chase isn't going to change."

"You forget, I was married to a bull rider. I'm well acquainted with the life," she responded automatically, but her mind drifted to the nights after Adam's death when she'd dreamed of him, waking with her pillow soaked with her tears, alone in her bed, knowing that he would never come home again. The ache of loneliness would tear through her, different than when he was just on the road, chasing his dreams of the buckle and championship. Slowly, the pain of his loss eased, but she never quite got used to being alone at night in her bed, and she *had* gotten used to feeling Chase's arms around her, holding her. What would happen when he left? How will she go back to sleeping alone?

"Shonda? What do you want?" Tara asked from behind Hailey.

The other woman stiffened then smiled over Hailey's shoulder. "Just apologizing for last week."

Tara pushed forward. "And what about me?"

"I wasn't sorry about that. Night, Hailey." Shonda turned and walked away without a backward glance, leaving Hailey with a lot of thinking to do.

CHASE WAS WAITING by the tent for the next batch of pulled pork, always a popular item from the firehouse at the fair. He was already salivating when he heard his name being called. A couple of young guys, early twenties maybe, were staring at him with something akin to hero worship. He didn't recognize them from town so he gave them a nod. That seemed to break their awe and they rushed over.

The dark-haired cowboy, skinny as a rail with a bruise on his jaw and a split lip, said, "Are you really Chase Summers? I saw you once riding in Amarillo a couple of years ago. You won that day. You inspired me to ride."

Chase thought back. "I remember that ride. I think I had Hard Tack. That bull was tough. He almost beat me, but I held on. Why did that convince you to ride bulls? I think I also broke a couple of fingers and got a concussion on the dismount."

The kid laughed. "It wasn't a pretty dismount, but you gave the bull the finger, basically telling him and everyone else 'screw you.' I loved it. I had been riding broncs, but that sealed it for me."

His friend rolled his eyes. "He liked the adrenaline rush better than broncs."

Chase gave an uncomfortable laugh because the truth was, he only remembered the victory. The bull had rung his bell just enough to scramble his brains like eggs, and he had forgotten some of that ride. But the guys were probably right because he did get penalized for a rude gesture. He grinned. Totally worth it.

"Did you compete today?"

That's all these kids needed. They almost fell over themselves talking about their rides, both somewhat disappointing that day, and their other rides on the circuit. Neither had been competing long enough to be at Chase's level, but through their comments and their questions, he could hear their curiosity and their willingness to learn. He remembered doing exactly the same thing every time the fair and a rodeo competition came anywhere near Granite Junction. He haunted the chutes and the hangouts where the riders gathered, begging for guidance and instruction. He had been lucky that a couple had taken pity on him, both here and on the road, and helped him improve his technique.

He looked at the baskets of pulled pork the firemen handed to him from the smoker and to the eager young faces.

"Need some help with that?" Hailey asked at his elbow in a light, teasing voice. "I wondered where you disappeared to. Should have known you'd find a place to talk shop." She took in the young men at a glance, but her smile never faltered.

Their faces fell, however, and they started to apologize, but Hailey held up her hand. "I can eat with West and Tara if you want to talk for a while."

He narrowed his eyes, waiting for the gotcha moment. What woman would be okay with being abandoned for a group of bull riders? What was the catch? She gave a low laugh and brushed a quick kiss across his lips, proving that she was probably the perfect woman for him. "Don't be too long. You owe me a dance."

She took her basket of food and sashayed away from him, her hips gently swaying, leaving him with the young men, who stared at her with mixtures of awe and lust. Chase whacked one of them not too gently on the head, the green-eyed monster of jealousy rearing its ugly head. "Watch it. She's taken."

"Dude, you really going to give her up for us? I don't think I could do that," the dark-haired one said, admiration in his voice.

Chase smiled smugly. "Well, I do get to go home with her so it's okay."

And it was, until he left in a week or two. But tonight wasn't for that.

MUCH LATER, HE finally extracted himself from the crowd of young bull riders that had grown as he had shared more advice from his years on the circuit. They had exchanged stories and chatted for a while, even as his food had gotten cold. He had forgotten how much he had enjoyed the camaraderie of the road, the easy banter and joking of guys and the bull talk about the next ride or the last ride or the best ride ever. Yet, he found himself looking for a certain redhead, hoping she would hunt him down and drag him back to her side. By the time the main attraction had started tuning their instruments, he ended the conversation and went on his own search and find mission with a few jeers and catcalls from the guys who had seen her echoing behind him.

West was standing a few feet away from the table with Cam Miller and a couple other ranchers, their expressions serious. Chase walked up quietly and joined them, hoping West would keep talking and not shut him out this time. Unfortunately, it was the end of the conversation but he'd heard enough. When the guys split up to grab their own women for the dancing, Chase grabbed West's arm, pulling him aside.

"What was that about?"

West shrugged. "The usual, Chase. Cost of beef is down and I'm looking for some ways to economize and liquidate some assets. It happens all the time, almost yearly. We've weathered this before, and we'll do it again. Cam and I are working on an exchange to strengthen our herds and see how to run leaner. We're fine." He clapped his hand on Chase's good shoulder. "Now, grab Hailey and show her how you two-step, since you didn't get the chance the other night. I got a date with my own pretty lady."

Hailey was at a table on the far side of the picnic area, laughing with Ty and Tara and Cam Miller and a couple of other ranchers who had lingered after the discussion, probably to flirt with his woman. He had left her alone for far too long and these guys needed reminding that she belonged to him. The music queued up and Tara grabbed West and dragged him onto the dance floor. One of the other ranchers stood and offered his hand to Hailey. Before she could take it, Chase stepped in the middle.

"Sorry, boys, this lady's dance card is full." But knowing better than to assume, he held out his hand and waited.

She gave him a broad smile and took his hand, letting him lead her onto the dance floor. Too bad it was a fast dance, but they kept up just fine until a slow dance came on and he had her where he wanted her, tight against his body, in his arms.

"We missed this at The Rock the other night. Promise you won't haul off and assault anyone tonight?" he murmured in her ear.

She tilted her head up and laughed. "No promises. Make sure your harem knows you're taken."

He threw back his head and laughed, generating looks from all of the people around him. "I think they got the word that night."

"Good." There was a wealth of satisfaction in her tone and possession, and he found he didn't mind because he felt the same about her.

She snuggled into his shirt, laying her head against his chest. He rested his cheek against the side of her head and they swayed slowly to the sound of the music, letting the rest of the world fade away. But questions nagged at him from his conversation with West, and he worried at it like a sore tooth even as one song faded into the next and another after that. He was going to have to go back on the circuit to help the family, but they could have tonight and a few more days at least. Enjoy this time before he had to go. He'd see where they stood at the end of the season. Hailey would understand. So would his family. This was what he did.

They danced almost nonstop, from slow to fast songs,

until the band took a break. Then they shared a beer and danced some more until the party finally ended at midnight, trying to get it all in before the end. He put the inevitable out of his mind and tried to enjoy the moment, the feel of her soft body in his arms, her sweet kisses as they danced, and her laughter as she tried to keep up with the faster dances. He'd miss the hell out of this on the road. Now that he had something to come home to.

Chase drove her home, his arm casually draped across the back of the seat, playing with the strands of her hair and her neck. This time, when he pulled into the driveway, he didn't go all the way. He stopped at the same small pull off as before and shut off the engine.

"Want to go for a walk?"

She stared at him. "Are you crazy? It's after midnight."

He arched a brow. "Do you have somewhere to be?"

She laughed and opened the door, hopping out. He got out and grabbed a blanket from behind the seat. He took her hand and headed for a small rise a short distance away. It didn't take long before they crested the hill and came to a watering hole. A river ran through the land, opening up just enough to create a little pool shallow enough for swimming on hot days, but it was a secret known only to his brothers and two others.

"Oh my God! I had almost forgotten about this. I wanted to bring A.J. here sometime but wasn't sure if I should. Wow, it still looks the same." She turned and looked at him, her eyes bright and shining in the moonlight. "Do you come here often?"

"Only when I need to think. I'm not home very much

and when I am, West puts me to work." He spread the plaid blanket on the ground and sat down, patting the space next to him.

She sat down and leaned into his body, shivering a little. "We used to come out here all the time in the summer. You, me, and Adam." She leaned away and looked up at him, a questioning look on her face. "You never brought another girl with you when we came here. Did you ever?"

He shook his head. "It's our place. It just seemed wrong to bring anyone else here, you know? But I think A.J. would like it."

She settled against him and sighed. "Let's wait until he's older and knows how to swim. He might come down here on his own and not be safe."

Chase gave a small laugh. "Yeah, good idea. I didn't think of that. I have a lot to learn."

She pulled his arms around her. "You've been great. He totally loves spending time with you. Thank you for that. He needed someone like you in his life. I never realized how much."

He tightened his arms until she squeaked a protest. "He loves you. You've done a great job. And I like spending time with him."

She laughed, a low sexy sound that kicked him in the gut every time. "You sound surprised when you say that. I don't know why. I see you working with Lew with the horses. I saw you tonight with the young guys from the rodeo. You're a natural with them."

He shrugged. "I guess I understand them, understand what they're feeling. It's no big deal."

She turned in his arms, going up on her knees and placing her hands on his cheeks, forcing him to look at her. "Chase, it *is* a big deal. Not everyone can connect with people like that, especially kids. You have patience and know how to teach them. It's a talent."

He laughed and pulled her to him, kissing her hard. "Okay, okay. I give up!"

She gave him a slight push so he fell backward onto the blanket with her on top. She straddled him, her hands braced on his chest, and his body reacted instantly, hardening under her. "Now I finally have you where I want you and you can't escape."

He dropped his arms to the side. "And what are you going to do with me?"

She became suddenly serious and leaned forward until her lips were next to his ear. "I'm going to love you."

His heart seized in his chest at her words, emotion filling him, only he wasn't sure if it was love he was feeling or panic. His blood pounded in his head, creating a roaring in his ears, and he felt a bit light-headed. Thank God he was already on his back or else he wasn't sure he would have remained upright. He swallowed against a suddenly dry throat and tried to speak, but she pressed her lips to his, effectively cutting off his speech.

"Don't say anything. Not tonight."

After that, there were only the sounds of moans and the occasional cry and Hailey fulfilled her promise to love him.

Chapter Twenty-Two

C HASE DROVE INTO town the next morning as soon as the horses were fed, needing a break from the intimacy of the previous night. After spending time at the watering hole, they had made it back to the house to make love again in his bed and fall asleep wrapped in each other's arms. Hailey hadn't repeated her words from earlier, but they lay between them, real and solid.

He had to throttle himself back last night to not say the words, to not lead her on. He was surprised how easy it would have been to say them, how quickly they had been on the tip of his tongue. Thank God she had stopped him, maybe knowing something he didn't, like his emotions were there but his head wasn't ready. He just knew she made it so easy to stay, and he needed distance to figure out what to do, what he really wanted.

Hailey was picking up A.J. at her parents' house and spending lunch there. He had begged off, saying he had duties for the ranch. She hadn't pressed him, though he had seen the hurt in her eyes. She had kissed him goodbye and drove off while he watched her, feeling like he was the one leaving, not her.

Damn it. He slammed his hand on the dashboard, pain radiating up his arm. He cranked up the music, hoping for a distraction, but in that moment, the music dulled to let the ringtone bleed through. He clicked over to the phone without checking the caller ID, assuming it was one of his brothers.

"Hey, Chase," J.D. McIntyre, one of his fellow riders and friends from the circuit, greeted him. "Where you been, man? We've missed you."

"J.D.! How're things?"

They shot the breeze for a few minutes, catching up on his injuries, then J.D. got to the point. "You heard about Tonio, right?"

Chase wracked his brain, but he'd been wrapped up in Hailey and the ranch, and he'd lost touch with the circuit. Damn, he'd never lost sight of the standings or the circuit like that before. Hell, he barely remembered when the next big competition was. What a fucking idiot he was.

"Nah, I've been getting rest and unplugged from everything. What's going on?"

"That Oleander's been a real devil since you rode him. He's been nastier than usual. Tonio drew him in North Dakota and got thrown bad."

Chase felt a chill run down his spine and nausea rose in his stomach. He almost didn't want to ask, but he had to know. "What happened?"

"Kicked bad and trampled. He's in a coma. Several ribs broken and internal injuries. He's bad, man."

"Fuck." Chase slammed his hand into the dashboard again. He wasn't close to the Brazilian, but he respected the hell out of the guy. "He's a helluva rider. When did this happen?"

"Few days ago. Wow, you weren't kidding about being unplugged." J.D. whistled. "Listen, the field's wide open. No one has really made any significant moves. You're still ranked pretty high since the summer hiatus. If you come back in Texas, you can claim the top spot. Then slide into the world championship. It's yours for the taking."

They chatted for a few more minutes, and Chase made a few vague noises about meeting up in Texas in a week for the next competition, the kickoff to the fall season, then ended the call.

He wasn't the type to dwell on the past, but he had a date with Oleander to show him that he could handle him. He'd ridden him once and he could do it again. Not to mention he had his goal in his sights: the world championship. He could almost taste the victory, the prize money being secondary, although that would give the ranch some breathing room with the taxes and other financial challenges that West was downplaying.

West and Tara had told them they would find a way with the estate tax bill that was inevitable once the ranch went through probate, probably by the end of winter, still several months away. But they were already squirreling away money, looking for ways to not only pay that bill but make sure the ranch stayed financially viable beyond then by diversifying with more than the beef cattle. The guest ranch was supposed to help bring in steady income, which is why the horses were so important. They'd be the start of a stable for guests to ride the beautiful land that made up Redemption Ranch and hopefully bring more people to them for vacations. After what he'd overheard the night before, his prize money was even more important now. Just a few more months of work. Then he could come back and rejoin the ranch and maybe settle down with Hailey and A.J.

He could have it all, right? Other cowboys did. There were other riders on the circuit with families. Adam had done it. Chase could too.

CHASE AND LEW pushed open the doors to the smaller barn set back from the house back on Redemption Ranch. This barn had been reserved for equipment storage, and years ago Douglas had set aside an area for Chase to practice. He paused to let his eyes adjust to the dim light in the barn before he turned on any lights. The midday sun filtered through the wood and the high doors from the loft above, enough to illuminate Theo, the mechanical bull Douglas had surprised Chase with more than ten years ago when he had expressed interest in bull riding.

Douglas had worked patiently with him every night after working the cattle all day, while Chase got thrown time and again. Then Douglas found a guy to teach Chase how to ride, and bought videos and tickets to events, too. He'd even sent Chase to a guy who bred bulls for the circuit, to learn about the bulls, to understand them.

Douglas had been generous with his time and money, never questioning Chase or telling him it was too dangerous. Instead, he did his best to make sure Chase had the best instruction and was as protected as possible. And when Adam was interested, Douglas generously brought him in on the lessons, too, only Adam hadn't been as intent on the education side.

Lights flickered on, and Chase blinked rapidly at the sudden brightness.

"Sorry, man. I didn't realize how bright the lights were. This is where you practiced? Cool." Lew came out from a small stall.

Chase nodded, and the memories retreated to the furthest reaches of his mind. He walked into the small ring, kicking aside the deflated cushioning, and pulled off the sheet from the bull. "Yup, this is Theo. He still looks badass."

Lew just laughed. "With glasses?"

Chase grinning. "I drew glasses on him because he seemed more like a teacher that way. He taught me everything I know about riding bulls. Let's get to work."

Within an hour, they had checked all the screws, wires, and connections. The ring had been inflated for protection and the bull was bucking away in the center. After showing Lew how to work the controls, he climbed on and they started slow, working their way up, to see how his body could take the jostling. He gritted his teeth. The bucking didn't feel great on his ribs or the arm that gripped the rope, but once his muscles loosened and remembered the motions, he settled in.

By the end of the first hour, he was loose and they progressed, slowly advancing through the levels, and Chase got tossed only a couple of times. Thank God for the cushioning Douglas had insisted on. By the end of the second hour, Chase's muscles felt like wet noodles and he was drenched in sweat. Lew tossed him a towel and a bottle of water that Chase opened gratefully and swallowed in a big gulp.

"That was awesome, Chase." The hero worship in the younger man's voice almost made Chase wince, but he hid it.

"It's a job and dangerous one at that. Use this with someone else here or not at all. That's why I came in with you. You should always have someone to watch out for you."

Lew nodded. "I don't think I'll ever get on that thing. I rode one at a bar over in Phillipsburg with my buddies once. My neck hurt for days after."

Before Chase could respond, A.J. came running over. "Chase, that was so cool! Can I try?"

Chase automatically looked around for Hailey but didn't see her. "A.J., where's your mom?"

"She said I could go down to the barn and see you. She said she'd be right down with some iced tea."

A.J. looked at him with big eyes completely free of any guile, but Chase still doubted she meant this barn, especially since he doubted she'd ever been inside it. But Hailey had been giving the boy more freedom when he was with Chase so maybe it would be okay, for a moment. But, if she was on her way, he'd rather keep A.J. with him than send him back out to roam the ranch.

He strode over to the controls for the bull and made sure they were all off. "Lew, unplug the controls then we can let A.J. on the bull." You couldn't be too safe.

Lew unplugged the control panel and Chase helped A.J. sit on the mechanical bull, bracing him with a hand against the boy's back. His legs stuck out to the sides a bit and he rocked back and forth with an arm in the air. Chase gave him a bit of guidance on proper bull riding technique, and that was where it all went south and fast.

"Momma!"

Chase had just taken a step back when A.J. jerked around. He waved his hands in the air wildly and lost his balance, falling forward toward the front of the bull, away from Chase. The inflatable ring was still there, but as luck and the fates would have it, A.J. clipped the horn of the bull with his chin as he fell. It took A.J. a moment to register the pain, but the adults were all reacting, with Chase reaching him first. Blood streamed down his chin and onto his shirt. As soon as A.J. saw it, he started to cry, reaching for his mother, pushing away Chase and the towel he was trying to put on the cut.

Hailey gathered him in her arms and rocked him gently, soothing him. Chase soaked the corner of the towel in the remainder of the water and held it out to Hailey. "Here. Lew, get an ice pack from the barn."

Lew ran at Chase's direction, but Hailey barely noticed. She glared at Chase, panic flaring in her eyes. "I think you've done quite enough. What were you thinking, letting him on that thing? He's just a little boy. That's just irresponsible."

He drew back. "It wasn't on, didn't even have power. And I was standing right there."

She pointedly looked at the blood soaking the towel. "Clearly not close enough. I need to get him to the emergency room for stitches."

"I'll drive you." He stood, brushing the dirt off his jeans.

"I can handle it," she replied, ice coating every word.

"Don't be ridiculous. He'll want you to hold him on the

way. You can't do that and drive. Let me drive you."

She gave a quick nod then stalked out of the barn without looking at him, grabbing the instant ice pack from Lew on her way out. He scrambled after her, running to the house to get his keys. By the time he came out, he saw the back end of her parents' car driving down the driveway and Hailey and A.J. were gone. He slammed his fist into the railing.

"Fuck!"

SEVERAL HOURS LATER, Hailey carried a sleepy A.J. into the house at the ranch. Chase was nowhere to be found, and she was grateful. She had timed their arrival for when he'd be feeding the horses, hoping he wouldn't hear the car coming up the drive or, at minimum, she'd be able to get inside before he got to the house. They had spent a few hours at the ER getting the glue for A.J.'s chin since, apparently, they didn't do stitches anymore. A.J. had been disappointed; he wanted to show off a scar to his friends at camp. To avoid the inevitable confrontation with Chase, she went with her parents back to their house for a quiet afternoon. For once, neither parent said anything about what happened, not even her father, which surprised her. Instead, A.J. took a nap and Hailey even fell asleep during a movie, worn out from the emotional highs and lows of the past couple of days.

How had things gone so wrong? Just last night, she told Chase she loved him. She had specifically told him not to say it back, or to say anything, because she wasn't sure she could handle him being awkward or, worse, saying "thank you" or "it's been great." She had to admit the facts. She was in deep with Chase, had fallen somewhere along the way, and was now faced with having to deal with the fallout and next steps, whatever those may be. She may have destroyed all of those chances when she blew up at him today then ran away like a coward.

She laid A.J. on his bed, deciding to forego the bath for the night. He was clearly exhausted. A.J. mumbled and shifted in her arms. "Momma? I want to show Chase my chin."

She smiled. "He'll see it tomorrow. He's busy with the horses. Now, time for bed. You've had a busy day."

A voice cleared from the doorway, and Hailey jumped. Chase stood there, his hat in his hand, and he looked hesitant, unsure of his welcome. A.J. struggled to a sitting position. "Chase! I got my chin glued."

Chase shot her a questioning look and Hailey stepped back, inviting him into the space. He walked to the bed and sat on the edge, looking sufficiently impressed. "How are you feeling there, buddy?"

A.J. thought for a moment. "My chin hurt for a while but I'm better now. I got ice cream too with Grandma and Grandpa. I don't think I want to ride that bull for real. Not like you."

Chase smiled. "That's good. You should never ride him, ever. I shouldn't have had you up there."

Hailey laid a hand on his shoulder then pulled back as if scalded. She wasn't ready for that conversation, not here, not now. She'd let them finish. She'd speak to Chase after. But he barely spared her a glance. "Now, you don't ever go in that barn. Understand? That's one of those rules of the ranch."

A.J. nodded solemnly. "Promise."

Chase ruffled his hair gently and stood. "Now get some rest. I'll see you tomorrow."

He strode out of the room without a backward glance. Hailey watched him leave, shocked that he would just walk away. "A.J., you can read one story then lights out, okay?"

She raced after Chase, but he was already out the front door, hat on his head, headed back toward the barn. "Chase! Where are you going?"

He never turned, but he did pause. "I think that would be pretty obvious. I have work to finish."

She tugged on his arm, but he was as immovable as a fence post. Finally, she planted herself right in front of him. "If you're mad at me, just say it. Don't give me the silent treatment."

He settled his dark gaze on her, jaw so tightly clenched she wondered if he'd break any molars. Deep within his gaze, it wasn't anger she saw but pain. "I think you made it clear how you felt earlier today. I put your son at risk and he got hurt."

She closed her eyes. Damn it, when would she learn to think before speaking? "Chase, he's a six-year-old boy. He's going to get hurt, something you pointed out to me not so long ago. Was I upset? Yes. Did I overreact? Totally. Will I do it again? Hell yes. You would too if you walked in on what I did. I was wrong to leave with my parents, but he was bleeding so much and they were here with their car. I just wanted to get him to the hospital. I made a mistake. I was wrong."

Chase stared over her head at the barn in the distance. "No, you weren't wrong. Hailey. I'm not the family kind of guy. I know nothing about being a dad or raising kids. Hell, I've never even been around them. I'm going to screw up often. And you'll hate me for it."

"And I didn't know what I was doing either. It's not like he came with an instruction manual. All of these things are a first for me too. He's gotten bumps and bruises before but never stitches. It scared the hell out of me." She wrapped her arms around herself and shivered, remembering that moment when her boy was airborne, falling forward right into the bull's horns. "I can't imagine the stunts he'll pull as he grows up, if he's anything like his father."

A ghost of a smile crossed Chase's face. "Adam was crazy. He sure pulled some crap, like the time he jumped off the falls out on his daddy's ranch. Or the time he thought he'd tried to be a matador with their crazy old bull."

"I can't believe he survived to adulthood."

"I can't believe you reproduced his DNA. Maybe you're the crazy one," Chase teased, tension slowly leaching from his body.

Hailey pressed herself against him and wrapped her arms around his waist. After a moment, he pulled her close in a tight hug. She sighed into his body. "I'm sorry that I overreacted. But I can't say I won't do it again."

"I don't blame you. He scared ten years off my life," Chase admitted quietly. "I just wish you would have let me take you to the hospital. I was going crazy worried about him here."

"I'm sorry," she murmured into his shirt.

They stood there for a long moment, enjoying the comfort from each other. Finally, she lifted her head. "What were you doing on the bull, Chase?"

He dropped his arms and stepped back, distancing himself from her. Somehow, she felt it wasn't just physically but emotionally too. "I got a call from the circuit. I'm still in the running for the championship. There's a big competition coming up in Texas, the start of the fall season. I could make up some ground if I have a good showing. I need to be on the road within a week."

The ice that had permeated her body all day and started to melt at his touch refroze and solidified deep in her soul, leaving her brittle and fragile. "What does this mean for us?"

He shuffled his feet and refused to meet her eyes. "Nothing. I mean, I'll still be on the road and I'll be back when the season ends in December, hopefully with the championship."

"And then what? Chase, I've already lived this life. There's always another purse, another title. When will it end?"

"Hailey, you knew this about me. This is my job. This is who I am. We can make it work. You made it work with Adam. But this time, you're around friends and family. We'll do it better. You won't be alone." He cupped her cheek with a hand, brushing a thumb over her lips. "You'll see. It'll be great."

She watched him stride toward the barn, holding in the sob until he was too far away to hear it.

Chapter Twenty-Three

H AILEY MOPED FOR a couple of days, staying sequestered in the office, putting the finishing touches on the website for the guest ranch. She did a lot of the initial layout and work herself, then they hired a web designer to finish the coding and the e-commerce side so it would integrate with the other programs they wanted in place for reservations and more. It was almost ready to be unveiled to the world, but first, she had to approve it with Tara. She had put off Tara, needing to lick her wounds in peace and find a way to put on a brave front. Her boss would be able to see underneath her mask if it wasn't perfect, and Hailey was just about ready.

She'd spent the past few nights in bed with Chase, savoring what may be her last time with him. She hated to be maudlin, but she, more than anyone, was so aware of how fleeting life could be, and while she was terrified that she was setting herself up for a heartbreak, she couldn't walk away now. Her heart was already gone, given to the cowboy she had come home to, and it wasn't going to matter if he stayed or left. That heart was his to keep, even if he took it with him. So, she took what stolen moments she had and treasured them and prayed that he would change his mind.

The front screen door banged, announcing Tara's arrival. Hailey stood, took a deep breath. Hopefully, her mask was firmly fixed. She didn't want Tara to suspect or to set Chase's brothers on him until he was ready to tell them. That was his decision, not hers. She could respect him wanting to handle his family. After all, he respected her enough to let her manage her own.

Tara breezed into the office, looking fantastic of course, her blonde hair pulled back in a single thick braid and her face slightly wind burned, probably from a weekend of riding with West—or something else.

"Tell me it looks fabulous. I've been dying to see it, and you've held out on me forever." That was Tara—being dramatic to overstate her case.

But Hailey smiled anyway and turned the computer. "Feast your eyes on this."

Tara clicked through the website, exclaiming over imagery, functionality, and making a few suggestions for changes, which Hailey documented. Finally, she sat back and pushed the computer away. "I'll want to look at it a bit more later, give another run-through, but that looks amazing! Did you take those pictures? Was that A.J. and some of our cowboys on the horses?"

Hailey nodded. "I thought we needed some photos that looked like people enjoying rides and other activities, and since we haven't exactly opened yet, this might be a good idea to show people how much fun it can be."

"I love it. It's brilliant." She closed the laptop. "Okay, enough work for the day. Celebratory lunch at the diner?"

Hailey laughed, although it sounded hollow to her ears. "You're going to turn into a giant waffle if you keep eating there."

Tara grinned. "West is going into town and he stops for lunch so I thought we could maybe catch up with him too."

"I see your strategy. It has nothing to do with me and everything to do with ulterior motives." Her stomach growled in that moment. "But I don't care. I'm starving. Let's go."

IT WASN'T LONG before they were sitting in a booth in the corner, just before lunchtime, so Emma was able to take a break and join them. Emma and Tara were joking about the dance and teasing Emma about how protective Cam had been over her.

Emma popped a french fry in her mouth. "He's been protective like my brother, but nothing more."

"What happened after the fight at the bar? He hustled you out of there quick enough." Tara waggled her eyebrows suggestively and laughed.

Emma growled. "He drove me home and made me drink a bottle of water with two aspirin. Then he tucked me into bed, alone, and left."

Tara leaned back in the booth and shook her head. "Girl, you need to take some initiative if you want that man. Seduce him."

Emma gave her a dirty look. "You don't think I've tried? Maybe I'm too much the schoolteacher and not enough the sexy seductress. Nope, I'm giving up on Cam Miller. There must be someone else in this town for me. What do you think, Hailey? You used your wiles on Chase Summers, got that wild stallion to settle down. How did you do it?"

As if all the pressure from the past week had built up, the words just exploded out of her. "He's leaving. Probably end of the week. Going back on the road."

Both women stared at her, mouths open and eyes wide. Tara had shot straight up in the booth, banging her elbow into the table with the sudden motion. Emma bolted around the table and gave Hailey a hug. Tara shoved a napkin in Hailey's face for the tears pouring down her face. Great, another public meltdown for Hailey Spencer. She honestly couldn't care less if her father was embarrassed by her actions now, although she did feel bad that she was letting Chase's news out to his family.

Tara remained seated across from her, eyes growing stormy and lips tightening. "When did he tell you this?"

Hailey wiped her eyes and sniffed. "Sunday. He was practicing on his mechanical bull. A.J. saw him and fell off and needed to go to the emergency room."

"He let A.J. on the bull? Is he crazy? I'll kill him." Tara's voice rose, the outrage causing the older guys, who seemed to have the counter stools surgically attached to their asses, turn in their spots to glare at them.

"Of course not, although I did overreact, just like that. The bull was turned off and disconnected. He was just sitting on it, but he fell when he tried to get off and run to me without realizing how far he was from the ground. He needed some glue on his chin. He's fine. But Chase and I fought. I was terrible." Hailey ducked her head, still feeling badly about how she had left Chase that day.

"So what?" Tara demanded. "Look, that was your son

and you were being protective. I'd probably do the same thing. He told you he was practicing to go back? What about you? What about the ranch and the horses? What about his brothers?"

Hailey shook her head. "I don't know."

Emma glared at Tara and made a cutting motion across her throat. "I think what Tara means to say is, how are you feeling about this, about him leaving?"

Hailey took a deep breath and let it out slowly. "I don't know. He says we can make it work, especially now that I'm home among friends and family. It won't be the same as when Adam left. I won't be alone."

Tara opened her mouth, but Emma shot her another look and Tara closed it with a click and settled back in the booth, folding her arms in front her, a mulish expression on her face. Emma sat sideways in the booth and took Hailey's hand. "That's not what I asked. I asked how *you* felt about it. What do you want, Hailey?"

Hailey shot Tara a look, worried about how her next words would be taken. Tara caught the look, pulled herself out of her funk, and leaned forward, grabbing her other hand. "Nothing will change, Hailey. You still work for us, and you're family. No matter what happens with Chase. That will never change, unless you want it to. You're in control."

She sighed. God, she hated being in the middle between Chase and his family. She'd worried they'd choose him over her and she'd be politely asked to find another position or, at minimum, another place to live.

But if there was one thing she'd learned after Adam's

death, it was that she was a survivor and could get through almost anything. This time, however, could she survive the broken heart she feared was in her future?

"I don't think I can go through it again. Waiting for the call, wondering if he's okay. I hated it when Adam was on the road. I didn't like the trips, the job, being alone all the time. I had a baby who needed all of my attention, which helped, but I don't want to do that again."

"Have you told him this?" Emma asked quietly.

Hailey shook her head. "I'm afraid to."

"Ah shit, honey. I'm sorry. I had hoped it would be different." Tara gripped her hand like it was a lifeline. "What are you going to do?"

"I need to talk to Chase. But I won't be left behind again."

CHASE AND LEW were in the stable, getting ready to take Cleopatra out for a workout when a man cleared his voice from the entrance to the barn. Chase turned. Ah shit. It was Hailey's dad. He gestured for Lew to make himself scarce, and the other guy scurried out the back to find somewhere else to be for a while. Chase braced himself and walked over to the man and held out his hand. He could do this. He could handle being respectful and not be an asshole, as long as Barnes played along. This was, after all, Hailey's father and he owed it to her to try to get along with the man.

"Mr. Barnes. I think Hailey and Tara went into town. Something about a celebration or lunch. I didn't quite get the details."

"I'm aware of that. I'm here to see you. Maybe we should step outside to speak?" His nose wrinkled as if he'd smelled something bad. Maybe he had. It was a stable, and there was no shortage of manure though they had cleaned all the stalls that morning, as they had every day. But the smell sometimes lingered, especially in the summer.

The man wore light gray dress slacks, a white buttoned-down shirt, and a tie. His leather dress shoes were the last thing anyone should wear to a horse stable, and he was picking his way carefully around the questionable droppings that hadn't been completely cleaned away. Too bad Barnes had chosen this spot for their discussion.

"I'm comfortable right here. Say your piece." Chase wasn't feeling too charitable and could only imagine what this conversation was about.

Instead, Tom Barnes walked over to the pony's stall. "My grandson loves this pony, you know. I hear it was his father's. I don't know how you found it or how it's still alive after all these years, but thank you for that."

Chase leaned on the stall door and watched Wildfire eat some hay. "Ponies can live a long time, even longer than horses, if they're well cared for. Cam Miller honored Spencer's request to hang on to the pony for Adam. You should thank him, not me. I just asked about him."

Barnes just nodded then cast Chase a sideways glance. "A.J. speaks of you often. It's bordering on hero worship."

"Well, that was never my intention. I'm no hero."

"No, you're not." Barnes turned and faced him. "I'd like to be frank. My wife and daughter don't know I'm here, and

I'd like it to stay that way. I'm well aware many people in town don't like me. It's hard to be liked or even nice when so much of the town's livelihood rests in your hands. Not literally but close. So, I try not to get too close to many people. They might find it uncomfortable."

Well, that was a surprise. He'd never thought of Barnes's position in quite that way, but it made sense. People had to go to him and share their financial details, making him privy to very sensitive details about people's lives. That would be uncomfortable for a small town. What did that have to do with him? It's not like he was asking for a loan or anything.

"I could see that." He kept his tone even, neutral, trying to figure out what his angle was.

"I love my daughter and my grandson. I may not have always shown it in the best way, and I regret that, but I love her anyway. I've come to believe that you might also love her. That's why I'm asking you. Are you staying or going?"

And the hits just kept on coming. That was yet another surprise he wasn't expecting. Since this was Hailey's father, he needed to throttle back irritation and be a bit more respectful, even if he choked on it.

He rubbed his jaw, feeling the stubble against his fingers. "Well, sir, I think that's really between Hailey and I."

The other man was already shaking his head. "I disagree. Your relationship is beyond the two of you. My grandson is involved too. And, if you want to bring other influences into it, the business requires your skill with the horses, so your brothers are involved. You are not an island, Chase, no matter what you might think. And your relationship has ripple effects."

Chase arched his eyebrow and crossed his arms in front of his chest. "Are you trying to protect the bank's investment, or do you care about your daughter?"

"Truthfully? My daughter. The investment will attend to itself. It's a bank loan and will survive or not. That's business. I wouldn't be here for business. I'm here about my daughter and grandson. She was devastated when Adam died; she had to work very hard to raise a child on her own. She's strong and determined, but I think you could break her."

Chase narrowed his gaze, anger slowly burning beneath the surface. "Where were you when Adam died? You should have moved her back here to support her, to help her. Instead, you stayed here with your precious bank, leaving Hailey to struggle on her own in Billings."

Barnes nodded. "You're right. I was angry that she married against my wishes and was still punishing her. And my daughter is a lot like me, proud, stubborn. We asked her to come home and she refused. She was determined to make it on her own. But where were you? Adam was your best friend. Hailey was your friend too. Why didn't you check in on her, help her? You also avoided her; you were also absorbed in your own world."

Chase turned away. He had stayed away. He had blamed himself for Adam's death, for leading him to the bull-riding circuit but not helping him be a better rider. And he blamed himself for caring about Hailey as more than a friend, and he knew if he saw her, he might want her in a different way than a friend should. And not only did he not have the right, but he was the completely wrong person for her and her son.

"I'm sorry," Barnes said. "That was uncalled for. She wasn't your responsibility. I should have been there and shouldn't have lashed out."

Chase swiveled back and studied the other man. "You don't know your daughter very well then. Hailey can take care of herself. She's strong, independent, fierce. But you're right. We both should have at least checked in and made sure she wasn't alone. I won't make that mistake again."

"But you're still leaving." The words fell flat between them, and Chase couldn't help but nod. "And that's why I'm here. I want you to let her go. Don't tie her to you. Let her be free to find someone else to love, someone to be there for her every day. She deserves that."

"Maybe I'll end after this season. This may be last one." He wasn't sure if that would be the case, if the ranch could survive without the influx of cash, but he'd figure that out. Someday he'd have to retire. This might be the right time, if they could get things going.

Barnes gave him a small, sad smile. "Can you really let go of the road, of the excitement? And what might happen in the meantime? She'll be waiting every night for a call like the one she got about Adam. It would be kinder to let her go now before she's in too deep."

Chase's heart felt like it had been stabbed and then twisted. "What about me? Maybe I love her too."

"I believe you do, but if you loved her enough, you'd stay. I hope you find someone you love enough to give up the road. But Hailey deserves a whole man, not someone who's given half his heart to traveling."

Chase stared at the man, his fists clenched at his side. He

wanted so much to haul off and hit Barnes, cause him the pain he had inflicted on Chase, but he knew he wouldn't. Not only would that hurt Hailey but Barnes was right. He was stringing Hailey along, forcing her to wait for him while he had his fun. He was no better than Adam, and he'd had huge fights with Adam over the exact same thing.

He had to let her go. He had to do it before he lost his nerve. And the rest of his heart. Because Tom Barnes was right, the fucker. He only had half a heart to give. The rest belonged to the road.

Chapter Twenty-Four

CHASE WATCHED LEW working Cleo in the corral. He had thought he was just mentoring the kid, but, on some level, he must have been preparing for this transition, even if he hadn't talked about it. Lew had good instincts; he would be fine with Cleo, especially since he'd been developing a relationship with the mare.

Chase was still reflecting on his conversation with Tom Barnes when Cleo suddenly reared and lashed out with her front hooves at Lew, knocking the young man to the ground, a hoofprint on the side of his face.

"Goddamn it. What the hell happened?" Ty came running out of the barn at the commotion and helped Chase herd Cleo away from Lew motionless on the ground.

"Call an ambulance. I don't want to move him," Chase ordered.

Ty grabbed his phone while Chase checked Lew's vitals, relieved to see the young man breathing and already coming around. Ty cornered the horse after calling emergency services and ushered her into the stable, leaving Chase to keep Lew company while they waited.

The ambulance crew loaded him into the bus while Lew protested the whole time. "Doesn't matter. I want to be sure you're okay. Concussions are nothing to mess with," Chase insisted.

"You've had like a dozen and you seem okay," Lew called back.

"Exactly, kid. You don't want to turn into this idiot," Ty cracked. "We'll be right behind you."

"Don't call my mom. She'll worry," Lew said just as they closed the doors.

"What the fuck happened?" Ty demanded as soon as the ambulance drove off.

Meanwhile, a car came screaming down the driveway, Tara's SUV, driving like a bat out of hell. The two women bolted out of the vehicle, looking white and shaken. They both ran to the men and were embraced immediately.

"We're fine. Cleo took exception to something, got spooked and reared, and clocked Lew in the head."

"Why the fuck was Lew working with Cleo and not you? She was your responsibility. Lew is just a kid." Ty's whole body was rigid, the adrenaline from the incident not having worn off yet.

"He wants to learn about working with horses. He's been working with me all along, and he'll need to get used to her when I'm gone."

It was like the whole world went silent. Shit. He hadn't told anyone other than Hailey that he was leaving at the end of the week. There would be hell to pay.

Ty's face went stone still and a muscle in his jaw ticked. Chase thought he could hear the molars grinding in his back teeth for a moment. Then Ty gently released Tara and shoved Lew's hat hard into Chase stomach.

"Here, asshole. You caused this. You fucking deal with

it." And he stalked off to the stable.

Chase rubbed his stomach and looked at the women who didn't appear to have an ounce of sympathy for him, although they did look sad. They shook their heads and walked into the house, leaving him standing alone in the dirt driveway.

CHASE SAT IN the emergency room with Lew until he was discharged. He went alone, his form of penance, guilt eating at him until he found out the kid was going to be okay. Ty had offered to come down, too, but this was something Chase had to do, since Cleo was his horse and the whole situation was his fault. Maybe they had rushed the training. Maybe Lew wasn't ready. Maybe Chase misread the situation. Hell, maybe Chase wasn't as good a trainer as everyone thought.

He had overestimated his skills and Lew had gotten hurt, much like when he'd thought he was doing right with A.J. and the kid had fallen off the bull. Maybe he should have stuck with what he knew, riding bulls, alone. He was good at that. Lew didn't blame him and neither did A.J., but the people around him knew he wasn't responsible enough to be trusted with mentoring or kids. That was more Ty or West's thing.

But he did take Lew back to his house for his mother to fuss over, then headed home to deal with the chores that remained. The horses had all been stabled and fed for the night. Chase walked down the center aisle to look in on

Cleo. She avoided looking at him, as if she knew the afternoon had been a clusterfuck. Or maybe she blamed him too.

"I checked her out and she seems to be okay. No injuries or anything. I think she just got spooked. She's got issues that won't go away overnight, you know?" Ty came up behind him and handed him a cold beer.

Chase shook his head. He didn't need alcohol fogging his brain, not when he needed to start focusing on the return. "She'd been doing great. I even rode her a little the other day. There was no reason for her to spook like that."

"Horses sometimes freak out. It happens. She'll never be a trail horse, most likely. She just needs time."

"Yeah, well, I shouldn't have pushed her or Lew. I'll see if I can find a trainer who will take her while I'm gone. Lew can't handle her."

Ty grabbed his arm and turned him around. "It was one time, an accident. Look, I shouldn't have said what I said. I was pissed, worried about Lew. I doubt the kid even blames you. Jesus, Chase. You don't have to take the blame for everything. Man up."

"What the fuck, Ty? Weren't you the one who just said that I fucked up? Now I didn't? Make up your goddamned mind." Chase ran a hand through his hair and stalked around the small space. "It doesn't matter. The horse needs more than anyone here can give her. She needs to go where someone can work with her."

Ty got right in his face, blocking his retreat. "Bullshit. You're cutting and running like always. Why is that? Why don't you stick around for more than a couple of weeks? I'm tired of us trying to find you a place here. You need to figure out what the fuck you want and make your own place. We can't do it for you anymore. I won't do it anymore."

Chase tried to push Ty out of the way, but Ty wasn't budging. "I don't know what you're talking about. I bust my ass on the circuit to send money to supplement this place."

"You can also die on the circuit. Or worse. Forgive me if I don't want anything to happen to you. Think about what you're doing to this family when you walk out on us. When you don't have to. We beg you not to. This is your home."

Chase slammed Ty into the barn wall, making the wood shudder under the impact. The horses snorted at the disturbance, but Ty didn't seem concerned, remained acquiescent under the elbow pinning his throat. "How long will we have this home if we don't have my winnings? What if the guest ranch or whatever the fuck it's called fails? What if we have a bad season? I think about this family every goddamned day. I send my winnings back to help this ranch so we have a fucking home."

"We'd rather have you than the money you send." Ty stared at Chase, his voice quiet in the night.

Chase dropped his arm, letting Ty down. "I don't fit in here, or anywhere. I'm nothing more than a cowboy on this place. West runs the ranch; he's the guy everyone looks to. You're his second-hand guy and the one all the calving and sick or injured go through. Me? I just do what I'm told. I need to contribute in my own way."

"Jesus, you're fucking dense. You're like a horse whisperer. We could make something of that. You could make something of that if you wanted."

Chase shrugged. "Maybe. But I get bored staying in one

place for long. This just isn't me."

"That's a damned excuse. You just don't want to take the chance." Ty pulled Chase's head down so their foreheads touched. "I know what it's like to lose a home, a family. We won't lose this one."

"You don't know that," Chase said, the words torn from his mouth. "I need to do this. It's the only way I can help."

Ty sighed and dropped his hand. "You're more valuable than this piece of land, brother."

Chase knew he was wrong. Chase Summers was never destined to have a home or a family. His whole life had been proof of that. No one ever stuck around for him and he had never had a home for more than a few months. Chase knew more than most how fleeting the illusion of a home was. First, he had to earn it. So back on the circuit he went.

Chapter Twenty-Five

T HE NEXT AFTERNOON, Chase was back at it, determined to be ready for the competition. He'd bought his plane ticket earlier that morning and was already registered for the competition. He'd actually been signed up months ago. Now, he just needed to be ready to ride. Lew was still a little sore and walking slow but was able to sit on a stool and man the controls for Theo, the mechanical bull. Chase had been able to avoid his brothers since the previous evening; hopefully, they were still out working the range and he could postpone the inevitable confrontation about his return to the road.

As before, he and Lew rechecked all the systems and made sure everything was safe before he started his ride, slowly increasing the difficulty. He hadn't been too sore after the last ride, his injuries feeling pretty well healed, so he was encouraged—as long as he didn't encounter the business end of the bull or any unforeseen accidents. He loosened up quicker and they ran through the experienced level designed for professional bull riders twice before he called a break.

When he looked over at the controls, Lew was gone, replaced by West perched on the stool. Shit, guess the confrontation had come calling sooner rather than later. Ty tossed Chase a towel from an old piece of equipment where he sat, then a bottle of water right after the towel.

"Think you got it out of your system yet?" Ty's voice was casual, but there was an underlying bite to the words that made Chase pause and lower the bottle of water.

"I'm done practicing for the day, yes." He deliberately chose to misinterpret his words.

Ty stood from his position on the abandoned tractor, stretching his lanky frame, and walked over to the inflatable ring. "When were you going to tell us you were headed back?"

Chase wiped down the sweat from his neck and face. "You always knew I was going back. Besides, I thought it was pretty obvious last night."

West slid off the stool and leaned on the side of the control panel. "When are you leaving?"

Ty's head whipped around. "You're just going to let him go?"

West shrugged. "I can't force him to stay. He's a grown-ass man. If he's too stupid to see what he's giving up and wants to bail on it all, well, I can't keep him here."

Chase just laughed. "Reverse psychology? It's too obvious. That may have worked when I was a stupid teenager to get me to stay away from a girl or to do my chores, but I've outgrown that."

West pushed aside the cushioning to let Chase step out of the inflatable area and onto the wood barn floor. "Nope. I've done everything I can. The rest has to be up to you."

"West, come on, you can't be serious. Tell him. He has to stay," Ty insisted, running his hands through his dark brown hair. "Damn it, Chase. Why?"

"We talked about this." Chase rested a hand on Ty's shoulder and peered into his eyes, willing him to understand what he was trying to say. "I'm not like you guys. You like your home, your roots. West has Tara now and is perfectly happy staying here. Ty, you always wanted a family, a home. Now you have that. You never have to leave the ranch. But me? I never stayed in one place for more than a few months until I came here. It's not who I am. I want to see places, more than Montana and the ass-end of a cow."

"Bullshit." Ty flung his arm off and stomped a few steps away. "This time was different. You were settling down here, making roots for maybe the first time ever. What are you hoping to find out there? Because I don't think you even know. And now, you have something here, not just cows but anything you want. Redemption Ranch is partly yours and you can do what you want."

"Maybe I want to be on the road." But even Chase knew the answer was bullshit, and he avoided Ty's knowing gaze.

"And then what? What happens when you're broken down, too hurt to ride? Chase, you can't do this forever. Or do we have to wait until one of those bulls kill you?"

West studied Chase solemnly from his position leaning against the control panel, arms folded across his chest. Chase threw the towel to the ground. "You're just a barrel of fucking laughs today, aren't you? Why do you assume I'll get killed?"

"Because you almost did." Instead of Ty yelling it, West's calm voice broke between the brothers. "I took the phone call in the middle of the night. I sat next to you for three days while you were in and out of consciousness. I was the one they asked for end-of-life decisions. It fucking sucked, brother."

Chase froze, all the wind taken out of his sails. He sank into the wooden chair by the empty stall and studied the scarred floor. "I'm sorry. If I could have spared you that, I would have. And I can't say it won't happen again. But can you understand that I need to do this? I'm so close to winning the whole title. It will help everyone, give us some breathing room for the taxes and setting up the guest ranch. You won't have to sell off more of the herd this year."

"And you get your championship, if you survive." Ty's voice was bitter.

Chase whirled in his chair, anger pumping in his veins. "Yeah, I get my championship, if I can win it. And why not? I've been working hard for this. I have my best shot right now. I can be someone, accomplish something. Do you have any idea what that's like?"

West laid a hand on his shoulder, a calming force as usual. "Will they let you ride with your concussions?"

Chase nodded. "It's been enough time and I've rested, not ridden. I'll have to be checked out, but I don't see a problem."

"Will you consider wearing a helmet? I know you don't have to, but we'd feel better if you did."

Chase started to protest, but he could see the struggle in the lines of tension in West's body, the way he was trying so hard to not demand or yell or force Chase to stay home. He was making an effort, and the least Chase could do was meet him halfway.

"It might reduce my peripheral vision," he warned.

"It would protect your head. Even your thick skull needs help." West laughed.

Chase nodded. "Fine. I'll wear it."

West gripped his shoulder hard, betraying his stress. "And will you consider retiring at the end of the season? Win or lose?"

Chase froze then leaned forward in his chair, letting his hands dangle between his legs. The request wasn't unexpected. It was one West made almost every year, in some fashion, but this was the most blunt he had ever been. And this was the first time Chase considered agreeing.

There was Hailey and A.J., two people who hadn't existed for him in the past. Traveling on the road, sleeping in empty hotel rooms, didn't hold the same appeal as holding a soft and sexy woman every night in the same bed, reading stories to A.J. after bath time, and eating breakfast with someone other than immature, foul-mouthed cowboys. He wouldn't miss the early morning plane rides, the broken fingers and bruises everywhere, the boredom between events while watching stupid daytime television.

He had told Ty he liked seeing new places, but Ty was right. He hadn't seen anything new in years. The competitions were held in the same places every year. When was the last time he went out sightseeing in any of those cities, if there was anything to really see? Ty had nailed it. What was Chase looking for? It was no longer exciting or fun; it was just a job. But he was so close to his goal, the one he'd chased for close to ten years now. He could almost taste it. Hailey would understand. He'd talk to her. And, at the end of the season, he could re-evaluate, decide what he'd do. And maybe, with his winnings, they could secure the home he'd always wanted, along with people to share it. If she didn't leave.

Apparently, he'd been taking too long because West cleared his throat. "Have you talked about this with Hailey? Does she know you're leaving?"

It's like West could read his mind. God, he hated when his brother did that. "Yeah, I told her the other night. She understands how it is. This is my job."

West and Ty laughed like he was an idiot, and Ty clapped him on the back. "Really? She's more understanding than I expected. I'll make up the couch in my cabin for you anyway, just in case. When do you leave?"

"My flight is in a couple of days. I want to get there early and get checked out so I'm ready."

A sound from the other side of the inflatable circle caught their attention. A.J. stood there, looking stricken, his eyes wide and his mouth hanging open. Tears welled in his eyes and his lower lip trembled a bit. Both West and Ty shot Chase a sympathetic look and stepped away.

"You're leaving?"

Fuck. This was not the way he wanted to tell the kid. He crossed the barn floor and knelt in front of A.J., placing a hand on his shoulder, but A.J. ducked out of the touch, glaring at him. Okay, so they'd passed from sad to angry.

"I have to. It's my job. I'm a bull rider. That's what I do."

"But my daddy was a bull rider and he never came home." A.J.'s words ended on a high note, almost a wail.

Shit, he hadn't known that Hailey had shared how Adam

died with her son. This was awkward. This time, when he reached for A.J., he grasped the boy's upper arms gently, not letting him wiggle out. "I know, but that hardly ever happens. I'll be fine. And I'll be back home in a few months. Promise."

A.J. blinked back tears. "You were hurt before. Bad." The boy threw his arms around Chase and held him tight. "Don't go."

Damn it. It's as if his brothers had coached the kid into what to say. He held him tight. "Everything will be fine."

A.J. tore himself out of Chase's arms and, with one last accusatory look, ran back to the house. Chase remained kneeling on the floor, his heart bruised and battered.

West laid a hand on his shoulder. "You shouldn't make promises you can't keep. You know you can't control if you get hurt."

Chase glared up at his brother and snarled. "What did you want me to do? Lie to him?"

West sighed. "I don't know. But that one's going to bite you in the ass."

Yeah, time to pay the piper. He may have told her about the upcoming competition, but Ty was right. It may not have been real to Hailey. How would she take the news when he told her he was actually leaving? He rose to his feet and headed for the house, hoping Hailey would take the news better. Somehow, he didn't think she would.

HAILEY STEWED AS she settled A.J. after he'd come running

from the barn in tears, saying something about Chase getting hurt like his daddy and going away. After momentarily panicking that Chase was hurt, she'd finally figured out that A.J. had heard Chase and his brothers talking about Chase leaving. Once she had calmed down from her initial freak out, she rocked A.J. until he fell asleep in her arms. Seeing Chase walking up from the barn, she put A.J. on the couch in the reception area and waited for him on the porch, her mind a jumble. By the time she saw he got to the path, she still had no idea what she was going to say. She only knew her heart was shattered.

He came up to the bottom step and rested his leg on the second step, took off his hat, and worried it in his hands. "How is A.J.?"

This was one area in which she knew exactly what she wanted to say. "He cried himself to sleep. He was so upset, Chase. How could you tell him like that?"

He tossed his hat onto the porch, stalked up the steps, and glared at her. "First off, I was talking to my brothers and didn't know A.J. was there. Second, A.J. was told never to be in the barn where the mechanical bull was, so he broke that rule barely one day after being told he couldn't be there."

She gave a short laugh. "Fine, blame the six-year-old. That's what they do, Chase. They forget things and they hear things." She looked away but couldn't see much with the tears blurring her vision. Damn it, she had wanted to be strong. "When were you going to tell us?"

He leaned against the railing across from her, blocking her vision of anything else, forcing her to look at him. "I had planned on telling you tonight, then figuring out the best way to tell A.J. Why didn't you tell me that he knows how Adam died?"

She shrugged. "He doesn't really know. He just knows his dad was a bull rider and didn't come home. He doesn't even remember Adam. I don't think he really understands it."

Chase snorted. "Well, he understands more than you think. He said he doesn't want me to go away and never come back like his daddy."

She stood and faced him squarely, feeling a strength and a decision she only just now had realized. "A valid point. Chase, you're not known for sticking around. You even say you have wandering feet. I can't just sit around and wait for you to come home when you want to, when it's convenient. I won't do that, Chase. I deserve more. I deserve a man who will be with me and A.J., a man who wants to be a husband and a father. I thought you were that man, but maybe you're not."

Chase straightened as if shocked, his face white, and he grabbed her upper arms, pulling her close. "Hailey, honey, I can be there for you both. I love you. We need the money, and I need to support the ranch the only way I can. I'd never forgive myself if we lose the ranch and I could have earned that money."

She lifted her hand and cupped his cheek tenderly, her heart aching for the pain in his voice. How could he feel that he had nothing to offer? "If you had earned the money, would you stay? Or would there be another prize, another purse, another competition? Chase, why do you really travel? There are other ways to make money, like training horses or helping run the guest ranch. You could contribute that way."

He shook his head. "Of course there's another purse. Always."

She dropped her hand, the truth settling in finally. "It's not the money or the job. It's the ranch itself. You are so afraid it won't be here for you that you keep running from it. You're afraid to stick around."

His hands fell to his side as if scalded and he backed away, glaring at her. "What the hell is that supposed to mean? I'm trying to save the ranch, my home."

"I believe you are. But you're too afraid to actually live here, to believe it's going to be here for you. You don't trust that you have a place." She stepped back and wrapped her arms around her body, hugging herself the way she wished he would hug her. "Then go, Chase. Be free. I never wanted to cage you, only love you. I wish you knew that love is not a cage, and neither is a home. I hope you find that out someday. But I won't be here for you. I can't be here for you. I love you, but I need to protect myself and my son."

She opened the screen door then paused. "Please find another place to sleep tonight. I'll make sure we're gone all day tomorrow so you can clear out your stuff."

She let the screen door slam shut behind her, leaving Chase and her heart on the outside.

Chapter Twenty-Six

THE NEXT FEW days passed in a whirlwind of activity. Hailey kept her word and vacated the house, moving to her parents' house and staying away while he was getting ready to leave. Tara refused to talk to him, although she did show up for his going-away dinner. Hailey and A.J. did not, even though they had been invited. Hailey had sent a message through Tara saying it would be too confusing for A.J. and not a good idea for any of them. He parked outside her house on the last night, but when she saw him from the upstairs window, she closed her curtains and turned off the light. He waited for thirty minutes, hoping she was coming down, but finally an older woman in a bright pink velour tracksuit and a yappy dog threatened to call the local police, so he left.

West drove him to the airport in Missoula to catch his flight. At the last minute, Tara slipped into the truck without a word. She played with her phone the whole way but gave him a tight hug and a watery smile at the curb, climbed into the truck, and gripped West's hand.

Fast-forward a day and Chase was medically cleared and just waiting for the first day of competition. God, he'd forgotten how boring the waiting was. The music rocked the stadium and the smells hadn't changed much. Cowboys milled about, talking about their time off since traditionally there was a couple of months' hiatus in the summer, although there were always competitions to increase points, including the one where Chase had gotten hurt. He caught up with a few guys and checked over the bulls, checked over the arena and chutes, then sat in the locker room to get in the right mental space.

He eyed the clock. A.J. would be getting home from camp, having a snack, maybe going to the barn to check on Wildfire, if Hailey had moved back to the ranch. Had Hailey moved into the ranch manager's apartments, the rooms he had occupied while recuperating, or did she remain at her parents' house? Who was teaching A.J. how to ride? Lew? He'd be a good teacher, if he had time to do it. Chase hadn't had time to find a trainer for Cleo, so he hoped Lew didn't get brave or stupid and take her out again. She needed a more experienced hand.

God, he missed them.

J.D. McIntyre plopped on the bench next to him with the ropes he was prepping. "Wasn't sure I'd see you here. Heard you found domestic bliss or something back home."

Chase winced at the reminder of what he'd lost and shook his head. "Nah, I won't subject a woman to this life. It's not fair to ask her to wait for a phone call or be alone while I'm on the road so much."

J.D. leaned to the side and eyed him speculatively. "But you did find a woman then? Because before you'd say, why limit yourself to one?"

Chase cursed softly. "Are we going to talk about our feelings or the bulls out there? Who did you get?"

"Nail Biter. Not a bad first rounder. You?"

"Ghost Dancer. I've ridden him before. A few twists but should be okay."

A commotion at the front of the locker room interrupted their conversation, but Chase couldn't hear what was being said. J.D. got up and went over then came back, pale and a bit shaken.

"Fuck, man. Tonio just died. They decided to pull the plug. They flew his family up from Brazil to say goodbye and make the decision. I guess he had no brain activity, so his wife and brother made the call."

Ice formed on Chase's chest, constricted his lungs. "His wife and brother? He had a family?"

J.D. nodded. "Yeah, a lot of them do. They come from Brazil to earn money for their family. His wife just had a baby over the winter, I guess. The guys all took up a collection to fly them up so she could be with him. His brother too. They're having a quick memorial in the arena before we start the competition tonight."

Chase nodded and waved him off, his mind preoccupied with thoughts of Tonio and his family. He couldn't help but think about his accident, waking up with West there, and the decisions he was asked to make for Chase. Hell, he remembered Hailey getting the call while dealing with a toddler, not having the chance to say goodbye or to make the choice for Adam. What if Chase had another injury like last time? He wasn't delusional. Bull riding was dangerous.

And for what? Another purse, money for the ranch, for his home where he wasn't living more than a few weeks out of the year? Damn, was Hailey right? Was he waiting for it to disappear like all of his foster homes before? Was he holding back, not putting down roots, afraid they'd be ripped out like they had every time he had dared to hope?

He had been the most at peace when he was at the ranch this last time, working with the horses, spending time with Hailey and A.J., being a family. Maybe he had been looking for that all along, even as he struggled against it.

And he'd thrown it away for what?

He tossed the helmet aside and leaned back against the locker, the sounds of cowboys talking about their night a low rumbling in the backdrop. Was this really what he wanted? When he could have his family, Hailey and A.J.?

God, he was a stupid ass to toss that aside. He'd had his wandering days. Now it was time he grew up and find his real home. Back on Redemption Ranch. If he hadn't lost everything that mattered.

Chapter Twenty-Seven

H E DROVE THE rental car like a bat out of hell to get home from the Missoula airport the next evening. It wasn't easy getting from Texas to Missoula last minute. Too many damned layovers, especially when he had finally decided he had to be home. Hell, he'd almost rented a car and driven the route, but he wouldn't have saved any time. He turned down the dirt driveway and found the ranch house dark, the rooms where Hailey and A.J. had stayed empty. They hadn't moved back after he left. He sat on the edge of his bed, the one where he and Hailey had spent so many nights and buried his head in his hands. He'd lost her. She'd told him she wouldn't wait, and she hadn't.

A sound in the doorway made him lift his head. Ty stood there, shock on his face, but he recovered quickly. He leaned against the doorjamb and plunged his hands in his jean's pockets. "When did you get back?"

"A few minutes ago. Where's Hailey?"

Ty pushed off the door and sat on the bed next to Chase. "She's with her parents, I think. She's been working here during the day but hasn't slept here since you left."

Chase studied his hands, clasped in front of him. "I've lost her then. I screwed up the best thing I ever had."

"Not necessarily," West said from the doorway. "That all

depends on you really. Are you home to stay?"

Chase looked up and nodded. "I'm done with the road, if you'll have me."

The relief on West's face sent a wave of happiness through Chase, but it didn't quite touch the empty place inside his heart where Hailey belonged. Ty clapped him on the shoulder and pulled him in for a manly hug.

"Well, I had to go to San Francisco to get my girl. You only have to go to town, though I think you might have more groveling to do. Are you prepared for that?" West asked.

Chase winced. "I've never had to do it. Any suggestions?"

West tilted his head and studied his brother, a smirk playing at his lips. "Cut the charm and flirting. Honesty and a little begging will go a long way."

Yeah, he had already figured that out.

CHASE PARKED IN front of Hailey's parents' house and killed the engine. Lights were still on in the windows, so everyone was still up, although her bedroom light was off. It wasn't that late, maybe ten o'clock, so he didn't think they'd call the police for disturbing the peace. He just didn't want to wait until tomorrow to see her, to talk to her. Of course, he still had no idea what he was going to say, provided she let him in the door.

The front door opened and he realized he had a bigger problem. Hailey's father was framed in the hallway light, the guardian of the family, and somehow Chase doubted he'd be open to letting him in or Hailey out, especially after Chase had done the one thing the man had asked him not to do: break his daughter's heart. Damn it.

He sighed and got out of the truck and walked up the brick walkway to the porch where he took his hat off and waited.

Tom Barnes remained blocking the doorway but didn't close the door. "You made her cry."

"Yes, I did, sir. And I can't tell you how sorry I am for that." This time, the respect was more natural. Maybe he could handle the groveling. It seemed he had a lot of it to do to a lot of people. Not just Hailey.

"Why couldn't you just leave?"

Chase refused to back down, refused to lower his eyes even as the shame pressed down on him. "I did leave, sir. And that's why she was crying." He walked up a couple of steps and paused on the top step. "I can't change that, but I can do something about the future."

Tom stepped out onto the porch. "You telling me that you're home for good, no traveling on the circuit anymore?"

"Yes, sir, I am."

Tom eyed him with disbelief. "You gave up the championship to come home and work cows? It doesn't say much that you gave up on a goal when the going got tough."

Chase rubbed the back of his neck. Damn, he hadn't really expected to have to defend his actions, not yet, considering his plans weren't fully formed. "First, the going didn't get tough; it's always been tough and I worked hard for it. But I gave it up for something better. And second, I'm not coming home to work cows exactly. I mean, I'll help where they need me but I'm going to work the horses for the ranch and maybe do some training. I've been doing it on the side already. It might take me some time to build the business, but I have a job. I may not be able to give Hailey a fancy life, but I'll love her better than anyone else and do my best to make sure she never cries again."

Tom's face was still set stubbornly in severe lines, but he gave a slow nod. "I hear you have a talent with horses. I'll be watching. And if you need financing, come talk to me. Provided you and Hailey work things out."

Chase heard the warning in his tone. He wasn't off the hook. He had passed one hurdle but had the toughest one yet. Before he could ask after Hailey, a woman's voice spoke from the hallway. "Tom, who is it?"

Hailey's mom came to stand by her husband, and A.J. poked between the two. His eyes widened but he didn't run to Chase when he once would have. "Chase, I thought you were gone."

And the second hurdle, the one he had almost forgotten. A.J. had been hurt almost as much as Hailey. Chase went to one knee. "I came back. For you and your mom."

A.J. looked down and clung to his grandmother, his lower lip stuck out. "When are you leaving again?"

"I'm not. I'm staying for good."

A.J.'s head lifted, hope radiating in his eyes. "Really? You'll teach me how to ride Wildfire and how to rope cows and will be my daddy?"

Tom cleared his throat and Chase glanced up. "Well, that all depends on your mom. Can I talk to her?"

"She's not here right now. She went out with a couple of

friends. Tara and Emma, I think," Hailey's mom said.

A.J. ran across the porch and hugged him. "You're really staying?"

"Yup, and no matter what, I'll teach you how to ride. Promise."

But first, he had to go get his woman. Then maybe pound his brother for not telling him that Hailey was out with Tara, because there was no way West didn't know that. Bastard. Having too much fun at Chase's expense.

HAILEY DOWNED ANOTHER shot, trying to ignore the way West hugged Tara to his side and the jealousy that speared her heart. He and Ty had walked in about ten minutes prior with shit-eating grins on their faces after stomping around the ranch for the past few days, grouchy as grizzlies after hibernation. Something had mellowed them out, and now West was all over Tara and she was climbing all over him, half in his lap, forgetting her girlfriends and Hailey's heart-break.

So much for girls' night.

Although, if Hailey had someone, she'd probably do the same thing so she couldn't really blame Tara. But right now, she wanted to haul off and shove West right off the chair just on principle. It really wouldn't matter who sat there. Any male would get the same treatment, but West was *his* brother, so he was fair game.

She reached for Tara's shot, since Tara was otherwise occupied, and a male hand covered hers, holding it to the table, not letting her pick it up. "Don't you think you've had enough, sweetheart?"

She glared up at Ty, the second brother. He'd always been nice to her, just like West, but right now he was a man and Chase's brother, so he was on the shit list. "Do you mind? Tara doesn't need it."

Ty hooked a chair with his leg from the neighboring table and dragged it over so he could sit on it, all without letting up the pressure on the shot glass and her hand. "You don't need it either, sweetheart."

She released the glass with a huff and turned away, studying the dance floor through the tears in her eyes that never seemed far away these days. Goddamn that Chase Summers, making her fall in love then breaking her heart. Ty rubbed her back and she leaned against him, angry at herself for needing the touch after being independent for so long, yet the comfort felt so good. Yet another charge to lay at Chase's feet. She had been doing fine on her own, strong and independent, until Chase strode into her life. Damn him.

Blindly, she fumbled for her purse. "I think I'll head home. It's too soon for this. I'm sorry, Emma, Tara. But thank you for thinking of me."

Ty held onto her shoulders, keeping her in her chair. "You can't leave yet. I'm going to be singing tonight, just for you. You know how rare that is."

She smiled at him. "And why is that? You have a beautiful voice. You should be in Nashville making loads of money and records, yet you're here chasing cows."

He shrugged. "It makes me happy."

She saw the sadness that she felt deep in her heart reflected in his eyes, hidden a little better maybe. "Are you, Ty?"

He pasted a smile on his face, but it still didn't quite meet his eyes. "Just stay a little longer, okay? Maybe Cam or someone else will dance with you. For me?"

She snorted but Emma and Tara took up the plea for her to stay and honestly, she wasn't quite ready to drive and she didn't want to pull Ty or West from their evening, since they were the only ones sober enough to drive her. So, she settled back in her chair and shot a glare at Ty who had taken the shot with him when he'd left. Damn him. If she was staying, the least he could have done was left the alcohol. Instead, she sipped her beer and moped. Emma shot her a look but shrugged and talked with Tara and West when Hailey wouldn't engage in conversation. Cam joined them, taking the chair Ty had vacated and watching Emma closely but not doing anything more. Emma seemed determined to ignore him.

The band started up, playing a fast song, and Hailey'd had enough of sitting on her ass. Tara had dragged West onto the dance floor and Emma was pointedly ignoring Cam in favor of another young cowboy, so if Hailey couldn't have the one she wanted, maybe she could play a little matchmaker and light a fire under the two who needed some help. She shoved her chair back and grabbed Cam's hand.

"Let's dance." He looked startled and glanced at Emma but followed her. Within a minute, Emma was out there with the young cowboy sending heated glares at both of them, more for Cam than her, but hey, you snooze you lose. The song ended and coincidentally, Emma was right next to them, sans cowboy.

Ty stepped up to the microphone and cleared his throat, his gaze finding her even in the crowded dance floor. "I hope you enjoy this next song, just for a special lady out there. So, grab your special someone and get on the dance floor."

Well, damn. Why did Ty have to single her out like that? He of all people knew she had no interest in finding anyone to dance with, especially now, yet he was also the one who insisted she stay. She turned to stomp off the dance floor, leaving Cam and Emma to stare warily at each other, when the crowd parted, revealing Chase. Her heart stuttered, stopped, then restarted again. The room seemed to tilt around her, though that could have been the Fireball shots, but she didn't think so. She started to shake her head and back away but there was a solid wall of people behind her, as if everyone in town were conspiring against her, forcing her to face her worst nightmare, Chase Summers's return and the heartbreak he'd inflicted on her.

West was right behind her and put his hands on her shoulders. He leaned down and spoke in her ear. "Just talk to him. If you don't want to, say the word and we'll drive you home."

She ran her eyes over Chase, looking for any new injuries. She knew he was riding in a competition this week, but she had intentionally avoiding looking at the schedule. She hadn't wanted to know the details, hadn't wanted to watch the event on television, to see him riding. "Why are you here?"

"I came back for you."

She shook her head again. "I told you before. I won't wait for you."

He took a few steps forward. "And you shouldn't. You shouldn't wait for anyone. You deserve the best and you deserve a whole man by your side every day, every night. I was wrong to leave, but now I'm back."

He was treating her like a skittish horse and it was pissing her off. She folded her arms in front of her. "You think that makes it all okay? Chase is back so Hailey will fall into bed with him again?" The crowd started murmuring, the small-town gossip train getting some momentum tonight, but she didn't give a shit about it. "What about next time, Chase? What about the next time you feel antsy or get wandering feet?"

He was shaking his head. "That'll never happen, sweetheart. I have no intention of ever leaving. I have a business to run."

She scoffed. "Yeah right. I don't think leading trail rides is quite in line with the adrenaline junkie side of you, Chase. It won't make you happy, and I don't want to see you unhappy just because of me."

He took a few more steps, still acclimating her to his presence like he did with Cleo. Seriously, she wasn't a fucking horse.

"Nope, I'm not conducting trail rides. God, can you see me with all those fucking people?"

Hailey cocked her head, the thought bringing some amusement to her. "Actually, I can. You're good with people. You'd be great at teaching them how to ride."

"And you're wrong about something. I'm not an adrenaline junkie. I never rode bulls for adrenaline. I rode them because they were my ticket to seeing new places, and maybe an escape. I was looking for something, a place where I belonged. I didn't let myself belong here on the ranch, didn't let myself be a true member of this family because I was always afraid it would be taken away."

"Oh Chase, I had no idea." Tara's voice was heartbroken from somewhere just to the back of Hailey.

Hailey turned and scowled. "You had your turn. This is mine."

The crowd laughed but it cut off when she shot them all a glare. When she turned back to Chase, he was smothering a smile . . . and stood only a few steps away. She narrowed her eyes and glared at him. Tricky, taking advantage of her distraction to sneak up on her. She tightened her arms, determined to remain strong. "See, I've realized finally that I have something else to offer. I'll work the horses for the guest ranch and do some training, turn that into a business. I even have an investor. And I can't skip out on that."

"Hallelujah. About damned time. I have a couple of horses that need breaking," one voice called out from the crowd.

"Shut up. They're having a moment here," Cam Miller yelled back.

Hailey narrowed her gaze. "An investor? Who?"

"Your father."

Her jaw dropped and her arms fell to her side. "My father? When did you speak to him?"

"Right before I came here. And I talked to A.J. I have their blessing, or at least I assume so. I just need yours." He took her hands in his and pulled her close. "I love you, Hailey. I'm stupid in love with you, and I can't imagine living my life without you."

"What about the championship? The money?"

He shrugged. "We'll figure it out. We're a family. We'll find a way. Besides, we won't be successful if I get hurt and we need to use that money for my medical bills, right? Anyway, I'd rather spend my time here with you and A.J., as a family, than on the road riding bulls. I'm done with that life. I had to go back to realize that it wasn't for me anymore. This is home, wherever you are."

She blinked back tears only to realize they were already streaming down her face. Chase looked panicked, his eyes widening, and he grabbed her. "Hailey, honey. What's wrong? What can I do?"

"Nothing. You've already done it." She hugged him, burying her tear-stained face into his shirt. "I swore I would never get involved with anyone again unless he was safe, and then you rode into my life and broke down all my walls and wouldn't let me stay there. I was hiding from the world, Chase. Damn it, you made me love you. Don't break my heart again, Chase Summers. I don't think I can take it."

He held her close. "Don't worry, baby. I'm going to spend the rest of our lives making sure that you never get hurt again. I love you, Hailey Spencer. Will you dance with me?"

She glanced up at the stage and saw Ty watching them from the microphone, a small grin playing about his face. She winked at him. "Play something slow, Ty."

"Just for you, Hailey. This is just for you." He broke into the Jimmie Allen song "Best Shot."

And they danced heart to heart, a bubble around them, as if no one else existed in the bar that night.

Epilogue

CHASE STOMPED HIS feet at the bottom of the porch, trying to get the last of the dirt off his boots, and A.J. did the same, even though he didn't have half as much dirt on his little boots. He was such a little mini-me for Chase these days, following him everywhere after school and asking more questions than Chase knew existed. But he answered them as best he could, even when his patience wore a little thin. It was worth it to have the family he loved. The family he'd been searching for his whole life, even if he'd never knew it.

Hailey came out on the porch, wiping her hands on her apron, eyes wide and looking a little frazzled. "I completely lost track of time and my parents will be here soon. Dinner is barely started."

He laughed. "What were you doing that made you forget something like that?"

"Setting up the schedule for your horse training. Do you know how many people in the county want your services? You're going to need a bigger barn and way more time. You may even need an assistant. I've been fielding calls ever since you made the announcement, foolishly, that you were putting out your shingle for horse training at The Rock. Don't you know better by now not to say anything at gossip central?"

He just laughed and swung her in his arms, planting a kiss on her lips. "It'll be fine. Besides, we have time. The guest ranch won't be open until next year. I can board the horses here until then."

A car drove down the driveway and parked next to his truck. "Perfect timing. I asked your parents to come early. I have something to show you. They'll watch A.J."

He drew her down to the truck, ignoring her sputtering protests, and waved to her parents. He may not be close to the Barnes yet, but they were getting there, slowly building a relationship. And Tom Barnes had made good on his word to offer financing, though Chase hadn't taken him up on it yet. He had a few plans to put in place first, and he needed the approval of his business partner, who was currently trying to smooth her hair and wipe the flour off her apron. She had no idea how absolutely gorgeous she was to him, no matter how she looked.

He drove down the lane to the small cut off they often used for the watering hole and parked. "Chase, we don't have time for a swim."

"I know. We're not going there. First, put this on." He handed her a blindfold and secured it behind her head.

"Well, we definitely don't have time for kinky sex games either," she said, though her voice had taken on the deep, husky tone that told him she was definitely aroused.

He got out of the truck and strode to the other side while she scowled in the seat, arms folded in front of her. He lifted her out of the truck, set her on her feet, and slapped her ass lightly. "Not this time, but maybe later."

He led her carefully over the rise but away from the watering hole to a flat area that already had some markers and string in the ground. He took off the blindfold and gave her a moment. She stared around at the flat valley in front of her, at the stakes and string, and her brows knit together. "I'm confused."

He took her hand and walked her over to the first spot. "This will be a stable for the horses. We can board them here and even have a place to rehabilitate ones that have been abused. I'd like to do more with abused horses, not just train local ones. Over there, we'll have an indoor ring so we can train year-round. We lose too much time with the winter in Montana, and I'll need the time and space for working the horses. We have plenty of space for grazing also."

She nodded slowly but frowned. "It's awfully far from the house."

He pointed to a spot near a copse of trees. "I thought we could build a house there. We'd have a separate entrance to your office for your consulting clients." She'd started adding new clients from the small businesses in town and couldn't keep working out of the house on the ranch, especially once the guest ranch took off.

He took a deep breath and let it out slowly, knowing the time had come to lay it all on the line. "When Douglas left us the ranch, Tara and West told us to pick out spots on the property. I've always wanted this spot because it reminded me of the happiest times I ever spent here. With you. I never thought I would marry anyone, have a space of my own. I never thought I'd have you."

He got down on one knee and pulled out a small jewelry

box. "Hailey, will you marry me and be my family?"

Tears streamed down her face and she tugged him to his feet, barely glancing at the ring. "You foolish man. Of course I will. I love it all! It's perfect. Absolutely perfect. I've finally come home."

He shook his head. "No, we've both finally come home."

And he kissed her right in the place where they would build their family.

The End

If you enjoyed this book, please leave a review at your favorite online retailer! Even if it's just a sentence or two it makes all the difference.

Thanks for reading *Coming Home to the Cowboy* by Megan Ryder!

Discover your next romance at TulePublishing.com.

TULE
PUBLISHING

If you enjoyed *Coming Home to the Cowboy,*
you'll love the next book in….

The Redemption Ranch series

Book 1: *A Cowboy's Salvation*

Book 2: *Coming Home to the Cowboy*

Book 3: *Coming in March 2020!*

Available now at your favorite online retailer!

More books by Megan Ryder

Lone Star Match series

Three Bridesmaids. Three lost loves. One match-making bride. Can a matchmaking bride reunite her bridesmaids with the ones who got away in the week before her wedding?

Book 1: *Something Old*

Book 2: *Something Borrowed*

Book 3: *Something New*

Knights of Passion series

The Knights of Passion. A team of team of sexy, dedicated men and women who love baseball and are filled with the competitive fire to win on the field and off the field. These are men and women who have been tested by life. They have found a place that they can call home and people they can call family.

Book 1: *Going All the Way*

Book 2: *Love From Left Field*

Book 3: *The Game Changer*

Available now at your favorite online retailer!

About the Author

Ever since Megan Ryder discovered Jude Deveraux and Judith McNaught while sneaking around the "forbidden" romance section of the library one day after school, she has been voraciously devouring romance novels of all types. Now a romance author in her own right, Megan pens sexy contemporary novels all about family and hot lovin' with the boy next door. She lives in Connecticut, spending her days as a technical writer and her spare time divided between her addiction to knitting and reading.

Visit her website at MeganRyder.com

Thank you for reading

Coming Home to the Cowboy

If you enjoyed this book, you can find more from all our great authors at TulePublishing.com, or from your favorite online retailer.

Made in the USA
Middletown, DE
25 August 2020